TREADING WATER

TREADING WATER

A SPARK OF LIFE NOVEL, BOOK TWO

by

GINNA MORAN

For Sarah Collier, my awesomely talented friend and critique partner. I'm so thankful to have connected with you two years ago. Much love!

1

HOME, SWEET HOME

SUNLIGHT TRICKLES THROUGH THE DEEP blue ocean, sparkling off the cerulean scales of my tail. I bask in the middle of the sea grass beds in the only place I can go to escape the watchful eyes of the inhabitants of Pearlestria.

It must be midday on the surface with the way the sun haloes up above in a white blanket of glowing light. It's the only time of day that I can pretend to be home on land in Azure Waters with the warmth of the sun on my skin, the crisp sea breeze in my hair, the soft sand between the toes I severely miss. But instead of the dry air, I have the swirling current of the ocean, the diluted light that can't even warm the water at this depth, and my tail that slaps the sandy floor in annoyance.

It's been forty days since I was dragged away from my human life and forced to accept a much less glamorous one under the sea. Without my family or friends, the time spent here feels like eternity. My only reprieve is when my boyfriend, Carter, sneaks me something from the shore. He tries his best to keep me connected to the human world, but I'm afraid the world will pass me by before I ever have the chance to escape the place that's supposed to be a haven but feels much more like a prison.

I flop from my back to my stomach, kicking up sand with my tail. It drifts through the water in a haze. Running my finger through the sand, I trace circles that wash away before they're complete. A school of mackerels casts a shadow over me, swimming through the water like a silver cloud. Dolphins circle the fish, wrangling them in the water to feast upon. This is as entertaining as it gets here within this underwater city's rock walls.

In this magical place, merpeople can live their lives without human interference, protected by whatever magic sets off the sparks within our chests. At the moment, I'm the only human-born mermaid in Pearlestria, but I've heard rumors of there being others at the different colonies throughout all the oceans of the world. I'd like to travel to them one day, if I'm ever forgiven for accidentally flashing my fins to a human—my best friend to be exact. No one knows it was someone I know. She'd be murdered for the sake of protecting our kind, though I highly doubt our kind needs any protecting most of the time.

"Ava, there you are," a feminine voice rings through my mind. It still unsettles me that anyone can just push their voice into my head any time they please, but it's especially unnerving to hear Starla, the mermaid responsible for my capture. "I thought you might've—"

I flick my tail, sending another sand cloud into the air. "Might've what? Swam away?" Running away isn't possible without legs. "You know I've come to terms with this arrangement." I force myself to smile, but I'm pretty sure I'm just baring my teeth. I wouldn't know. I never knew I could actually almost forget what I look like without a mirror.

"I was going to say found some friends. You know there are plenty of mermaids your age here. It'd be good for you." *Yeah. No, thanks.* As it turns out, I have very little in common with the merpeople of Pearlestria for the simple fact that the majority have never been to the surface.

"I'm fine, Starla. I've never been much of a people— merpeople?" I fumble over my words. "I'm not much for socializing." *Says the girl who has a close group of friends on land who think you've run away to travel the world with a boy you just met.* Thinking about my friends makes me miss them more than ever. Giselle, my best friend, promised she was pretending to be me to everyone, but I'm not sure how long that can even go on—I'm sure Sapphire, Chloe, and Daisy will realize it soon enough when she can't produce the photos they want. Matty and Logan are probably taking bets on whether or not I'll ditch them all eventually.

"Ava? Did you hear me?" Starla asks. Of course I heard her but my mind wandered to the place I want to be, and I shut off the sound of her voice in my head.

"What? I'm sorry."

"I think you've been here long enough. I'd like to start planning the coupling ceremony for my son."

Oh, that. Before I was transformed into a mermaid, Carter worked on the yacht I had vacationed on with my friends. In a freak accident, I fell overboard and drowned. Carter gave his one opportunity to transform someone into a mermaid to me, giving me his spark along with the bond that came with it.

"Why? Shouldn't that be up to Carter and me?" The coupling ceremony is some weird tradition that's supposed to involve the transformation for a human, but since he did things a bit out of order, it'd be a ceremony to make our coupling official—which is basically marriage in the mer world. A marriage I'm not even close to being ready for. Carter understands. He's lived on the land. Merpeople traditions mean nothing to him, but for Starla, his mom, they mean a whole lot.

Her brows scrunch. "This is important, Ava. How will you ever fit in if you don't at least try to pretend you care about our traditions?"

"I don't care about fitting in. I care about getting the control I need to stay on land so I don't have to live here. I don't even see how that's possible if I can't have my sea stone ring back. How am I supposed to practice?" I flop back, flicking my tail hard enough that she has to swim to stay next to me. The sudden current widens her eyes, but she doesn't project to me the thoughts clearly written on her face for me to decipher. She just flicks her tail harder to stay close enough. Always too close for comfort.

If it weren't for Starla, who stole the sea stone ring right off my finger, forcing me into a permanent mermaid form, I'd probably have gotten the hang of not transforming at random. Carter and I had managed to convince my parents that traveling before college would be good for me. We were going to find somewhere I wouldn't have to worry about being seen by someone I know. We had everything worked out and the means to do so. But Starla wouldn't hear it. All she cares about is turning me into the perfect mermaid bride despite her own self living among humans most of the time.

"It's not about practicing, Ava. It's about knowing who you are and where you belong. You have to be anchored to the ocean before you can live on the land as my husband and I do. Being born a human makes things a little harder. Your feelings are all over the place. Your heart and mind have to be in agreement at all times. It's something that will happen eventually. Give it a few years."

Years? I don't have that kind of time. I have a human family waiting for me to come home before I leave for college in the fall.

"Whatever you say, Starla." I swim from the sand to meet her eyes dead on. "My heart and mind are in perfect agreement.

Neither wants to be trapped behind these walls. For one, I feel like I'm in a tank. And two, how can I be grounded to the ocean if I can't even enjoy a good swim?"

"You want more freedom," she says, confirming what I've wanted all along.

"Is that so hard to believe? I can't even swim without strangers watching me, some even stalking my every move. You tell me to make friends, but no one even attempts to talk to me here. They treat me like an outsider. Like I'm here for their amusement." What makes it even worse is I can't hear the whispers. I can assume they talk about me telepathically. It's easy enough to cut people out of our mental conversations. "You want to plan the coupling ceremony, but for what? No one would come."

She twists her lips to the side, sending her voice into my mind. "Everyone would come, including King Attilonious, since this is his home colony. And to be fair, you don't look approachable with the scowl you constantly wear—" She twirls her finger at my chest. "And the bikini top is a constant reminder of your difference. If you're really uncomfortable with your body, I could fashion you something that doesn't make you stand out in a crowd."

Heat rises into my cheeks. Carter always found it funny I wore half my bikini, but he never bothered me about it. While some mermaids here choose not to cover up, some still do for fashion, I guess—like Starla. She wears a grass woven, strapless bra, and while it doesn't look out of place, it looks uncomfortable. My bikini top is like a baby blanket. I'd feel lost without it.

"Thanks, but no. I'm fine." I hate that I'm having this conversation at all. "And don't you think it'd be kind of weird to invite the king...or anyone else for that matter? Can't it be a private ceremony?"

For this being the king's home colony, I've never actually seen the merman. He feels more like the king in a fairytale and not the actual ruler of the seas that contain me. It's his laws and traditions that put me here. I'm not so sure I could even force a smile.

"I'm starting to think you don't want to be with my son at all," she says, her nose crinkling.

I roll my eyes. "Can you stop?" I don't have to prove anything to her. "If planning the stupid ceremony is so important to you, then do it, but I'm not going to pretend like I want this now. I'm only eighteen."

"Which is the perfect age."

I rub my hands across my face. For living on land most of the time, she really doesn't understand what I'm going through. "You're impossible. I don't even know why you're pushing for this. I know how much I bother you. Why would you even want to claim me as your family?"

Her forehead furrows with a frown. "Ava, you *are* my family. You're my daughter now, and I care about you immensely. If I didn't, I wouldn't have fought so hard to make sure you'd survive in this world. I wouldn't be here checking to make sure you're okay. I wouldn't worry about you fitting in."

Ugh. How can I even respond to that? She infuriates me one second and then makes me feel guilty the next. Sorrow washes over me as I think about my own mom on land. Isn't this something she should be included in? I never imagined going through any of my big life stages without my parents. *It's only a coupling as merpeople. It's not marriage in the human sense. You'll manage. Do what makes life easier.*

I close my eyes for a moment. "I'll try harder, okay?"

She smiles. "And I promise to allow you to have more freedom. But it has to be supervised by either me or Carter. I can't allow you to leave the colony on your own."

It's better than nothing, I suppose. I won't be asking Starla anytime soon, but Carter will be thrilled to be able to take me out of here.

Pulling me against her, Starla hugs me, petting my floating hair down to my back. She leans away with a smile before hooking her arm through mine. For the first time in over a month, I don't want to strangle her with kelp. I never would, but I have imagined doing so a dozen times.

"Thanks. You don't know how happy this makes me." Officially coupling with Carter isn't the worst thing in the world. Our bond is deep-seated and irrevocable anyway. We share a life, a heart—everything—split between our two bodies.

She guides me along. "Good. Your happiness is important to me, too."

I lounge on a kelp-wound rock in the corner of our small living room. The pearlescent walls shimmer through the bubbly current that drifts in from the cutouts in our walls. A few bright orange and white clown fish dart through the colorful coral lined perimeter that makes the space feel less empty. Without the need of furniture or the luxuries that come from the human world, there's not much I can do to make this home-like. I took advantage of having everything at my fingertips as a human so adjusting to a simple life hasn't been pleasant. It's been downright maddening sometimes, especially knowing the human world above us goes on without me.

"Ava," Carter calls into my mind before I see him drift through the archway. "I'm back."

I swim through the water and tackle him before he even has the chance to clear the entryway. We spin together, flying to the sandy yard in front of our underwater house. He lands on his back with me on his chest, and I lean down and shower him with kisses.

"You must've had a good day," he says into my mind, sliding his arms around me, pulling me closer to kiss me deeply, sending chills over my skin. His happiness drifts over me, extinguishing the despair I cling to in the lonely moments when he's gone.

I'd never admit it to Carter, but I feel utterly pathetic my life has resorted to me constantly waiting on him to return. He's basically my sole form of entertainment, and it's something I never want to get used to. The ocean stripped me of my identity, of my ability to do things for me. My sole existence shouldn't be for a boy no matter if I'm in love with him.

But if I told Carter, he'd hold onto the guilt I think he's finally let go of about transforming me. Just because I'm miserable doesn't mean he has to be. It was my devastating mistake that put us in this position.

"It was the same as usual, but I've missed you," I say, smiling against his lips. I don't have to fake it with Carter. My smile comes easy enough the moment I see his jewel-like eyes holding me in their intensity. "I thought you might've decided to stay on land."

His smile fades, a darkness flourishing in him like a sudden storm on the horizon, a reminder he can see past my smile into my mind. He knows this life isn't for me—for either of us. "Never without you."

"I'm teasing." Mostly.

Flicking his tail, he propels us from the sandy floor and carries me with him back inside our home. He swims with me in his arms through the quaint living area to the bedroom before setting me on a bed of woven kelp. The sand is soft enough beneath us that we don't need much more, and I'd be comfortable in Carter's arms regardless.

The vibration created by his moans against my lips ignites shivers through me. His fingers trail down my sides until they graze the backside of my tail. Pulling me closer, he presses against me, sending me images from his day, including images I've waited over a week to see.

He finally made it to the surface to check on my family,

and through his eyes, I take in the scenery in front of my house, a remodeled Victorian, with my mom sweeping the sand off the patio. After that, another image floats into my mind of Giselle's smiling face as she uses my phone to snap a photo of Carter.

A bout of envy sneaks into my heart at the sight—I would give anything to hang out with my best friend. It sucks that Carter gets to and I don't.

He eases away to peer into my eyes. "You're upset," he says after a moment.

I shift my gaze away. "I'm sorry. It just doesn't seem fair I'm always down here. That I have to accept a fate under the water and you can still go to the shore."

His eyebrows knit together. "I'll stop if you want me to. I don't have to go."

"No, I'd never ask that of you. I just miss home is all." This is the reason I try to hide my feelings the best I can. Carter, while he loves the land, would give it up in a heartbeat. He was born in the water after all. This isn't new to him. But if he did stop going to the surface, I'd have no one to watch over my family, and Giselle would have a harder time keeping my disappearance into the sea a secret.

Reaching around, Carter pulls his waterproof bag from the floor beside us. "I brought you some things."

My sadness melts into excitement. This is one of the better things about him returning to shore. I still haven't gotten used to a mermaid diet, and I'll spend days without eating, because I can't get up the nerve to tear into the freshest form of sushi.

Carter did manage to get me to try some seaweed, which was basically like chewing on a slimy salt rope with a hint of lettuce. I couldn't exactly survive on the stuff.

Rummaging through the bag, he pulls out a variety of fruits and vegetables in a few separate plastic pouches. The water is cool enough to keep them for a couple days so I don't have to gorge myself. In another, I find some deli meats and cheese without bread or crackers since those turn to mush the moment they hit the water. As long as I eat them quick enough, everything just tastes a little like the ocean.

He hands me another bag with a broken chocolate bar, and I grin, shaking it in my hands. I never knew I could miss so many things until I no longer had them. The final baggie he gives me contains a few photos of Giselle standing in front of a white wood condo on the shore of a beach. On the back of one of the pictures, she wrote, *Home, Sweet Home. Three bedrooms, two baths, walk-in closets, beach front. Our home for college.*

My eyes widen as I look at Carter. "Carter, you didn't give her hope I'd be home for college did you?"

He laces his fingers through mine. "She holds her own hope, Ava. She said even if you couldn't live there, she wanted you to have a place to stay for when we can return."

If I could cry freely without the water interference, tears would be running down my cheeks. Giselle and I had plans—we were going to rent a house while going to college at UCSD. It was supposed to be the time of our lives. And now, she's still moving forward with the plans without me. The last thing I want is for her to be alone, holding out for something that most likely won't happen anytime soon, if ever.

"You have to tell her the odds are slim," I say.

He shakes his head. "I'm not going to burst her plans when we don't even know that. Maybe we'll get out of here sooner than you think. I've—"

"Carter, Ava? I'm home." The sound of Starla's voice cuts through our minds. At least she can't hear anything unless we direct our thoughts to her. It's a lot of fun having our own conversations in front of her without her even knowing what's on our minds.

Starla stops in the archway to our room. When she sees us lying together on the small bed, she smiles. "I see you've told Carter already."

What? I think for a moment. Oh, crap. The coupling ceremony.

Carter shifts his gaze to mine, keeping a straight face. He sends his thoughts only to me. "Told me what?"

I bare my lower teeth in an awkward smile. "I might've agreed to the coupling ceremony."

He blinks in surprise before a smile crosses his face. "You what?"

"Yeah," I think to him. "Looks like this is going to be official."

2

MEET THE FAMILY

STARLA GRINS AT THE SMILE on her son's face. It's the same one he saves just for me, the one where he's all dimples and squinty eyes—all the happiness in the world lighting his face. It's the one that makes my heart race, makes me forget that the world still spins outside the two of us.

But now, the smile feels different.

Carter laces his fingers through mine, lightly squeezing my hand. "I'm assuming you've agreed to plan the ceremony?" Carter asks his mom.

"It's my job as your mother. Your father will be thrilled—

the rest of the family, too," she says. "Everyone's been dying to meet you, Ava."

I shift my eyes to my glittering scales. I knew Carter had other family down here, but I have yet to meet anyone personally. I haven't wanted to for the simple fact I don't want to learn to like it in Pearlestria like Starla hopes. Not to mention how awkward it is.

"Then why haven't they come by?" It's a simple enough question. Starla's always pushing me to socialize, but no one has ever dropped by. That is, unless this little prison of mine doesn't accept visitors.

Her smile falters. "You're not exactly approachable, Ava."

"Mom!" Carter snaps.

Oh, great. Another fight. It's all too often Carter gets into it with his mom over me. It mostly ends with him sending her away.

I touch his hand. "Carter, it's okay. She's right." I only say it to diffuse the situation. Carter is fiercely protective of me, and I sort of feel bad watching as Starla's eyes widen, looking like two giant saucers the same color as the ocean around us—the same color as Carter's eyes.

"She's far from right, Ava," he thinks only to me.

"Please," I whisper in his mind. "Not tonight."

He frowns in defeat, but he doesn't argue. Instead, he says, "Ava's doing the best she can. If it would make you feel better, I'll take her to meet some of the family."

Starla's smile returns. "What a wonderful idea! You two

should go out this evening instead of staying home like always."

I can't stop the frown from pulling my lips down. "I don't know..."

"What if I allow Carter to take you for a swim after? Would you do it then? You really don't want to show up to your coupling ceremony and know no one." She's bribing me. Not because she wants me to make friends but because of the coupling ceremony. Everything constantly revolves around the mer-traditions and ways. I should know this by now.

"Outside of the walls?" I ask. She did promise earlier. I just didn't think she'd allow Carter to be the first one to take me.

She nods. "And I trust you not to do anything stupid or dangerous."

I roll my eyes. "I really had my heart set on breaching in front of some tour boats."

Carter laughs while pulling me from our bed. "She'll be on her best behavior." As we swim past Starla, Carter stops to kiss her cheek. "Don't wait up for us."

When we exit the house, I can't stop the fear from slowing me down. Meeting people has never been hard for me before, and the old me would've never stayed home so much, but this is different. Who knows what the other mers think about me. Starla already made it clear I don't fit in.

It takes Carter a moment to realize he's the only reason I'm moving. I float behind him like a balloon tied to his wrist. He swims in a circle around me, causing me to spin in a small whirlpool. The fast movement makes me laugh until he catches me in his arms. The gesture is something he does when he's unsure what to do with himself...or me for that matter.

"You're nervous." He doesn't have to ask. My fingers tremble against his chest.

"They're going to think I'm weird," I say.

"Why do you say that?"

"Because I'm wearing a bikini top." I still can't get over Starla's remark from earlier about standing out.

"Well, you know I won't complain if you take it off," he says with a grin.

My cheeks flush, and I slap my palms against the hard muscles of his chest. "You're so not helping."

He wraps me in his arms. "I just want you to do what makes you comfortable. No one will say anything about your top. They all know you're human-born. If anything, they probably wish they had something like it. Why do you think some mermaids create tops? The human world is fascinating."

"Your mom said—"

"My mom says a lot of things, Aves. You know this. Don't let her get to you."

I sigh, blowing out a small bubble. "She already has."

Sadness crinkles his eyes in the corners, but he doesn't say anything. Instead, he flicks his tail, propelling us toward the center of the colony where it's busy with life. Watching the merpeople feels as scary as it was to watch the ocean after my sister, Bailey, was swept away years ago. I can't put my finger on why it's so scary to immerse myself in the world I'm clearly now a part of, but it might have to do with the fact that I didn't choose to be here.

When we reach the main stretch of houses, I say, "You should probably let me swim or they might think you're forcing me to socialize against my will."

The seriousness in his eyes fades as he half smiles. "I like holding you in my arms. Plus, I'm afraid you might swim away if I don't."

I laugh, tilting my head forward until my blond hair floats between us like a veil. "Okay, you might be right, but you can hold my hand."

Reluctantly, he releases me to only twine his fingers through mine. We don't swim long before Carter slows in front of a house twice the size of ours that looks to have been carved out of a huge, glittering boulder. The entrance sits halfway up the dome shape through what looks like a porthole on a ship.

Carter stops just before entering. "My grandma lives here. But I have to warn you, so does my—"

"Carter, my boy!" A deep, familiar voice reverberates through my head, and I recognize the merman before I even see him. "You finally brought Ava."

Anger snakes through my mind when a merman with long, dark hair pops his head through the hole. It's one of the merpeople who helped Starla drag me away from the shore. And I can't help the hate I feel for him. I wish Carter had brought me anywhere but here.

Carter side glances me. "Easy, Ava. He was acting under

my mom's authority when she asked for help. Uncle Tobias isn't a bad man," he says only to me. He turns his gaze to the merman. "I figured it was time Ava met our family. My mom tell you about the coupling ceremony yet?"

The merman, Tobias, grins. "She spent all afternoon here talking about it."

Carter pulls me up toward the entrance to the dome house. Tobias pops back in, giving us room to enter. My mouth falls agape at the sight before me. Decorative stones line the walls and ceiling in a kaleidoscope of colors, swirling in an intricate pattern that looks like a sunset on the water. Faint light trickles in through the circular cutout in the middle of the ceiling. Large rocks create partitions throughout the home, so that even though it's divided into rooms, each one has a view of the magnificent walls. The sandy floor appears pink from the reflection of the deep red stones, which resemble rubies. Who knows? Maybe that's what they are.

Large flat rocks, covered in the softest looking sea grass, form a circle in the living area so when you perch on them, you have to face one another. The room is filled with all sorts of interesting things. A gigantic anchor rests near a partition, and next to it is a metal chest with a few vases sitting on top. The steering wheel to a ship hangs out in front of one of the window cutouts, making it so no one can exit that way, and on the floor, half stuck into the sand are various different glass plates. It's like they've scavenged shipwrecks to decorate the place.

I run my fingers over the jeweled wall. "You have an interesting collection," I say to anyone willing to listen.

"Thank you, Ava," Tobias says. "Humans are such interesting creatures. The pieces always give me something to talk about when we have visitors."

I blink a few times at his comment but don't respond. He doesn't consider me human. As far as he's concerned, I'm a mermaid—which is hard to forget with my tail.

"Carter? Is that Ava with you?" A mermaid rises from behind the partition behind the anchor. Her golden brown hair, streaked with blue, is tied in a long braid that stops halfway down her tail. Her blue eyes, the same as Carter's, crinkle in the corners. Though her skin is relatively smooth, I can tell she's probably older than Starla with the way she carries herself in such wise confidence. A woman who has probably seen all that the ocean has to offer.

"Yes, Grandmer," Carter says, tugging me along with him. "Ava was finally feeling up to visiting."

The mermaid swims closer and pulls me away from Carter, wrapping her slender arms around me. I'm so surprised by the gesture that I don't hug her back. Instead, I force myself to smile when she releases me.

"Well, I'm delighted to meet you, Ava. Are you two hungry?" she asks, swimming back. "Tobias was about to bring in some dinner."

My stomach lurches at the thought. "No, thank you. Carter might be hungry, though."

He kisses my cheek. "Starved."

"Starla mentioned your difficulty transitioning your diet, Ava," Grandmer says.

Great. I'm about to get another speech about how I need to get over my food aversion, because this is the mermaid life.

"She's making progress," Carter says, interjecting.

"I hate it all," I say, shrugging. "Don't get me wrong. I like some fish but not raw. Even if I did like raw fish, humans prepare it differently. I'd rather starve than eat something that's trying to swim away from me."

Grandmer laughs like I've said the funniest thing. "I appreciate your honesty, dear." She motions for me to join Carter on one of the sea grass beds.

Carter wraps his arms around me, pulling me against his chest so I'm sitting on his lap. The one thing I've come to notice is how affectionate merpeople are. And it doesn't bother anyone. Public displays of affection are so common that people notice if a couple isn't at least holding hands.

"Thanks for not thinking I'm being ridiculous. It's just been really hard on me. I can't do any of the things I loved down here." I don't know why it's so easy to open up to Carter's grandmother, but she just seems to understand.

"What did you like to do?" she asks.

Tobias leans back with his hands behind his head, just listening without interrupting.

"I like to bake," I say. "Can't exactly do that here. My best friend isn't here either. We'd always hang out."

Tobias waves his hand at Carter. "Carter's right there."

"Carter's my boyfriend," I say.

Tobias raises his eyebrows. "But you've coupled."

This gets a laugh from Carter. "Uncle Tobias, relationships work differently on land."

"Is it not normal that I don't call you my best friend?" I think only to Carter.

"It's fine, Ava," he says to me. He turns back to his uncle. "While Ava might be my best friend and mate, it doesn't mean I have to be her best friend."

"But that friendship is over," he says. "You're not a human and those relationships don't matter anymore."

I stare at Carter's uncle, speechless, for what feels like an excruciatingly long moment. How can he even say that? Do merpeople give up their relationships if they choose the land over the sea? Obviously not. If they did, Carter wouldn't be here.

To stop myself from giving him a piece of my mind, I tug away from Carter and swim up toward the exit. This was a bad idea coming here. I should've just forced Carter to let me keep to myself. This merman doesn't even care that he helped Starla rip me from my life. He thinks everything is all good.

Well, it's not.

"I'm sorry. It was nice meeting you, but I have to go." Without waiting for a response, I dart from the house to the channel of sand running between the houses. A few mers stare in my direction, but I don't meet their gazes.

Instead, I swim. I swim as fast as I can toward my favorite

place near the boundary wall of Pearlestria. I don't even wait for Carter. I just swim up toward the surface until I can dart over the wall.

And then I'm in the open sea.

3

OUTSIDER

NEARLY FLYING THROUGH THE WATER, I ascend closer to the surface. I have no idea where I am or where I'm going. All I know is I won't feel better unless there's at least a dozen miles between me and Pearlestria. I obviously can't make my way to land, and I'm sure if someone were to find out I rose to the surface, I'd be in trouble because I have no idea what lies above the magical underwater city.

So I remain thirty feet below, just high enough to catch a glimpse of the white moon rising above. The sea glows with its magical light, allowing me to see through the pitch darkness. I doubt any humans would see me if I surfaced now, but I'm already worried I won't ever get my sea stone ring back.

A bale of sea turtles, caught on a current, drifts over me. I startle at the sheer size of them. I had no idea how big the creatures were, and they're at least half my size. I swerve in and out of the turtles, taking in how graceful they look as they move together. After following them for a few good minutes, I dip back down deeper.

A massive coral reef extends the bottom of the ocean the shallower the water becomes. From my place, it glows in vibrant colors, and all sorts of animals move around the fascinating reef. A few black tip reef sharks swim toward the surface, not straying far from where I catch them feeding on a school of gray fish. One of the sharks propels in my direction, swimming right toward me, but it darts around me at the last second to head back toward the reef.

I float in the water, hovering with the mild current. My hands circle at my sides, and my blond hair drifts around me. A spiky, striped fish swims near my head, tangling with my hair. I shake my head as it tries to yank free, but it ends up getting stuck worse.

After a minute of it pulling and tangling my hair, I finally wrap my hands around it to stop it from trying to rip free.

"Need help?" Carter slips up next to me, smirking as he watches me struggle to free the fish.

I shake my head not only to respond to him, but to spread my hair through the water. "I'm fine."

"You don't look fine."

I slide my fingers through the hair around the fish. "I don't need help, okay?"

I sink lower until my tail smacks against the sand. Carter continues to smile at me, flashing his dimples. Just watching him watch me struggle infuriates me. I don't want his help, but he doesn't have to mock me. I'm plenty capable of managing things on my own.

After another minute of tug of war with the pesky fish, I throw my hands out and give up. The fish swims in circles around my head, tightening its hold. Crossing my arms, I fall back to the sand, lying on my hair, shortening it enough that the fish can't pull it far. Carter silently swims closer before easing onto the sand above my head.

In one quick motion, he jabs the fish with his sharp nails, killing it right in front of my face. He unwraps my hair from the poor dead fish and then proceeds to peel the skin away and takes a bite right from it.

I cringe at his unexpected actions. "What are you doing?" My voice rises in my mind. His actions shouldn't bother me. This is how things are for us now, and eating the freshest fish is part of the merpeople diets, but it's like he's purposefully reminding me.

"What does it look like?"

"You killed it."

"I had to. I couldn't get it otherwise unless I cut your hair. Plus, it's not like I'm wasting it." Carter uses his nail to cut off a square of meat. He holds it in front of my face. "Want to try it?"

I squirm away, knocking his hand from my face. "You know I don't."

I can't take my eyes off him as he carves away at the weird fish, popping small bites into his mouth. It's ten times better than how Starla eats, just biting the fish—most of the time while it's still moving—but the thought still grosses me out.

"That's fine. More for me." He continues to eat right over my head.

I sit up, but I don't swim away from him. My tail thuds against the ocean floor, and I continue to watch him pick apart his catch—well, technically my catch. When Carter finishes, he feeds the rest of the dead fish to one of the black tip reef sharks that eats it directly from his hand like a dog getting scraps at the dinner table. The shark circles us, expecting more, but Carter waves his hand, shooing it away.

Carter turns his gaze from the shark to me. He props his body on his arms, resting his palms against the sand. His blue eyes sparkle in the glowing ocean, and he doesn't say anything as he watches me.

I know he's waiting for me to say something first. He always does when I'm in one of my moods. And it drives me crazy how calm he is when all I want to do is yell and scream my frustration.

"Are you not going to ask me why I ran out of your grandma's?" I ask after a moment. I'd rather him drag the information out of me. It's easier to voice my thoughts that way.

"Nope. I know you well enough to know why, Ava," he says.

I sink my fingers into the soft sand. "It's just—I can't get used to the social norms and customs. And it makes me feel awful. Am I hurting you, Carter? Does it bother you that I only consider Giselle my best friend? People are going to think I'm the crappiest mate in the world. Maybe—" I sigh. "Am I really the *one*? Your *one*. You deserve better than—" The words are more difficult to form than I expect. I pull my hands from the sand and wave them in front of me. "You deserve better than me."

He doesn't say anything for a long while. "You're having doubts about the ceremony."

"It's just—your mom was pestering me. She made me feel like I was a huge disappointment to you. And I think I am."

The face he gives me, pouty lips and pinched brows—a look of complete despair—nearly causes my undoing. He wears the hurt of my words for me to see and take in unlike his usually stoic expression when I complain about how tough things are. It's enough to tighten my chest, squeezing at my heart that beats in sync with his.

"Ava." The sound of my name coming from him into my mind sits heavy on my very being. "You mean everything to me. *Everything*. I don't give a damn what my mom thinks or what anyone else thinks. But I do care what you think, and hearing you say that I deserve better than you kills me. There is absolutely no one better in the world than you are for me."

"I'm sorry," I whisper into his mind. "I feel like I'm failing all of this—because I want to fail."

"And that's okay. We're not staying here forever."

"It feels like it."

"I swear to you, Ava. I'll figure out how to get you back to shore, even if it means I have to give you my ring to do so." He holds the chain that carries his sea stone ring in front of my face.

"That would mean..."

"It's the worst case scenario."

I bury my face against his chest. I couldn't imagine returning to land to only leave Carter behind in the sea. He doesn't have to tell me he'd do it now if he thought we could get away with it—if he knew I could manage on my own without him. But I'm not even confident in myself to push for such a thing. Not to mention how awful the idea of returning to land without Carter makes me feel, like I'd be leaving half my heart in the ocean. It'd be enough to tear me apart. It'd probably make it impossible to get my heart and mind to agree, not when Carter would be bound to the sea.

"I can't leave you," I finally say. "I don't think I could even if I wanted to."

He holds me tighter. "I don't want you to leave me, but if that's what it takes to fix things. I'll do anything for you, I'd—"

"I said I'm not leaving you," I say, cutting him off.

Bringing his lips to mine, he sends a dozen images flashing

into my head. Along with his thoughts of me comes a wave of emotion. Emotion that swirls and mingles with my own. Feelings I've known were inside him all along, but it's different when he projects them directly to me. He's never done it before, and the sheer warmth of our bond as mates pushes away the cold lingering in my once human bones despite having already adjusted to the freezing waters.

"Whoa." My voice barely sounds like a whisper in my own mind. "That was—" I can't even come up with words to describe what that was or how that felt for me.

"I'm sorry. I didn't mean to do that," he whispers. "I already know your own feelings are enough for you to handle."

"You can feel me?"

"Sometimes"

"I'm sorry."

He laughs in the water, pushing tiny bubbles from his lips that float up toward the surface. "Don't apologize. It's mostly the good stuff...well, except today."

Twining my fingers with his, I hold his hands, bringing them up to my mouth so I can kiss his knuckles. I can just imagine the feelings I sent into him, especially at his grandma's house. No wonder he always knows what to say to me in moments like those.

"Is there anything I can do to stop that?" I ask.

He shrugs. "Maybe try not to let my mom put doubt in your mind about me again."

I purse my lips. "That's impossible."

Frowning, he says, "Then things are going to have to change."

"What do you mean?"

He pulls me off the ground with him. "Come on. Let's head back. You'll see."

If an argument could heat the water, our living room would be boiling right about now. I hunker in the corner of the room as Starla and Carter have a mind shouting match with each other. To me, it's mostly random words thrown in here and there because they're directing their heated thoughts at each other, leaving me mostly out of it, but they're both so angry that some things slip through.

"This is *my* house, and I want you out!" Carter's voice trickles through my mind.

My eyes bulge, hearing the words. I didn't know this place belonged to Carter. I had assumed it was Starla and Mateo's, and that we were just staying here for the time being.

"You're being unreasonable!" Starla flings out her arms.

"Unreasonable? You're jeopardizing my life with my mate!" Carter's eyes flicker to mine before he reins his voice in so I can't hear the next words directed at his mom.

She whips her head to look at me, but Carter swims between us, blocking her view. His towering form is like the perfect protective wall, sparing me from whatever she was about to aim at me.

All these weeks, I knew Carter had been on the outs with

his mom. I just assumed we didn't have a choice. She told me she was the one who was supposed to help me adjust. It's why she left her home on the land with Mateo.

"Ava," Starla says to me even though I can't see her past Carter. "Please, you have to say something. He listens to you. I know I might've said things that hurt you, but it wasn't my intention. I'm just trying to help. How can you fit in if you don't know that you're acting like an outsider?"

I frown. "That's because I am an outsider. I agreed to the coupling ceremony to make you happy. Isn't that enough?"

Carter turns to peer at me from over his shoulder. He heard what I tried to send only to Starla, but she left me flustered and I usually always include Carter in my thoughts. His fuming expression melts to one of concern, but just as quickly as it came, it disappears. "Is that true, Aves?"

I don't respond. I can't. Because it is the truth. At least it was when I agreed to it with Starla. At the time, I didn't know how happy it'd make Carter. He never made it seem like a big deal that I didn't want to participate in what I thought was a silly tradition. But now, I can tell it was a façade. Carter is a merman after all. He might've adapted to the land, but he still follows the rules of the sea.

Pushing from the floor, I swim the few feet to Carter and wrap my arms around his taut shoulders, resting my chin on the crook of his neck. He relaxes under my touch, running his hands down my back until he tightens his grip around my waist.

"Ava?" he asks just to me because I still don't answer.

"It's true," I finally say. "But it doesn't matter. I see how happy the idea makes you."

I expect him to smile, but he doesn't. He blinks a few times, like he's trying to process my words. The two of us just float together in silence for a long while. Starla doesn't speak either, or if she does, I can't hear her. The anger they shared has fizzled out, and I swear the water cools around me.

Lowering his shoulders, he turns his gaze back to his mom. "Do you think you could stay with Grandmer?"

She silently nods and swims toward the exit.

"Hey, Mom," Carter says before she can leave.

"Yes, son?"

"Can you let everyone you've already told know that the coupling ceremony is off?"

Her face falls in disbelief, but if she says something, it's not directed at me. She darts from our house without another look, leaving me alone with Carter. My heart thuds in my chest as his words sink in. He just called off the coupling ceremony, which I know is a huge deal. I doubt any merperson has ever done such a thing.

I thought I didn't want to go through with it, but now that I don't have to, I can't stop myself from feeling awful. A part of me already accepted the silly ceremony, and while my relationship with Carter is brand new, I can't even imagine being with anyone else.

Would it be possible to change my mind one day? I'm

young. I never even thought I'd get into a serious relationship until after college. I had questioned if I was good enough for Carter but never the opposite. Carter is perfect for me. His spark lies in my chest. How could I ever be with someone else if it's his heart that beats in sync with mine? If it's his thoughts and memories that I carry in my mind? If it's his life that allowed me to live? I couldn't...could I?

"You know, you lied to me about the coupling ceremony. You said it didn't matter. You said it wasn't a big deal to you," I say, looking into his aqua eyes, trying to figure out what he's thinking before he even says it to me. I wish he'd push his emotions into me again, but even his face remains expressionless though our hearts beat faster than usual and not in a good way.

"It isn't, Ava," he says.

Pulling away from him, I cross my arms. "You're lying again. I saw the look on your face when your mom told you I had agreed. You were so happy."

His eyes soften. "Of course I was happy. The girl of my dreams wanted to officially be mine in the eyes of the merpeople and the ocean."

Confusion settles over me. "So why did you tell your mom to call it off? If it makes you that happy..."

"Because how can I really be happy if I know you only agreed to the coupling ceremony to please my mom? Seriously, Ava. What kind of guy would that make me?" He swims back, putting distance between us. "What were you even thinking?" Hurt lines his words, and I feel even worse.

"I—" What am I even supposed to say? I'd give anything to call Giselle to ask her what I should do.

Had I known any of this—how I'd make him happy just to accidentally devastate him, I'd have never relented to Starla's annoying persistence. But I'm also irritated that Carter wasn't honest. Sure, he says none of this is a big deal, but it clearly is or we wouldn't even be discussing it.

"I'm sorry." It's the only thing I can say. "I just thought going through with the ceremony would make things easier on everyone."

He nods his head once without smiling. "I get it, but that's not what it's about."

"I know, I—"

He cuts me off with a kiss. Locking his hands around my back, he pulls me closer until our bodies are touching completely. His smooth skin radiates warmth through me, and I moan when he slips his tongue in my mouth, gliding it over mine.

"Ava," he says, still kissing me, his voice wrapping around my mind. "If we go through the ceremony, it's going to be because we want to be together for the rest of our lives. It's going to be because you have absolutely no doubt in your mind, and because you want to do it for us—not just me."

He swims back with me clinging to him, guiding me to our bedroom. Gently lowering me to the sandy floor, he lies on top of me with his hands pressed into the kelp bed on both sides of my head.

Slowly pulling away, I lean all the way back to gaze at him.

"Not *if* we go through with it. I do want to go through with it, Carter. I don't envision my future without you. But, I want to be excited about it. Right now, I'm not."

He hugs me, sinking me deeper into the sand. "I promise to change that, Ava. Things are going to change around here."

His certainty should be enough for me not to question it, but I can't stop myself. I purse my lips in a half smile. "Really? How?"

"Well, for starters, my mom's not going to interfere in our relationship anymore." Just hearing that Carter's going to stop Starla from trying to get us to do things her way is enough to make me lock my fingers around Carter's neck to kiss him sweetly.

A thought lingers in my mind though, Starla's own words digging into my soul. Without her, I won't learn what I'm supposed to learn to get out of here to resume my life on shore. "But who'll teach me the mermaid ways? Isn't it against the rules for you to do it?"

"I have an idea, and we'll worry about that later. Right now, I just want to be with you, if that's okay?"

It's more than okay. Smiling, I gaze into his eyes, focusing on intentionally sending all the intensely good emotions rushing through me to him.

His eyes widen, and he leans in to kiss me, but I raise my hand up, pressing it to the spark in his chest to stop him for a second. I might've agreed to the coupling ceremony to get Starla off my back, but I also had agreed to it because I'm in love with Carter—words I've yet to say to him not because I haven't wanted to, but because our love resonates enough that we've never felt the need to do so. But I feel the need in this moment. I've never felt it so desperately.

"I'm in love with you, you know?" I ask.

And I thought agreeing to the coupling ceremony made him happy. The smile he gives me is brighter than the sun reflecting off the crystal clear ocean. His joy and pleasure nearly smother me in all the goodness that he is. They're enough to push away anything negative that was lingering in me.

He kisses me deeply, his skin hot against mine. We lay together, our hearts beating against each other, and I shiver, excitement rushing over my skin. Carter's fingers explore my body, slowly making their way around my back to untie my bikini top. It floats away as he trails kisses down my neck to my collarbone.

His love washes over me, drawing me in. I lose myself in his kisses and desire. I lose myself to him completely.

4

NEWFOUND FREEDOM

CARTER BRUSHES HIS LIPS AGAINST my bare shoulder, holding me from behind. Tingles rush down my tail like a small jolt of electricity courses through me. I moan, turning over, and stretch my arms up before embracing him. Memories from last night linger in my mind, but only the good stuff. The memories that make my heart race and my mouth smile.

"God, you're beautiful," he says, resting his forehead against mine. An image of me lying on the sand under him flashes through my mind when he kisses me. "I could stay here all day if you'd let me."

I grin, sucking in my bottom lip. "You know I would."

Leaning closer, he kisses me again. "Then it's settled."

I laugh, tilting my head back as his lips tickle my jaw and trail to my neck. His fingers grip my waist, pulling closer until my chest presses against his.

"Carter? Ava?" The sound of his mom's voice echoing through my mind forces me to frown. Of course she'd show up now despite everything that happened between us. "Can I come in?"

Carter's jaw twitches as he stiffens. "Give us a minute."

Reluctantly sitting up, Carter peers around the room before he finds my bikini top stuck to the coral under the cutout that's supposed to be a window. He helps me tie it around my neck and back before twining his fingers through mine. I'm tempted to tell him to face her alone, but we're stronger together when it comes to her persistence. She's probably going to try to change his mind about the coupling ceremony.

When we enter the living room, Starla floats outside the archway in our front yard. She holds one arm over her chest, slowly rubbing it up and down her other arm. Her blue eyes line with sadness, and I can't help feeling a tiny bit bad about the tension between us.

"What is it, Mom?" Carter asks without greeting her.

"I thought long and hard about things last night, and I think it's best if I go home for a while. You were right about a lot of things. I'm sorry to have caused either of you pain. I realize that you already have hard feelings toward me, and I had hoped that we could work past them, but staying here isn't helping any. I don't want you to grow to hate me more than you do."

"I don't hate you, Mom," Carter says.

She glances at me, but I don't say anything. I don't do it to be mean, but I just can't find it in me to coddle her with fake feelings after everything she put me through. Not to mention how jealous I am that she can just choose to leave and go back to live her life on land like she wasn't the reason I lost my chance to do so.

"Thanks for being here all these weeks, but you're right. It's best if you return to Dad. I know he has to miss you. I think it'd be better if someone less invested in me were to help Ava adjust as well. She doesn't need your motherly pressure right now." Carter squeezes my fingers.

She frowns. "So, the ceremony is still off?"

He nods. "For now."

"You know the king will be unhappy," she says. "He's been overly generous allowing Ava to take her time, you know."

"And I can deal with that if he has something to say," Carter says.

All hail King Attilonious for claiming to be a kind and fair king when it's his rules that have stolen my life. It's his rules that would be the death of my best friend if anyone were to find out she knows of our kind. It's his stupid rules that want to force me into a ceremony for the sake of fitting in. I couldn't care less about the king's happiness when he has no regard for my own. He shouldn't have anything to do with my relationship to Carter in the first place. I'd never say that to his face, though. If he's anything like I imagine him to be, I'd probably force myself to stay in control of my disdain toward him so he doesn't assure I never see the human world again.

"If there's no changing your mind..." She rubs her hands together.

"There's not."

"Then I guess you know where to find me."

Carter hugs his mom for a long moment, and I can see an exchange of words I can't hear through their gazes when they pull away. Starla reaches out and takes my hand in hers instead of hugging me. I'm glad she doesn't try to because I'm pretty sure I wouldn't allow her the opportunity.

She smiles with sadness in her eyes. "I hope you can find it in your heart to forgive me someday, Ava. This was never how I imagined things would be between us, and I hope they'll change eventually."

"It is what it is," I say. I don't respond about the forgiveness. Petty? Totally. I don't care.

"Please, take care of my son."

I nod. "You know I will."

Starla lets me go and swims away, looking back only once as she reaches the end of the row of houses that lead to the main channel of Pearlestria.

Turning my eyes to Carter, I study him for a moment to decipher his serious expression. I'm sure it can't be easy for him to have this kind of strain on his relationship with his mom. It stressed me out more than a dozen times over the weeks.

"What now?" I ask when he doesn't move from my side.

"I have an idea," he says.

"Okay..."

He pulls me from the house. "Come on. It's going to be fun."

I cling to Carter's back, the world zooming by us at a speed I haven't felt since we had arrived at the merpeople colony. He propels us through the water, swimming away from Pearlestria and the walls that have been my prison. The bright sun shines fifty feet above us, but I swear I can feel its warmth on my skin as the rays sparkle through the clear blue water around us.

"Where are we going?" I ask, my hair flowing behind me from the speed of his swim.

"It's a surprise," he responds, turning his head to peek at me while I rest my chin on his shoulder. He didn't even wait a few minutes after Starla left to return to San Francisco before taking advantage of our newfound freedom away from his mom's ever-present need to control us.

He ascends toward the surface the shallower the water becomes. Through the rippling waves, I see the azure sky reflecting above us, making everything even bluer than it already is. A smile crosses my face, excitement and relief washing through me at the realization of what we're about to do.

"Are you serious?" I ask, nearly trembling in anticipation

against Carter.

"Get ready."

Seconds later, I spit out water and suck in a deep breath of fresh ocean air. Saltwater drips down my face, and I blink as my eyes adjust to the surface light that blinds me for a moment. It's been so long since I've seen or felt the world from above, it's hard looking around. I close my eyes, absorbing the sudden heat of the sun and the feeling of the breeze against my skin. I had almost forgotten how good it feels to be out of the water. My hair sticks to my already drying cheeks, and I push it behind my shoulders.

I float on my back, trying to get out of the water as much as possible. Carter slides his hands under my back and lifts me higher, flicking his tail so we're treading water. The air circles around me, caressing me in a feather light touch that I want to cling onto forever.

Reaching my arms over my head, I stretch out, arching my back. Carter spins me around, sending my hair splaying out in surprising soft tendrils on the wind, and I laugh. Hearing the sound of my voice makes me laugh harder. Who knew such a simple thing could make my heart feel ten times fuller and lighter.

Carter lowers me down, flicking his fin to keep us at the surface. "I've missed your laugh so much, Ava."

I shower him with kisses all while laughing again. "It feels so amazing to use my voice."

He cups my chin in his hand, brushing his lips against

mine for a long while. Kissing him above water is a thousand times better. All my senses feel so much more intense—the sound of his breathing in air, the scent of dry saltwater on his skin with a faint hint of sunscreen, the weight of his body heavier without the buoyancy of the water—everything about him so familiar of our time on land.

"Want to see your house?" he asks after a moment.

I press my lips together, tasting the saltwater more now that I'm not submerged underwater. "I don't know."

While the thought of swimming close to shore to see my house with my own eyes is what I've dreamed about for weeks, the idea depresses me. How can I be so close but unable to transform into my human form to walk the beach? It might be better to just stay right here in the middle of the vast ocean with the sun on my skin and happiness in my heart.

"It's just not the same," I finally add.

"I know it's not, but I want to do something for you—something I haven't been able to manage since your ring was taken." He smiles as he says it, flashing his dimples. The smoothness of his voice wraps around me like a comforting embrace, and I'd probably agree to just about anything he says at this point.

I slowly nod. "What is it?"

He lowers me back into the water. "You'll have to wait and see."

Taking his hand, I swim next to him in the direction I assume is toward Azure Waters. We cut through a school of yellowtails, some of the larger fish bumping against me, and I graze my fingers over their silvery backs. The shallower the water gets, the more we swim under the shadows of the boats off shore.

Fear tickles the back of my mind as we weave in and out of a couple of fishing lines. I slow down when I catch sight of a leopard shark struggling to free itself from the hook of one of the nearby boats. It struggles to swim forward with the line dragging it backward in a tug of war for freedom. Carter glances at me in the water in silent question, and I point to the shark.

He lets go of my hand, and I swim away from him, careful not to catch myself on the other few dozen lines hanging off the medium sized vessel. In one quick motion, I slice my nail across the line hooking the shark and cut it free.

Before I have a chance to do anything, the shark speeds away. Carter propels forward, snatching me around the waist from above me. We fly through the water as one, my arms outstretched in front of me, quickly catching up to the shark. Carter dives down, weaving us through a kelp forest, after the fleeing shark.

Carter releases me, bolting ahead to carefully hold the shark. I expect it to put up a fight and thrash, but it just rests in Carter's arms as he slowly turns it over onto its back. It reminds me of a puppy with how it lets Carter stroke its belly, nothing like the scary white sharks you see trying to devour unsuspecting humans in the movies. This one isn't even half my size.

"I need you to unhook the line," Carter says, sending the thought into my mind.

Nodding, I swim closer, peering closely at the metal circle hook sticking from the side of the shark's mouth. The shark's tough skin makes it difficult to slide the hook free, and I frown, afraid of causing damage.

"Use your nails," Carter says after a minute.

My nails are tough, but not tough enough to cut through the metal, so instead, I make a tiny cut near the hook and slide it free. The shark isn't fazed by the tiny incision, and the moment Carter rights it and loosens his hold, it swims off toward the sandy bottom.

He takes the hook from me and hangs it from his necklace instead of dropping it into the current.

Looking around once more, he laces his fingers through mine and pulls me through the kelp forest and back to where the boats block out the sun on the surface. This time, he guides me away from them and toward the shallows that lead to the shore.

"You can't tell anyone about the shark, okay?" he says into my mind, swimming next to me. "It's against the king's law to meddle with human affairs, especially in what he considers their territory. He considers all the coastlines to be part of the human world, so we're only ever to observe. Fisherman would notice if we started cutting all their lines."

"Is there a list of laws or something?" I ask. I feel like I should attend some sort of mermaid school for this information.

"That'd make it easier, wouldn't it? The king, while

mighty, also is forgiving. It's why he's ruled all the oceans for over a hundred and fifty years without an uprising."

"What? You never told me we live longer," I say.

He shrugs. "That's if we plan to live in the sea. We age at a human rate on the land. My parents plan to return to the sea at the end of their human lives."

"We can do that?"

"If that's what you want."

Maybe by then, it wouldn't be so hard to let go. It's a strange thought to even consider.

He smiles, watching me process the information. "We have a long time to consider it, Ava. Our whole human lives."

He's right. I need to focus on the present and not the future.

The water grows warm the closer we get to shore, and I search around the familiar shoreline. Carter slows down when we near some huge black rocks—rocks I never thought I could be so happy to see—and he stops in the water, staying just below the surface.

"If I ask you to wait here, would you?" He pulls my hand to his lips and kisses my knuckles.

"Where are you going?"

"It's a surprise."

I narrow my eyes while smiling. "I guess I can."

Carter kisses my cheek before he takes off, disappearing into the surf. Sinking to the bottom, I relax on the sand, curling my tail to my chest. There's no way I'm going to break the surface now without Carter, especially not this close to home.

A few fish swim by, but the water remains pretty empty around me. Waiting here is excruciating. I propel myself from the floor after what feels like forever and swim a few anxious circles like I'm stuck in a tank.

Come on, Carter. Whatever he's doing is taking longer than I expected it to, and I'm starting to wonder if he's ever going to come back. I descend a few feet and tilt my head up to gaze at the surface only a few feet above me.

That's when I see them. Two people share a surfboard, fighting against the bubbling waves about thirty feet away. All I see are four legs as one person straddles the board and the other kicks behind it. The surprise of seeing them sends me swimming backward and deeper into the water. We're pretty far from shore, too far to catch the swells that the surfers of Azure Waters love.

Just when I'm about to bolt, the surfer straddling the board swings its leg over to sit sideways before jumping off the board to dip under. From this distance, I can tell it's a brunette girl with perfectly tan skin but not much more than that.

She spins in the water once, like she's searching for something, and then stops when she faces me. She shouldn't be able to see me as I am, but I still worry. Maybe I'll scare her away. Instead of trying to get away, the girl lifts her hand and waves in my direction. The only thing I can think to do is flee.

5

DOUBLE LIFE

CARTER WAS CRAZY FOR BRINGING me near the shore while it's still daylight. Not only is he risking my safety, he's risking the safety of the poor humans. Unlike him, I can't just transform into a human to wait.

And I'm pretty sure the surfer saw me—the real me. If someone from Pearlestria followed us, they would probably drown the person. The only reason I got away with accidentally flashing my fin to Giselle before was because Carter told his parents it was a stranger, and it was already after the fact. Now, it's easy enough to get rid of my spectator. The ocean is a dangerous place. Drowning happens. I could never go through with it, though.

"Ava?" Carter's voice drifts into my mind. "Where are you? Come back to the rocks."

"I can't. Someone saw me. This was a terrible idea."

"Just come back. It's safe."

Reluctantly, I swim back toward where the surfer girl had spotted me. Carter waits for me underwater. His glittering teal tail sparkles in the light penetrating through the sea. The spark in his chest glows brightly, drawing me in, and there's no sign of the surfers.

Meeting me halfway, he hooks his arm around my waist. He studies me with his brows knitted together like my thoughts project from my eyes for him to see. My bottom lip quivers, fear still gripping me in a hold that makes me want to flee. Bringing his hand to my face, he brushes his index finger over my lips. Then, he hugs me.

His lips brush my ear as he holds me. "Ava, it's okay. You're safe. A stranger didn't spot you." His voice is utterly certain in my mind.

"The surfer waved."

"What else would you expect from Giselle? She can see you as you are, you know, because she knows of our secret."

His words swirl through my mind, sending my heart racing. My eyes widen when he nods his head, and I stare at him in disbelief. I can't believe he just told me the surfer I spotted was my best friend. I was too scared to recognize her—Carter for that matter.

"Are you crazy?" I ask. "You're jeopardizing my best friend." All I can think about is how someone might find out that Giselle knows our secret. I could never forgive myself if she got hurt or worse. I'd probably end up the same because there's no way I'd ever allow that to happen.

Carter's smirking face melts into a frown. I guess this wasn't the reaction he was expecting from me. It's obvious he had hoped to make my day, to make me feel better after all these weeks, and I'm grateful he tried, but at the same time I'm upset.

"I've taken precautions. I swam the area to make sure it was safe. Please, trust me when I say it's safe. I'd never do anything to put Giselle in danger." He tries to take my hands, but I cross my arms over my chest instead.

"But this *does* put her in danger. I worry enough as it is about you visiting her on land. I'd rather just go home and hope for the day I can return to land with my legs. I'd rather wait years to see her safely than risk everything." The words kill me to say. I feel physically sick as they leave my mind. Because I want so badly to see her, to hear her voice, to talk to her about everything. But I can't.

I turn away from Carter. "Can you tell her I'm sorry, but I can't see her?"

Carter grabs my shoulder, spinning me around in the water. "No. You tell her yourself, Ava."

"What?"

"I said tell her yourself," he repeats. "Because I know you'll regret it if you don't. I know you're trying to do the right thing by her, but I can't stand to see and feel you so sad all the time. Giselle is willing to take the risk. If she wants to visit with you, then let her. It's not only yourself you're hurting."

"Carter..."

His forehead wrinkles as he stands his ground. "Ava, please. I'm trying my best to do right by you. I don't ever push you, and I always let you have the final say. But this—" He waves his hand behind him. "I'm making you do. So, you can either go tell your best friend you don't want to see her, or we can both leave together right now and leave her waiting."

Anger sneaks up on me, and I narrow my eyes. Heat crawls up my neck, my hands shaking as I curl them into fists. I can't abandon Giselle while she waits on the rocks so far from shore. She could get hurt paddling back to the beach. Carter knows this.

"You can't be serious," I say. He has to be bluffing. I don't understand why he's doing this. If something happened to Giselle, I'd blame him. I'm not sure I could ever forgive him, either. The fact that Carter is definitely aware of that makes this even worse. His confidence is the only thing that makes me swim past him in Giselle's direction. He's betting on our relationship that everything will be fine—and I know how important I am to him. It still pisses me off, though. I've never been this angry at him before.

I spin to face him, sensing him right behind me. Pressing

my hands to his chest, I stop him in his tracks. "Uh-uh. You stay here and keep watch."

He clenches his teeth, his jaw twitching in his annoyance. "Ava it's—"

"I *said* stay here." With my words, I flip in the water and flick my tail to swim back to the rocks where Giselle waits for me.

The surf near the rocks is empty, and bubbles drift through the water as waves crash against the rocks. I peer at the surface for a moment before I ascend and spit out water to take a breath. Giselle grins as she perches on the back side of the biggest rock, the spot where no one can see her from the shore. Her surfboard sits next to her, and she offers out her hand to me.

I don't take it.

She frowns. "You look mad as hell."

She knows me all too well. We've grown up together. Giselle can read me as good as, if not better than, Carter, just like I can read her. Concern crosses her face, and I know she knows why I'm pissed without me even having to say anything.

"Of course I'm pissed off!" My voice sounds out through the air louder than I expect it to. "How could you even agree to this?"

She glares at me. "It was *my* idea. I told Carter if he could ever get you to the surface that I'd better be the first to know. It's my fault you're down there in the first place. I can't just forget about how my insecurity sent you to mermaid Hell."

I can't help the smile that lights up my face. "That's a bit dramatic. It's not even hot there."

"But you live in a rock!"

I laugh. "Carter told you that?"

She reaches out her hand again. This time I take it while flicking my tail to propel myself onto the rock next to her. My cerulean blue tail shimmers in the sunlight, my caudal fin smacking against the waves that hit the rock, splashing cool water onto me, keeping me damp.

Giselle stares at me with wide eyes. It's hard to stay mad at her. I can't even tell her that I don't want to see her while I'm without legs. All my arguments fall away as my best friend reaches up her hand and holds it above my tail.

"Can I touch it?" she asks. "You don't even know how mesmerizing you look. Remember how I used to pretend to be a mermaid in the pool with that slip-on tail? God, this is so cool—" She runs her fingers across the side of my tail before I have a chance to agree. "And so flippin' insane. Ugh. I hate it and love it at once. It's so beautiful, but it keeps you away."

I sigh. "Right?"

She touches one of my pectoral fins on my arm. "This is kind of freaky, though."

I spread my fingers in front of her face, showing off the short webbing that ends before my knuckles. "This is, too."

"Whoa!"

I snort at her amazement. "You don't even know how much I've missed you—missed talking with you. I have nothing in common with the merpeople, and it's as exciting as dirt. I basically lie around all day and stare at the fish."

"That's gotta change. I'm going to look for more water-proof stuff to have Carter give you." She taps her fingers against my tail, like she still can't believe it's real. "I wish I could give you your phone."

"Even if you didn't have to use it to keep in contact with my parents for me, it'd just die. Can't exactly charge it." Being underwater is like living how I imagine a caveman would live. But we don't even have fire.

"I'll figure something out," she says. "Oh, and speaking of phones...I brought yours." She moves her board off a small pouch hooked to the tether of her surfboard. She pulls the lock up the string and uses her fingers to widen the opening before digging out my phone still in the waterproof case she had given me.

My heart smacks against my ribcage at suddenly being able to be connected to the world I was ripped from. I never knew withdrawals were possible when it came to disconnecting from technology, but they're very real, and I still have trouble not being able to just turn my phone on and have access to all my friends all the time. And now, I can finally call my parents.

I open my favorites in my contact list and hit my mom's name. Giselle quietly listens as the ring echoes over the ocean air.

"Ava, what a nice surprise. You usually just text." my mom says. "How's Seattle?"

I side glance Giselle. "Found some free time, and Washington is beautiful." I have nothing else to really say because I've never actually been to the state.

"I could tell from the pictures you sent. The postcard's stuck to the fridge with the others." My mom's voice triggers sadness to wash through me. She thinks I'm having the summer of my life, and there's no way I can ever tell her I'm absolutely miserable most days.

"I'll keep sending them."

"Send more of yourself, too," she says.

I blink tears away. "Will do."

"Great!" There's a short pause. "Hey, Avie. I hate to do this, but can I call you back later? I'm in the car about to leave to meet Ruby and Anaya for a late lunch."

My lip trembles as I say, "Okay, sounds good, Mom. If I don't answer, I'll call you back when I can."

"Love you, Avie."

"Tell Dad I love him, too."

I smother a sob with my hand when the line cuts off. Giselle slides her arms around me and hugs me against her as I try to get myself under control. That was a lot harder than I had expected it to be. I'd give anything to see my mom right now—to hug her, to smell her floral fragrance. But I don't even know when or if that'll ever happen again.

"Ava," Carter's voice echoes into my mind. I blink, almost forgetting he was in the ocean still. "Is everything okay?"

"It's fine," I think back to him.

Turning my attention to my best friend, I smile at her through my tears. "Seattle, huh?"

"I pay people online to take cell phone pictures so I can send them to your parents. The same goes for postcards. They mail blank ones to me with my address stickered on so I can peel it off and write in your parents names and forge quick notes. The location stamps make it look legit." She grins as my mouth falls open. "People will do anything for cash."

"It's really scary how easy it is for you to fake my existence on land," I say.

"It's shocking how many people live double lives, Ava. I found a message board with so many ideas. Since I'm an expert at your writing, your parents have never even second guessed it. The only problem is the pictures of you they ask you to send." She holds up the camera. "Speaking of pictures. I should take a few of you."

I raise my brows. "Like this? No way."

"Just your head. I'll pay someone to photoshop you onto a different background," she says.

I tilt my head back and look at the sky. "I don't even know what to say. You're way too good at this."

She laughs and points my phone at me. "Just look happy, okay?"

I force myself to smile.

"I *said* look happy."

I practically bare my teeth.

She snaps a few photos. "Good enough, I guess."

A wave crashes over both our legs, and Carter pops his head above water. He glances between the two of us, like he's interrupting a private moment, but then he turns his gaze to me.

Panic seizes my chest. "What's wrong?"

He wraps his fingers around the base of my tail, stopping himself from getting taken back under by the tide. "Nothing, we're fine, but we need to head back home. We'll be missed."

I frown at Giselle. "I hate that I have to leave."

"We'll meet again, okay? I don't care if you think it's dangerous. I'll rent a boat or something. We'll make this work." She squeezes my hand. "Promise me you'll see me again."

The words stick in my throat, but I nod my head.

Wrapping my arms around Giselle, I hug my best friend one more time before I jump back into the waves. I don't resurface. I can't find the will to say goodbye. I'd rather just end things with a hug and a promise.

"Go ahead and start swimming home, Ava," Carter thinks to me. "I'm going to make sure Giselle makes it back to shore, and then I'll catch up."

I don't move. "I'm fine waiting."

He reaches out and brushes my floating hair away from my face. "I'm going to transform."

"And you don't want me to see," I say, finishing his thought.

"This is hard enough on you as it is. I can see it in your eyes." His voice is soft in my mind, like he's afraid that his words could break me.

He's right, though. I'm jealous enough as it is that he can do something I can't. Just knowing that he's about to take on the form I so desperately miss depresses me. I can almost close my eyes and imagine what it would be like to kick my legs instead of flick my tail.

I suck in my bottom lip and drop my gaze to the sand a few feet below me. "You don't have to always protect me, you know. I'm not made of glass."

"I'd protect you even if you were made of steel," he says in my mind, kissing my cheek. "I'll be quick."

He waits for me to pull away and swim. I propel through the water, diving deeper, and head back toward the open ocean. When I'm just far enough away, I stop and turn around, straining to see Carter in the water.

With a heavy heart, I stare as his body transforms before my eyes, his scales disappearing into bronze skin before it splits apart, and he kicks his legs to reach the surface. He's breathtaking in his human form, everything I remember him to be from our time on land. It's enough to force me to look away.

I do the only thing I can.

I swim.

6

KING ATTILONIOUS

CARTER'S STRONG HANDS WRAP AROUND my waist when I'm already a few miles away from shore and past the few fishing boats. He spins me around with him like we're rolling in the water, and then he flicks his tail, pushing us faster as one. I'll never get over the feeling of swimming with Carter pressed against me, feeling the heat of his skin as he propels us faster than I could ever dream. I still swim on the slower side, but I can't blame myself for that. It's not like I've had the chance to build my speed and stamina while hiding away in a merperson colony.

Stretching my arms in front of me, I pretend to fly underwater like Superman. Carter's lips brush my shoulder, sending tingles through me. It's hard to still be mad at him for the ultimatum he'd given me regarding Giselle, but just because it worked out, and I've cooled off, doesn't mean I'm going to easily forget.

Carter bends forward, and together we dive through clear blue waters for another few miles. He doesn't say anything to me as we swim, and it reminds me of all the times we spent enjoying just each other's presences while navigating the ocean.

A pod of sperm whales dive down to our level. Their giant, round heads cut through the water, creating a current strong enough to catch us in. Carter weaves around one of the young whales, and I slide my hands across the top of its smooth back.

Carter dives deeper when we reach the front of the pod, and they follow along behind us for a few dozen feet, creating turbulence that rocks me against Carter, but he never loses his grip on me. His laughter echoes in my mind as one of the larger whales opens its mouth next to us, displaying a row of big teeth as if its smiling.

Bending forward, Carter descends down, but the whales stay together and ascend back to the surface.

In moments like these, I wish I had an underwater camera. Ocean photography could totally be my new hobby, but I wouldn't really be able to show anyone. Instead, I have to just imprint it in my mind and hope I never forget. Unable to share this new world with the people I love most takes its toll on me.

"You sure we have to go back? I forgot how good it was to swim with you," I say, sending my thought to Carter.

He shifts his hands, flipping me around so my back faces the sea floor, and our chests press together. He grins at me, his eyes full with hints of desire—the same look he gives me when he comes home after being gone all day.

I brush my lips against his throat. His Adam's apple bobs as he holds me tighter. Bringing my hands to his neck, I run my fingers up to his head and into his hair. He meets his lips with mine, sending me an image from what feels like forever ago—one from my vacation up the coast to San Francisco on the Ocean Jewel yacht with my friends. It was the long swim from the San Francisco Bay to the yacht hours away.

It was when I had almost given myself to him right on the sand before my transformation was triggered. It was also when I met his parents, but neither of them stay in my mind for long. All I can think about is swimming forever like this in Carter's arms.

The water suddenly shifts, warming around us, and I force my eyes to open. Below us lies the colony of Pearlestria. It looks even more foreboding than ever even though it shimmers and glitters with colorful rocks and merperson-made houses with pearlescent walls—the reason for the colony's name.

The sky blazes orange far overhead, casting an eerie glow around us as the sun sets on the surface. I haven't spent much time outside my little rock house later in the day, and I can't even remember if I've ever really seen a sun set from down here.

It's just as amazing as from on land, but more intense and vibrant, the water rippling in warm colors with the current overhead.

Fish pepper the water above us, like black spots among the fiery surface. They swim around, some in large schools and others all alone. The sea life above makes it hard for me to go back to what awaits me below on the sea floor.

"I promise to take you out again as soon as I can, Ava," Carter says, navigating us down and into the center of Pearlestria.

At least a dozen merpeople swim the sandy channel, making their ways back to their homes as the night falls upon us. The looming castle of King Attilonious shines like polished gold in the dimming light, and I wonder what it looks like on the inside, behind the gleaming walls.

I expect Carter to let me go so I can swim myself next to him, but he doesn't. Resting my chin on his shoulder, I take in the view of the small colony with a few dozen houses all made from the same shimmery rock material. With a clear view of the castle, I notice a few merpeople exit from different cutouts, before I catch sight of a merman with flowing salt and pepper locks adorned with a silver crown on top his head, muscles twice the size of Carter's—bulging arms, ripped abs, a sturdy chest—and a sparkling golden tail that glints like tiny diamonds are embedded in his scales. He holds a golden staff in his hand, leaning on it, and I swear he's watching me watch him. He's far enough away that I can't tell what his eye color is, but he's obviously smiling. And then, he raises his hand and waves.

Lifting my hand from Carter's neck, I hold it up and wave back.

The king smiles wider before offering me a bow from his place above on his balcony.

"Carter," I say in his mind. "The king."

Carter lifts his head to follow my gaze. I practically stare upward along the shimmery wall outside the castle where the king watches me. Slowing down, Carter arches his back so we're vertical in the water. I ease myself away from Carter and bow when he does. The king nods his head before he winks. Then, a moment later, he turns around and disappears into his castle.

I turn my wide eyes to Carter. A million thoughts circle through my head, but I can't form a single sentence. I've met royalty before—my mom was declared a countess for all her fundraising by a prince of Malta—but I never dreamed of meeting a merman king—my king. The man responsible for me being here. And I suddenly feel no hatred toward him. I'm actually a little star-struck.

My cheeks burn in embarrassment. "I can't believe he waved at me."

"He complimented me on my choice in a mate," Carter says.

My eyes nearly bug out of their sockets. "He talked to you?"

"I'm just as surprised as you are," Carter says, hooking his hand around my waist to pull me along in the direction of our home. As we swim, he nods to a few people in greeting, and I offer a small smile when they direct their words to address me.

It feels like everyone's staring at us. I'm sure they've already heard about Carter cancelling the coupling ceremony and kicking Starla out. This is a small colony despite having the king here. Just over a hundred merpeople live within these walls, which Carter says is half the size of most of the other colonies.

I tug on Carter's hand, pulling us faster. "Can we hurry? I feel like I'm under a microscope."

"It's because we are. People are already talking."

I knew it. They're probably judging me, because there's no way Starla would've told everyone it was Carter who called off the coupling ceremony. She probably blamed it on me to save herself from embarrassment.

"Ugh!"

"No one will be brave enough to confront us, though. We don't owe them an explanation, either," he says, squeezing my fingers.

A few bright blue fish swim around us from one of the reefs outside our little house at the end of the sandy channel. It's on the outskirts of Pearlestria, which makes it easier to hide away from the curious eyes of the others.

"That's easy for you to say." My voice echoes through my mind. "You're not the girl breaking the heart of her mate for denying him such a tradition."

He tilts his head back, laughing not only in my mind, but in the water, causing a few tiny bubbles to escape his mouth.

He pulls me to him. "Do I look heartbroken, Ava?"

I shrug. "No, but people will assume."

He shakes his head, his short hair floating in the water. "If they're talking about anyone, it's me. Everyone knows I had taken the unconventional route. They feel badly for you. It's why no one is intruding on your space, forcing you to adjust and enter society before you're ready. If anything, I'm the merman who stole the human girl's choice."

I relax in his embrace. "I'd have chosen this."

"Would you have really, though?" he asks, his aqua eyes boring into mine.

I think about his question for a moment. Who would choose death over a second chance, even if it is in a new body, in a new home, in a new life? I'm pretty sure had Carter taken me away the moment I had fallen off the boat, I'd still have fallen in love with him. I'm thankful he didn't do what would've been the right thing according to his mom, because losing my family and putting my parents through the loss of another child to the ocean would've hurt me for the rest of my life.

"Yes," I say.

The suspicious look he gives me speaks volumes. He obviously doesn't believe that I'd have chosen to be a mermaid if the circumstances were different and it wasn't an option between life and death and only a decision between one life or another. "But you had to think about it."

I gently pinch his chin between my index finger and thumb. "Not about whether I'd choose to be a mermaid. I was thinking about everything after."

"Oh." I'm sure he's thought about it a dozen times as well. "I don't regret taking you back to your friends. I'd do it exactly the same all over again—except I would've fought harder to stop my mom from stealing your ring."

As much as he can replay that terrible day in our minds, I don't think there was anything he could've done to change my fate. If it wasn't that night, it would've been one of the many after. We were outnumbered, and it would've been impossible to hide on land forever—not with the rise of the full moon that forces us back to the sea once a month.

I smirk, kissing him. "I know you would. But let's not dwell on the what-ifs. They just make things worse. Trust me."

"That sounds like something I'd say, Aves." He wiggles his nose against mine as he pushes us through the archway that leads into our living room.

I kiss his nose. "Don't let this get to your head, but you might just say some really smart things to me, even if I pretend to ignore them half the time."

We don't even make it to the bedroom before Carter lies on top of me on the floor. His elbows dig into the sand on each side of my head, and he presses his weight against me, keeping me anchored.

Bending down, he kisses me deeply, desperately—the kind of kiss that would've left me breathless on land. Tingles blossom from my stomach and zing down my tail. I smack it against the sand, kicking up a small cloud, and he sucks my bottom lip between his, grazing his teeth over it in such a way that makes me shiver.

He cups the back of my head with his hands, combing his fingers into my blond hair. My fingers explore the curves of his shoulders as I work my way over his solid chest to his muscular stomach. I slide my finger along his skin right along the ridge of his tail, and he reacts with a moan reverberating through the water from deep in his throat. I don't hear it, but I feel it vibrate against my lips.

"I could stay with you here forever as long as we can stay like this," he says, flashing an image of me beneath him into my mind.

His words send my heart fluttering. Spending eternity in Carter's arms in our own private world helps keep the sadness away. How can I be sad when he says stuff that makes me swoon?

"You make me happy, you know? Even when I'm sad and homesick, just you holding me and whispering in my mind, sends the grief away. I love you, Carter. I love you so much that I look forward to my future with you. You might not feel it, and I'm sorry if it comes across like I don't want this sometimes, but you do make things good for me."

He smiles the smile he saves just for me. "I thought I might've messed things up this afternoon."

I kind of wish he didn't bring it up. I stiffen in his arms. "What you did..."

"Can you forgive me for my lapse in judgment?" he asks instead of arguing.

"You make it incredibly hard to stay mad at you."

Smiling again, he leans forward and brushes his lips against my temple. "Good."

I let the conversation drop for the sole fact that I don't want to think about it. I loved seeing Giselle today. I loved talking to my mom. I loved that Carter forced me to go against my decision and made me do something I didn't want to for the first time since we came here. Maybe it's what I need to adjust. A little more pushiness and less coddling. I won't tell him that, though. I like being coddled—and cuddled and loved like I'm the most important mermaid in the world.

"Carter?" A voice sounds through both our minds from outside our house. I recognize it as belonging to his grandma.

Carter doesn't get off me. Instead, he thinks, "Come in," projecting his voice to her.

Grandmer swims into our living room, her hair neatly braided as it floats behind her. She eyes us on the floor but doesn't look anything other than happy when she greets her grandson with a smile.

"This doesn't look like two mers who just called off the coupling ceremony," she says, raising her eyebrows.

I blush. "That was Carter." I don't know why I say it, but I feel like he should take the blame. He was the one who called it off even if I agreed for the wrong reasons.

Carter crinkles his nose at me in a fake glare. "It was a mutual agreement for now."

"Your mom is extremely disappointed, you know," she says. "But I understand. She couldn't believe how you stood your ground. I thought I'd never hear the end of it last night." Grandmer flicks her gaze to the ceiling. "No wonder you asked her to leave."

Carter's smile melts into a serious expression. "You have no idea, Grandmer."

Her lips pull up in the corner. "I think I do. And that's why I'm here. I'd like to take over as Ava's teacher if you'd allow it. You won't have to worry 'bout me pressuring you into the ceremony either."

Carter turns his gaze to mine. "How do you feel about it, Aves?"

I shrug. "I guess that would be okay."

"Then it's settled." She turns her attention to Carter. "Why don't you get us some dinner, and we can get started tonight."

I frown. "Tonight?"

She plops in the sand next to me. "Actually, now."

I lean my head back on the sand as Carter pulls away from me. It seems so sudden, and I had planned on spending all night in the soft sand with Carter, but his grandma doesn't look like someone I can argue with.

Instead of complaining, I remember it could be much worse with Starla. "Okay," I say to Carter's grandma after a moment. "Where do we start?"

7

GIFTED

GRANDMER STUDIES ME AS I pick through one of the bags of fruit I had hidden from Starla under one of the few decorative rocks in my room. She'd have thrown a fit had she known Carter brought me food from the surface. Grandmer, on the other hand, couldn't care less. She even takes an apple slice from me when I offer the bag out to her.

Carter sits a few feet away, picking apart a bright red snapper. I try not to watch him carve his sharp nail through the fish, but I can't help it. After a few minutes, he steals one of my small bags of lettuce and wraps a leaf around a small piece of meat.

"I want you to try this, Ava," he says.

"No thanks," I say.

Grandmer watches us quietly. A smirk pulls the corner of her lips up, amused by us. Her deep blue tail matches the blue streaking her golden brown hair. Wound around her chest are a few pieces of long seaweed strung through a bead-like rock that gives it shape. I expect her to tell me to stop being stubborn and to try the damn fish, but she doesn't. Instead, she takes the piece from Carter and pops it into her mouth.

"Carter, offering Ava a fish you killed and cut in front of her, especially after she's already stated she can't stomach the idea of eating something she was swimming with a minute ago, isn't going to make her want to try it even if you disguise it in lettuce." Smart mermaid. I can already tell I might actually enjoy spending time with her. She might've chosen the ocean, but she told me she spent years on the land with her husband before he passed away, which is why she returned to the water.

"Yeah, Carter. You know how cute I think our fishy friends are," I say, grinning. "If I could talk to them, I would."

He covers his forehead with his hand for a moment. "So, if I bring something back you haven't seen and disguise it in something you like, will you try it for me?"

I play with my floating hair for a moment. "Only if it's something I can pick up at a human grocery store. And it has to be tiny."

"Really?"

I shrug. "Only because of the trouble you'd have to go through for me."

He smirks before swimming closer to kiss my cheek. Wrapping my hands around his muscular bicep, I stop him from swimming away. I lean up and kiss his lips for a long moment to show my appreciation. I'm not exactly looking forward to whatever he brings back, but if he does this, I have to at least humor him.

"I'll be right back. Will you be okay with Ava, Grandmer?" he asks.

I wrinkle my nose, because part of him still thinks I might be a little bit difficult. Maybe for Starla or some poor merperson who doesn't understand my human ideals and culture.

"I'll be better than fine, dear. You picked a lovely mate, and I've been dying to get to know her since the moment she arrived." Grandmer reaches over and pats my hand. Her smooth skin contrasts the age and wisdom in her eyes. I could only hope to look as good as she does when I'm a grandmother.

"You have?" I ask, watching Carter swim through the archway, leaving us alone. "I thought Starla might've ruined my image for everyone."

"I know it doesn't feel like it, Ava, but Carter's mom does care about you. She hated she had to be the bad guy in all this. Your situation with Carter is rare—non-existent. Most merpeople wouldn't know how to deal with it in the first place. The king himself has never had to deal with a human turned mermaid who was given the mermaid life on a whim. Most merpeople choose mates within their colonies, or if they do choose to live on land, they spend years with a human to make sure they're the one. We can only choose once, you know. That's why the coupling ceremony is quite the affair. It would not only have been where you'd vow your life to Carter, but it would've been the moment you had given up your human life as well. In most situations, the gift of his life wouldn't have worked because of your initial lack of bond. But clearly, you're special. You two—" She pauses, gathering her thoughts. "You basically eloped with my grandson, and no one was invited."

I don't respond to her comment about being special. I don't even want to think of the loss of my life had Carter's spark not worked to transform me. "Kind of like a drunk couple in Vegas?"

She snorts. I wasn't sure she'd get the reference, but Grandmer seems to know the human world well. "Exactly. Except there are no annulments under the sea."

"It's a good thing I love Carter then. At least we had one date before I took the plunge," I say.

Grandmer's smile widens at my words. "A lot of folks 'round here have been concerned about your feelings for my grandson, but I've always known not to doubt Carter's choice."

"Maybe you could spread the word," I say. "I grew up in a small town—well, not as small as this—but I know how people talk."

"Don't you worry about anyone else but you and my grandson. Everything will fall into place how it should be. I think without Starla interfering and pressuring you, you might actually start enjoying yourself. Who knows, maybe you'll figure out what you like to do here. Mermaids are gifted with certain affinities. I think yours might have to do with the ocean animals."

"Starla never mentioned that," I say. Well, she technically didn't mention much besides the coupling ceremony and whether or not I'd eat something she brought me.

"I'm sure she'd have gotten around to it," Grandmer says.

"What's yours? What about mermen?"

"Like Starla, I'm a healer. I'm gifted with the ability to help those hurt or injured. I was a nurse on land," she says. "Very few mermen have affinities. King Attilonious is gifted with the power of ocean magic. It's he who now creates the sea stone that allows us to change. He's the only one who doesn't need it to transform. He's also the most powerful mer in existence. It's why he's king. He controls the sea."

I nod my head even though I never questioned that the king wasn't powerful. He'd have to be in his position. Just the sight of him screams power. It's Carter that I wonder about.

"My grandson was gifted with the speed and strength of a warrior, just like his dad. They're the protectors of our colonies—the ones who the king will look to first," she says. "Well, not Carter just yet. He has many years to go."

I always knew Carter was a fast swimmer, but I always thought it was because he's been doing it all his life. I guess that means I'll never be as fast as him.

"No wonder I always feel safe with him," I say with a smile.

Silence falls between us for a few minutes. Grandmer continues to explain how merpeople tend to spend their time doing the things they enjoy, which also serves to better the colony. There are mers who hunt, those who keep humans from discovering our secrets, healers like herself, caretakers, and even merpeople who do their best to care for all the creatures of the ocean.

Carter's voice drifts into my mind after what has felt like a long, informative evening with Grandmer.

"Close your eyes," he says into my mind. "And no peeking."

I shift my gaze to Grandmer, who has taken it upon herself to braid my hair as she speaks of all the endless possibilities of being a mermaid. She nods with a smile before I close my eyes. Carter swims into our living room, creating his own current that sets me adrift. He gently takes my hand, stopping me in place. I can't see him through my closed eyes, but I can feel him hovering in front of me.

"Now, open your mouth."

I cringe at his words. "Do I have to?"

"Yes. I spent the last two hours hunting and preparing this dinner for you, so open your mouth." His voice is teasing in my mind and not annoyed like most people would be after jumping through hoops to make something only to be greeted with complaints.

I slowly open my mouth and brace myself for the worst.

My only saving grace would be the fact that the salt of the sea masks the fishiness of everything, blocking my sense of smell completely and dulling my taste buds.

Carter chuckles, his voice echoing through my mind. He takes an excruciatingly long time to stick whatever it is he brought me into my mouth.

"Seriously, you better hurry or I'm just going to spit it out," I say, sending the thought only to him. The anticipation doesn't send my heart racing in a good way.

And I'm sure he feels it, because a second later, his fingers brush against my lips as he holds something to my mouth. "Take a bite," he says, waiting for me to decide how much I'm willing to try.

Skimming my teeth against another lettuce wrapped piece of fish, I take the tiniest bite possible, not even sure I got a piece of its meat with the lettuce. I open my eyes when I move the piece of lettuce over my tongue, not really tasting it with the saltwater.

Carter holds up the lettuce square again, and I notice the deep red color of the piece of fish within it. He brings it to my lips, his eyes narrowing as he smiles, and I lean forward and take a bigger bite. It's surprisingly mild and meaty, and not as gross as I expected it to be.

Carter unrolls the lettuce from the fish. "Raw tuna actually tastes better with seaweed. You can find it at most sushi restaurants."

It's probably why I *think* I like it. I eat tuna pretty regularly. I just never really wanted to eat it raw. "It wasn't so bad. I still wish we could cook it. I miss warm food." What I would give for a plate of steamy enchiladas with their melted cheese goodness. I'd probably be happy with a piece of toast fresh from the toaster at this point.

Grandmer pats Carter's shoulder. "I think you have things under control. Your parents would be proud, Carter."

He smirks, staring at me take another small bite. I really want to hate it and hold a grudge against the undersea eating habits, but Carter looks so cute with how he grins, his shoulders straight, his chest nearly puffing with pride. He'd probably give himself a high five if I wouldn't laugh at him for doing it. Who knows? He still might.

"People will now think I'm the spoiled mermaid," I say. "How do you even deal with me? I'm not even sure I'd deal with myself."

He wraps his arms around my shoulders, stealing a bite of the piece of tuna from my fingers. "I'd be bored if you made things easy." Turning to his grandma, he says, "Let me see you home, Grandmer. It's getting late."

Grandmer smacks her deep blue tail against the sandy floor to propel herself up. I swim closer and give the old mermaid a hug, happiness settling into my soul for one of the very few times since I came here. She's so easygoing and understanding that I wish it was her who had taken me under her fin from the beginning. It'd have eased the tension with Starla, and I might've actually grown to like my future mother-in-law. Now,

I'm not sure I ever will. I'll be cordial for Carter's sake, but I won't seek anything more from her.

Carter kisses my cheek. Holding his arm out to his grandma to take, he guides her from our house and into the glowing night waters shimmering with the magic created from our sparks. Their forms blur the farther they swim until they disappear, leaving only a swirl of sparkling sand in their wakes.

It's so strange not having a fight with Starla before heading to bed. Tonight actually felt normal—something I could get used to if I had to. *You do have to...*

Turning my back on the door, I peer around the room at my simple house. It's weird to think of it as mine and Carter's. I almost wish I could figure out what else to do with it. Like Giselle said earlier today, I live in a damn rock.

Sighing, I finish off the few pieces of tuna Carter spent all evening preparing for me and continue to think about my best friend, missing her just as much now as I did yesterday before I got to see her again—if not more. Giselle would be so proud that I ate the tuna and would exclaim how she couldn't wait to take me to Sushi Days, her favorite sushi restaurant in Azure Waters.

I can't help thinking that maybe this life would've been better suited for my best friend. Not only does she love the ocean—she does basically every water sport—she also loves raw fish. She'd probably be brave enough to eat it mermaid style. I imagine bottling up Giselle's essence to hold with me. I'll get through this. I know I will.

"Ms. Ava?" An unfamiliar voice sounds through my head, calling my name. I spin in my living room, almost disoriented by the foreign thought that doesn't belong to anyone I've begrudgingly met so far in the colony.

It takes me a moment to see the figure floating a few feet from the front cutout. "Yes, come in," I say, projecting my thought to the unfamiliar merman. I'd never invite a stranger into my house in Azure Waters, but it feels weird hearing this man in my mind and not being able to confront him. I've never been one to talk on the phone with anyone other than my parents or my friends, so it feels just as awkward as that but worse.

A merman with short black hair and a thick black beard pokes his head into the archway of the living room, gripping the frame in his hand without swimming completely in. His dark eyes look like two black onyx stones in his face, and two fish hooks hang from his ears.

"I'm sorry to bother you so late. Is your mate home?" he asks.

I shake my head. "No, Carter swam his grandma home. Is there something you need?"

He swims a foot into the room through the archway. Even without seeing him extend to his full height, I can tell he's a good few inches taller than Carter, nearly hitting his head on the roof. He sweeps his deep indigo tail across the sand, creating ripples through the room that force me to flick my own tail to stay in place.

"I'm here with a message from King Attilonious. It's only

respectful to wait for your mate to arrive before I deliver it." Peering around our small room once, he then shifts his gaze to me. His eyes flick over my bikini top for a split second in curiosity, but it's not in a creepy or mocking way. Just taking notice that I'm wearing something out of the ordinary compared to the rest of the mermaids in the colony.

I wave toward one of the kelp wrapped rocks. "He'll be home shortly. Have a seat if you'd like."

The merman glides through the water before lowering himself on the rock, splaying his tail out in front of him. He leans back on his palms, making me feel all sorts of awkward with his silence. It's the first time I've had a strange guest in my house, and I'm freaking out just a bit since he claims to have a message from the king.

Fear trickles in my mind. "I hope everything's okay," I finally say after a long moment.

The merman sits up straighter, nodding his head wildly. "Oh, yes. Sorry if I made you think otherwise."

I find a place near him on the sandy floor and curl my tail to my chest. "You'll have to excuse me. I'm not exactly sure of the mer etiquette. I'd usually offer a guest a drink, but—" I shrug instead of finishing my sentence.

The merman smiles. "This is perfect. Thank you. Most mers don't even invite me in to sit."

"Oh," I say. I hope I didn't break some rule by letting a strange merman into my home. I doubt it, though. Everyone is treated equally here. "I'd hate to be forced to wait outside." *Like it's much different from inside here.*

His smile widens. "You're a lot nicer than I expected."

My lips turn downward in a frown. "Thanks, I guess." I knew people were probably thinking the worst of me, especially since the whole colony probably believes it was my complete decision not to go through with the coupling ceremony, not to mention I hide in my house all day.

He waves his hand. "I'm sorry. I didn't mean to make you upset."

Things are getting awkward really quickly. I knew I'd fail at having a normal conversation with a merperson, especially one who I'm nearly certain has never even been on land. "No, it's okay. I was just caught off guard." I know people are curious about me considering the circumstances, but to actually have to sit here and think about how someone didn't think I was nice is torture.

I wish I could bury myself in the sand until Carter gets home, because the more I sit here, the more uncomfortable things get. The merman's eyes train on me, studying me a lot harder than any normal human on land would do in these circumstances. I regret wanting to be polite. But now I can't even ask him to wait outside in fear of him changing his mind about my nicety and then spreading the word about how everyone was right. I'm Ms. Unapproachable.

"Carter, where are you?" I project my question to the sea.

I'm so flustered that the merman picks up the thought intended for Carter. My feelings must be splashed across my face, because he moves from the rock in front of me and takes my hand between his.

"My apologies again, Ms. Ava. I really didn't mean anything by it," he says, twisting his mouth into a frown.

Instead of accepting and since it couldn't possibly get any more uncomfortable, I ask, "So people assume I'm mean?" I have to know what people think of me and if it's as bad as I imagine. Carter doesn't tell me anything except not to worry about what others think. But how can I not? I've cared about what others thought all my life.

"Forget I said anything." The merman's thoughts come through my mind laced with something that sounds like worry.

"No, please. I'm not upset. I just want to know."

Releasing my hand, he backs up and blows a small bubble through his lips. "It's not that I didn't expect you to be nice. I expected you to act differently. Everyone knows how Starla dragged you from the shore and that you hate this life."

"I don't hate—"

"It's been a long time, Tide." Carter's thoughts interrupt what I was going to say.

Of course people think I hate the mermaid life—I do—did. I mean, I have mixed feelings. I like having a tail...sometimes. I do miss my legs though, miss all the little things about the land that I didn't even know I would miss. But the last thing I want is for people to think I hate their way of life. Because I don't. I just hate it for me. There's a huge difference.

"I imagine you're not here to just say hello," Carter adds, pulling me from my own thoughts.

The merman, Tide, swims the distance to Carter and gives him a half hug before they tap their tails together in a gesture I haven't ever seen before. I equate it to a fist bump on land, like the ones my friends Matty and Logan give each other.

"You know it's the king's order not to come here without an invitation," he says. What? The king ordered people to stay away unless invited? While I'm sort of thankful for the lack of interruption from strangers, I'm also annoyed that no one told me people were commanded by the king to stay away.

I tilt my head to the side. "Why's that?" This whole time I thought they were staying away for their own reasons—mostly because Starla said so—but I had no idea it was an actual order. I feel a little bit better about things with the knowledge that people aren't just avoiding me at all costs.

Tide turns to me. "In ordinary circumstances the whole colony would stop by to meet the newest resident, but he didn't think overwhelming you was a good idea. Our king is very kind and empathetic. I'm sure you'll be as fond of him as everyone here. Which brings me to why I'm here uninvited."

"The message from the king," I say, anxious to hear it.

Tide turns his gaze to Carter. "King Attilonious requests that you bring Ms. Ava to the castle at first light."

My chest clenches. I never dreamed of meeting the king, and now he's requesting my presence. But why? It's been weeks since I've been here. He's had plenty of time to summon me.

I'm excited and scared all at once.

"Thanks for the message, Tide," Carter says, patting his old friend on the back.

With a quick nod, Tide leaves without another word to me, though I think he and Carter share a few private words I don't hear.

Carter crosses the room to where I slide to the sand, piling it over my caudal fin with my fingers. He settles next to me, trailing his hand along my tail, brushing off the sand I've nervously buried myself in.

Sliding his arm under me, he lifts me onto his lap. "This is a great honor, Ava. King Attilonious doesn't just invite anyone over."

"I'm going to make a fool of myself," I say, resting my head on his warm chest while listening to the rhythmic sound of his heart beating. It sounds as if it does so only for me.

Carter runs his hand over my braided hair. "I highly doubt that's possible."

"Your friend expected me to be mean or something," I say. "What if the king's already formed an opinion of me? He already knows I disagree with his stupid laws."

"The king complimented me, remember? I highly doubt he thinks so little of you if he went out of his way to say such nice things. As for Tide, he's terribly sorry and embarrassed for upsetting you. He was more nervous meeting you than he let on. He's never met a human-born before." Carter rests his chin on my head. "Don't let any of it bother you."

That's easy for him to say. He's merely the talk of the town by association.

"Think we can get out of it?" I ask. "I think I'm feeling sick."

He holds me tighter. "We'll be fine."

But he doesn't sound as certain as he should be. It's enough to leave me feeling afraid. "I hope so."

After a minute of silence, he uses his tail to propel us from the sand and toward the entrance to the bedroom. "How about I distract you for a while? Take your mind off things." He nuzzles his face into the crook of my neck, and I tilt my head back.

"I'd like that," I say.

Unfortunately, even Carter's kisses can't calm the unease settling through me. I don't think anything can.

If only I could flee.

8

TREADING WATER

I SLEEP WITH MY TAIL curled to my chest like always since it's one of the few circumstances where I can sort of pretend that I still have legs. Carter kisses me awake, pressing his body weight against me from behind. His hands brush my tail where my hips would be if I had legs, and he runs his hands over the ridge that separates my tail from my stomach.

It's not even light out, and I wish that the king would've invited us later in the day. Whether I'm in the sea or on the land, I'll never be a morning person. Carter does make waking up a bit easier because I'd rather have him wake me up instead of an alarm any day. I just can't figure out how his body knows when he needs to be up. It might be instinctual like he has an internal alarm, something I definitely don't have.

Flipping in his arms, I press my chest to his to feel his heart beat against mine. The glow of our sparks lights the water around us, and I'm tempted to close my eyes to fall back asleep. I'm dreading heading to the castle. I'd rather bite a chunk out of a swimming fish.

Carter grins into my lips. I must've sent him that thought in my tired state. He leans his forehead against mine, his closeness blurring my view of him in the rippling water. After a moment, he pulls away and stretches out, nearly touching the opposing walls at the same time, one with his caudal fin and the other with his fingertips. I don't let go of him, though. I cling to his side as he swims from the floor and circles the room a few times.

Sliding his hands under my arms, he practically peels me away, laughing the entire time he does. I sink to the floor, crossing my arms over my chest all while pouting my lip. It makes him laugh harder in my mind. I only glare at his amusement.

He scoops me up for another kiss, and I comb my fingers through his dark hair, sliding my tongue into his mouth, sending a dozen images of all the fun we could have if we skipped our summons to the castle.

The images tempt him enough that he sets me down, rubbing his eyes for a moment, trying to clear his thoughts without saying anything to me. I reach out and try to touch his tail, but he swims circles around me a few times, making me spin in the center of the room. I can't stop the smile that crosses my face. I know how hard it is for him to resist me, especially since he only swims circles like this to keep himself in control.

Closing the distance, he swims up to me and nudges me back into the far wall until my body rests against the pearlescent rock. "It'd be terribly rude to not show this morning."

"I'm okay with rude." I cup his face in my hands and hold him in place.

"Ava…" His voice fades in my mind. I know he wants to give into me, and it bothers him that he can't.

I rub my nose against his. "It's fine, Carter. I'll survive."

He smiles but sadness furrows his brows. "I'll be with you the whole time."

"I know."

He touches my chin, kissing me gently, sending a wave of love over me. Within the love lies an ounce of desire that he suppresses to keep himself together.

I send him a few images of all the things I'd rather be doing, including staying here with him for the rest of the day, making him smile.

"Don't think I'm not saving those thoughts for later," he says.

I respond by sucking my bottom lip between my teeth. If I were on land, I'd take the time to get ready, to dress up, prepare, but there's not much for me to do. I pick the knot out of the end of my braid and unravel the work Grandmer did on my hair last night as my only form of getting ready. I'd rather have my hair to veil my face since I've grown so used to hiding behind it.

"Ready?" he asks, brushing my hair behind my ear.

All I do is nod and take his hand. He pulls me through the house like a half deflated balloon being tugged around by a string. When we reach the door, Carter glances at me before hooking his hand around my waist only to flip me onto his back.

I tighten my hold around his shoulders when he jets off, speeding through the sandy channel that sits between the houses. He navigates the colony with ease, weaving in and out of the few fish that dart around.

A few merpeople peek their heads from their homes as we pass—some even waving to Carter. I force myself to smile at anyone who shows me any interest. I don't want to be known as the mean girl who hates the merpeople way of life. That's a terrible reputation to have. I don't want to be pitied either.

It doesn't take long to reach the looming castle, which is nothing like the castles I've seen pictures of on land. Morning light gleams off the pearl-like stones giving it an almost ethereal, magical feel. Decorative stones embedded throughout the walls create a pattern that looks like the sea around us. Two tall rock towers sit on each side of a rounded center that raises a few stories tall. Underwater, it's hard to judge just how massive the castle is. There are dozens of cutouts, leading to different parts of the palace, but Carter swims directly through the arched entrance in the center. Unlike the castles on land, this one is unprotected and open. Only one merman guards the place, but he looks half asleep, leaning against the wall by the entrance. I doubt the king even needs his protection. According to Grandmer, he's the most powerful in all the sea.

Carter flips me off his back, and we enter a cavernous room that looks like the inside of a diamond encrusted, blue walled cave. The deep midnight color mimics the night sky and diamond-like stones sparkle like stars. In the center on the high ceiling is a circular cutout and from this angle, it looks like a sparkling blue moon as the sky lightens way above us on the surface.

Along the far wall lies a huge coral reef with all sorts of rainbow fish dancing through colorful sea plants, some I've never seen before. A few human artifacts decorate the vast room, from the broken bow of a small vessel to a gold-plated treasure chest; all of the things that seem to be lost to the sea end up among the merpeople.

Trailing my eyes over every detail of the place, I shift my gaze up the wall to a small balcony two stories up. King Attilonious grips the banister while peering down at me. When our eyes meet, I smile before bending forward to bow just like yesterday. The king's salt and pepper hair floats around his head, and he offers me a huge smile, one that speeds up my already racing heart.

"Welcome to my home," the king says, thrusting his arm out over the cavernous room. "I'm so pleased to officially meet the newest mermaid in my kingdom."

He motions for us to join him, and Carter laces his fingers through mine and ascends until we swim in front of the king.

"Your majesty," Carter says with another bow. "Thank you for having us."

I tilt my chin down, finding it hard to meet King Attilonious' eyes. "It's an honor to meet you, my king. Thank you for accepting me into your kingdom." I've rehearsed what I was going to say a dozen times, using my knowledge of movies to reference how I should greet him. But all the rehearsing over night didn't prepare me for how ridiculous I feel in this moment.

King Attilonious might tower before me. He might wear a jewel encrusted crown on his head and carry an air of regality. But he still doesn't truly feel like *my* king. None of this life feels like mine, though. I should be used to it.

"It was not me who has accepted you into my kingdom, Ava." His words dance in my mind, his eyes holding me in their curious gaze.

Reaching out, he takes my hand and brings it to his chest. He presses my palm over his heart, startling me, and I feel it thrum under my fingers. I hold utterly still, his strong hand covering mine, forcing me to feel the smooth muscles of his broad chest. I'd like nothing more than to pull away, but I just gaze at him until a subtle glow arises from under my fingers, revealing the king's own spark. It disappears as quickly as I saw it, and I blink, unsure if it was even there to begin with. I shouldn't have been able to see it. The intensity of this moment might be making me go a little crazy.

"It was the ocean that accepted you, Ava, but I'm happy it did. You're such a lovely girl. No wonder Carter had impulsively given you his life." The king doesn't say it in a way that'd make me feel bad for being alive, though I hope he thinks I'm more than a pretty face.

"Thank you, my king. I couldn't have asked for a better merman to love me," I say.

"And do you love Carter?"

I'm taken aback by his question. Too many people underestimate my feelings for Carter. Yes, in the beginning, all I felt was a strong attraction to him, but it's grown into something much more in a short period of time.

"Yes." The answer is simple enough to say, but I feel like King Attilonious is expecting more.

It's easy to say you love someone—it's proving it to the world that is harder for me. Carter feels my love—he knows it's there. But the colony? All they see is the once human girl, who barely leaves her house, refuses to participate in the coupling ceremony, and the mermaid who fails at most mermaid things.

The king studies me for a long moment before turning to Carter. He slides his arm over his shoulder and pulls him away in a conversation I can't hear. The two of them swim away from the balcony, descending toward the entrance, and I remain in my spot.

With curious eyes, I gaze at the king escorting Carter to a

cutout that leads to some other part of the castle. A mermaid greets the two mermen, and Carter shifts his gaze to me. The mermaid bows to the king and Carter before motioning Carter to follow her, leaving me desperately wanting to follow him or swim right through the cutout in the ceiling to make my escape.

"The king wants to speak with you alone, Ava. I'll be waiting in the dining hall." Carter's voice drifts through my mind as he leaves me alone.

Panic seizes my chest. "Why?"

"I don't know, but it's okay. You have no reason to fear King Attilonious."

King Attilonious' massive figure appears before me, blocking my view of the cutout Carter left through. He hovers in front of me, his tail glittering in the faint morning light shining on him from above like a spotlight. His caudal fin expands out three times the size of mine, thick and powerful, yet breathtaking as it waves to keep him floating before me.

My eyes trail up the king's ripped stomach to his boxy jaw and sharp nose. For the first time, I notice his deep sapphire eyes that look like the fading night sky. His silver crown sparkles on his head, decked with precious jewels that I didn't think could be found in the water unless the crown was retrieved from a shipwreck. I wouldn't put it past him. Even so, it's perfect for him.

"You're nervous," the king says, sending his powerful voice into my mind.

I clench my shaking hands. "I'm sorry, my king."

"Don't apologize, Ava. You're allowed to feel and process things in your own way. The transformation opens you up to the mermaid way of life—it's ingrained in your very essence to feel things more intensely than you did as a human." King Attilonious waves his hand to get me to swim next to him, and his fingers brush against my lower back, guiding me along.

We head through the cutout in the balcony and into another great room, but this one contains a throne grand enough for the king. Decorated in thousands of pearls, the high-back throne looks like it was made from the shell of a giant clam, though the seat is made from a smooth black stone. It sits atop a flat rock that looks like a platform. Behind it, the water glitters as thousands of pinprick holes pierce the rock that curves up into a dome, allowing in sunlight from the surface as the sun rises.

In here, the floors are made of smooth, deep brown stones, the first time I've been inside a place without sand for the floor. A curtain of seaweed hangs over another cutout to the right, and I realize it leads to his private living quarters. He pulls the curtain aside, motioning me to enter a living room with what looks like a pool filled with black sand from somewhere that isn't Pearlestria. A big rock, wrapped in woven seaweed, sits against the far wall. Above it, hooked to the wall, is a sheet of metal etched with a wave pattern. I spin around the grand room, glittering with stones like the rest of the palace, and then tilt my head up to look through a series of small holes that make the place feel open because I can see the surface. The silhouette of a boat crosses overhead, and a trickle of fear seeps into me.

"Your palace is breathtaking," I say, swimming forward to run my fingers over the black sand pool.

"Thank you. It's stood here for as long as anyone can remember." He settles down on the edge of the sand pool. "How do you like Pearlestria?" he asks, his sapphire blue eyes watching me sit down across from him.

I'm not sure whether or not I should lie. My mind says yes, lie, lie, lie, but my heart tells me I had better be honest. "It's not bad." It's sort of the truth. It's not awful, but it's not enjoyable either.

"You're unhappy," he says for me.

"Not always."

"What makes you happy here?" This seems more like an interrogation than anything. I guess it's better than the king assuming things or hearing it from someone else.

"Carter." *Blah.* The answer sounds so lame as I say it. I hate that the only happiness I find in this endless ocean world revolves around another person. My mom would tell me I had better work on finding happiness within myself like all the characters in the novels she reads—the ones who find their own happily ever after.

But in this moment, I don't even know how to do that. My happiness lies in the world I was dragged from. It lives and breathes with my friends, with my old human life, with being able to do things I can't do down here.

I can't exactly tell the king all that. Well, I could, but

there's no way I would.

"Yet you won't agree to the coupling ceremony with him. Why's that?" I wish he'd say something more than ask questions, and I definitely wish he wouldn't ask what's on basically all the merworld's mind.

"It's complicated." I didn't want to get into it with Starla, and I definitely don't want to get into it with King Attilonious.

He rubs his chin, annoyance clearly written on his face. "You're going to have to give me more to work with than that."

Can I get away with denying the king answers to his questions? I have no idea. I'm not sure I'm willing to risk it.

"I care deeply for my merpeople, Ava," he continues without letting me attempt to respond. "I have all of your best interests in my heart, and I want nothing more as a king than to make sure my kingdom lives happily and safely. Unfortunately for you, those two things don't seem to coincide. I'm well aware of yours and Carter's decision to live on land, but due to the strange circumstances you've found yourself in, that isn't possible at the moment. And I'm sorry I have to hold firm in my decision. With saying that, I need a better answer to why you're unwilling to couple with the merman who clearly would do anything for you, one you claim to love." His serious expression sends me curling my tail to my chest.

I don't push my floating hair from my face, letting his words sink in. Would he even understand my argument? Would he understand Carter's? Does any of it even matter in his eyes? He's about his kingdom as a whole. We're the first to do things differently around here. Maybe that's a bad thing.

I grip my tail tighter. "I don't only claim to love Carter, your majesty. I do love him, and I want to couple with him— just not now. Carter doesn't want to go through with the ceremony if my heart's not in it. He wants to do it when the idea makes me happy. And in all honesty, I'd only be doing it for him and your kingdom's ways. I could not happily go through with it until I'm happy in my own scales."

He leans his elbows on the rocks beside him, stretching his tail so far forward it rests on top of mine. "Ava, you've been given a tremendous gift most humans will never understand. Turning your back on our ways will always leave you feeling unsatisfied in your new body. I hate that it has to come to this, but as your king, I'm commanding you to agree to the coupling ceremony with your mate, and you will not tell Carter about this. You will tell him you're ready to accept who you are and your position as his mate."

My brows furrow. Everyone has always gone on and on about what a fair and kind king King Attilonious is, but he wouldn't command me to do this if that were true. "What? Why are you doing this?"

His chest heaves, pushing water from his gills. "Because it has to be done. I can see how much you resist the mer way, and I don't think you'll ever be happy in your skin unless you do. That makes you a risk to my kingdom."

"But I can't lie to Carter," I say. "He's my mate."

"Then you better come to terms quickly so you don't have

to lie to him."

I dig my fingers into the sand, turmoil threatening to leave me broken. I can't even respond to the king.

He takes my silence as agreement. "I'm doing this for your own safety, Ava. The call of the land seems to have pushed the call of the sea from your mind. Until they're balanced, you'll never be able to live the life you want."

If I could cry, I would. "But I—"

"This is final. The ceremony will fall on the next full moon. It's time for you to accept your true place in my kingdom and under my rule."

Any respect I had for King Attilonious disappears with his serious expression. I can't stand to be under his gaze a moment longer, so I flick my tail, knocking his tail off mine and bolt toward the closest window cutout. But even if I could swim as fast as Carter, it doesn't compare to how quickly the king swims up and blocks my way, forcing me to stay in the room with him. He waves his hand, knocking me back, his lips twisted as he loses his composure.

Fear and anger threaten to consume me, stealing away everything good I desperately cling to so I don't lash out and make things worse for me. Without Carter here to protect me, to guarantee my safety, I'm not so sure I'd actually make it from this room if I were to act out on my frustrations. But I might if the king won't let me leave.

I turn away, covering my face with my hands. "Why won't you allow me to leave? I need to process this. It's not like I'm going to leave the colony. I have nowhere to go."

"Because you're upset, and it's in my best interest that no one sees you like this." He reaches out and latches his strong fingers to my elbow. "Now, sit back down. We're not through yet."

He doesn't really give me the choice as he pushes me to the black sand pool. Taking my place across from him, I sit silently, thinking about how the full moon is only days away—it's the time where every mermaid must leave the land to rejoin the sea. Starla will be over the moon excited, thinking I've come to my senses.

And now, I'm just going to have to suck it up and remember it's not the end of the world. I've grown to love Carter, but it's just hard to swallow that I've lost control of my life. That's my biggest problem. Being a mermaid, I don't have the privilege to live how I see fit. Carter swears it's only for now, but how can I trust that? Giselle can't pretend to be me forever.

"You know, Ava, I'm not as bad as you probably think right now," he says, filling the silence.

"You don't know what I'm thinking," I snap, turning sideways and pulling my tail to my chest so I can rest my chin on it. It stops him from resting his tail on top of mine, from dominating the space I need to calm down. It's one thing to force me to comply with his wishes, but to also force me to lie to Carter about all this—if Carter were to find out—I don't even know.

He leans back like he's sure I won't try to bolt again. And

he's right. "I understand Carter has managed to maintain your human life on land—something no other human-turned-mer has ever accomplished and I—" He pauses, gauging my reaction without finishing his thought.

Great. Just great. He's going to force me to cut ties to my family, and I won't stand for it. Heat travels from my chest to my hands, and I shake my fingers out, causing the black sand to swirl from the pool in a whirlpool and into the air without touching it. A strange feeling washes over me, the water seeming to move around me in a comforting blanket despite the natural current, like I caused it to move more than it should've with my motion. One look at King Attilonious' intense gaze sends the reassuring feelings fleeting, drifting away from me, leaving a chill in my bones.

He still doesn't continue but just watches me and the sand, making me completely uncomfortable in his gaze. Something lingers in his eyes—curiosity? Intrigue? Surprise? I'm not sure. But he doesn't speak or do anything except watch the swirling sand between us.

I force myself to fill the silence with more important matters. Creating tiny whirlpools is nothing exciting or important. "So, you're going to make me give up my human life now?" The question burns within me, my voice resonating from my mind and to the king in a sharp wave.

He jerks his attention from the sand, surprised by my tone, and smacks his tail once to push the sand in the water away. "It's what I should do."

My chest tightens with his words. I consider calling out to Carter, begging him to find me, to take me away from here, but we have nowhere to go. And if Carter sees me like this, he might do something that would make things terrible for the both of us. I wouldn't put it past the king to take his ring as well.

"But I think doing so will only hinder your ability to adjust to the sea. You still have a lot to learn, but you can't with the constant desire to return to the world above," he adds, his hard voice softening in my mind.

Hope rises in front of me so close that I can imagine grasping it. Going through with the coupling ceremony might be worth it if the king doesn't rip me away from my family forever. "So, what are you saying?" I ask.

"That I'm going to proceed with caution. You do understand the consequences that happen if humans discover our kind, right?" he asks. "For the sake of your family—your entire town—I cannot allow you to return to live your life as you had planned. You cannot go home because it would put everything at risk—"

"That's basically forcing me to sever my ties then," I say, cutting him off. I was stupid for even trying to hold onto an ounce of hope. I'm sure the king is capable of wiping Azure Waters off the map. If that were to happen, if anything were to happen to my home, I don't think I'd survive.

He raises his hand. "Let me speak!"

I cringe under the wave of heat that comes with his words.

But once again, he reels in his anger quickly. I don't like his unpredictability. One second he's calm, nice even, but the next it feels like he'll strike me with the staff he rests next to him—all for the sake of his precious kingdom. I bet no one has ever questioned his authority like I have. But I can't stay silent. It's not right.

He draws a pattern in the sand with his finger, drawing out the silence longer than necessary before he says, "Because this has never happened, I'm going to allow you to return to land once a month for a few hours. You may not see your family, though. I know there are other ways of communication, and one of those must suffice. If it turns out to be too difficult, or they start to question too much, then I'll insist that you cut your ties."

I frown. I can't help it. "I can't ever see them? Like forever? Then what's the point?"

His brows furrow with a glower. He rubs his chin, thinking about what he has just said. "I'll allow you one visit a year under my supervision."

"You? How would I explain that?"

"You should be grateful, Ava. Would you prefer to not go at all?"

I shake my head, forcing my grief away the best I can even though I don't feel right about the situation. I don't know what I was expecting. I should appreciate the compromise. I should be satisfied to be alive. But now having to live my life by the rules King Attilonious creates on a whim? It's awful.

I'll never get to live how I wanted now. I had planned to eventually go home after everything was under control. I wanted to go to college with Giselle. That future is as lost to me as my human identity. My future feels non-existent.

Swallowing the lump in my throat, I direct my thoughts back to the king. "I appreciate your thoughtfulness, my king. I didn't mean for my concern to come off as ungrateful. You've been nothing but kind to me when you don't have to be." It's half a lie. He doesn't feel kind to me. He feels like he's pretending to be nice only to talk badly about me behind my back. But at this time, all I can think about is faking my way through this so I can leave and be alone. I'll agree to anything if it gets me out of this room.

King Attilonious smiles, showing off his slightly pointy yet straight teeth. "Every merperson is important to this kingdom, whether they choose to live on the land or not. I know you didn't choose this life, but I'd like for you to choose to accept it. You have the potential for great things but also terrible things if you don't learn our ways."

"I already have accepted things."

He leans over and takes my hand. The gesture feels too personal for my liking, but I can't tell if it's customary to intrude on someone's personal space. I'm still lost to everything. Unfortunately, he's right about all I need to learn. "Now that all this is settled, I'd like to make a formal announcement about the coupling ceremony. Once that takes place, I'll grant you your first adventure back to shore. Is that acceptable?"

I nod, thinking about how Carter will be so angry if he ever finds out I'm not going through with this by my own freewill. It's just as bad as agreeing to it to please his mother—this time, it's for the king. Someone neither of us can deny.

"Yes, your majesty," I say.

He grins. "I'll put the ceremony into my court's hands. It'll be a royal affair. It's been a long time since we've had such a celebration."

Starla's going to have a fit when she finds out, but I'm secretly satisfied it won't be in her hands. I just hope I can get through this without losing my mind.

"Sounds wonderful," I say, though my heart's truly not in it. "I guess I should tell Carter."

King Attilonious propels up from his spot, pulling me with him. "Don't look so defeated, Ava. You should be excited you're going to make your mate the happiest merman alive."

I know he should be right—I should be happy—but it just feels so wrong. I feel like I'm treading water, trying to stay afloat, trying to get through this, but eventually I'll get tired and sink to the ocean's depths.

I can't think about that though. I can only hope that instead of sinking, I'll learn to swim in this strange new world.

9

OFFICIALLY COUPLING

CARTER CUPS MY FACE IN his hands, smiling through another kiss. His joy is contagious, and it's easy to forget how just an hour ago, I was breaking inside as all my freedom to make my own decisions was ripped away by the king who has taken great interest in my life as a mermaid.

I haven't even had time to process things and just go where the current takes me.

"What changed your mind, Ava?" Carter asks through another eager kiss.

King Attilonious watches with a stern expression from behind Carter, daring me to go against his command. Guilt nudges into my mind at Carter's question, but I force it away like all of the other nagging feelings threatening to be the cause of my undoing.

I suck in my bottom lip, soaking in his palpable excitement like a sponge. "I promised I would when I found my happiness here, and I *am* happy. I love you, Carter. I can't think of anything else that would make this life even better."

He frowns for a second when my voice hitches in his mind, but I kiss him again so he can't see the worry that flickers on my face.

His doubt fizzles out when he leans away, and I've pulled myself together to act genuinely thrilled. "We're going to have an amazing life, you know. I promise."

I believe him with every fiber of my being. It's the one thing that keeps me from turning around and swimming away. The ceremony might be happening sooner than I'd like, but it's also the key to my first approved trip to the shore, one I probably wouldn't get otherwise.

"I know. The king has everything planned out." I wish I could take back the words, but it's already too late.

He holds his lips against mine without pulling away, blocking anyone from seeing the look of concern flitting across his face. To the several onlookers, including the king, we merely look like two merpeople in love, showing our affection for the world to see.

"Ava..." The sound of my name coming from his thoughts

nearly ruins everything.

"It's okay, Carter. Really. It's not exactly what I had in mind, but it's better than the alternative."

"Which is?"

"We'll talk about it later. I'm fine, though. I couldn't be happier to be here with you."

Slowly detaching myself from him, I beam my brightest smile. Carter blinks a few times, hiding his oncoming emotions with a smirk. He knows me all too well to accept that everything is fine, but he won't question it. Not here in front of the king.

Carter turns his attention to King Attilonious. "Thank you, your majesty. I haven't seen Ava this happy since—" He doesn't finish his sentence. No one needs to be reminded that my happiness comes from the land.

I twine my fingers through Carter's, tugging him close enough to wrap my arms around his shoulders. "I've never been so happy."

Carter bows to the king, but I don't. It doesn't seem to bother King Attilonious either. He just peers at me with a small, approving smile. One that tells me I've done a great job and that he's satisfied with my acting. If only I could be as convincing to myself.

The more I think about the situation, the less it becomes about the coupling ceremony and more about how the king basically threatened me into doing what he wanted. It's nothing short of unsettling how my fate lies in his hands, in his rules, in a merman who could very well destroy me if the mood occurred.

A familiar black-haired merman swims into the room, drawing my attention away from the king. Tide stops in front of his majesty and takes a deep bow. They have a silent conversation for a quick moment.

King Attilonious turns his attention back to me. "Ava, if you'd please follow Tide, he'll show you to your changing quarters where Luna will help prepare you for the coupling ceremony announcement."

I consider arguing, telling the king I'm fine how I am, because all I want to do is leave and hide in my house, but my desires fall flat with a pointed look from my ruler.

My eyes dart to Carter's for a split second, but he doesn't say anything. He doesn't know what's going on in my mind, because for what feels like the first time since I've come to Pearlestria, I've built a wall around my heart and mind to protect the both of us.

Nodding my head, I bare my teeth in what I hope is an acceptable smile. Things are happening too fast, and I have no idea what the king means by preparing me. It's not like I can do my makeup underwater.

I reluctantly let go of Carter to follow behind the merman. Tide doesn't say anything, swimming in front of me from the king's quarters. He's probably afraid he might say something to upset me like last night. At this point, I'm pretty sure anything anyone says might get under my skin.

We swim through a narrow tunnel that leads to a small room with a human mirror attached to a wall. In front of the mirror rests a smooth, white rock meant to be a seat. A shelf cut into the wall holds all sorts of colorful stones, bright coral pieces, and pretty shells. A young mermaid, no older than me, with black hair and a golden tail, sits in the sand with a dozen pieces of long, bright green sea grass strewn across her lap.

Tide stops in the middle of the room, and she brings her eyes to his and smiles before offering me one just as bright. With a slight nod, the merman leaves us. Wringing my hands together, I float nervously in the middle of the room, taking everything in.

"You must be Ava. I'm Luna. The king told me you'd need some help getting ready for your first real public appearance." The mermaid motions for me to swim closer.

I can't take my eyes from the mirror. The only time I've ever seen myself as a mermaid is through Carter's eyes, and to see my reflection now is mesmerizing. I feel like me, but I look like a stranger. I don't remember my hair looking this light while wet or my face being completely blemish free. Even though the sea has been hard on me mentally, it's at least made me look good while feeling bad inside.

"If he says so, then I guess I do." I perch on the rock next to her, finally answering her.

"You seem nervous," she says, weaving a few pieces of grass together without looking at me. Moving from her place on the floor, she rests on her bended tail in a kneeling position behind me. She loops the sea grass around my chest before cutting off the excessive length with her nail. "But there's no need to be."

"Why do you say that?" I shift my tail so it doesn't knock into the mirror in front of us.

"You're trembling." Her fingers move so fast, my eyes can barely keep up with them as she braids a few pieces of grass together. Without asking, she hooks her fingers on the clasp of my bikini top and snaps it open.

I brace it against my chest. "Hey! What are you doing?"

She twists her lips to the side. "You can't wear that for your big announcement."

"But—"

"I'm going to make you something much prettier, unless you'd prefer to go without. It's your choice. Either way, the human top has to go. The king was clear about that." Luna unties my top strap, leaving me holding my hands over my chest. I don't think I'll ever get used to how nonchalant merpeople are about their bodies. I know I shouldn't care, but swimming topless in front of a bunch of strangers is fitting for one of my nightmares. I'd die of uncomfortable embarrassment.

"I'm not going topless," I say.

"I like to dress up, too," she says, motioning to her own sea grass top with shells woven through it.

All I do is nod instead of tell her it's more than a fashion choice, but I doubt she'd understand. Instead, I force myself to pull my bikini top away so she can measure a few more strands of the sea grass.

While she works on my new mermaid-approved top, I gaze at my reflection more in the mirror. My long blond hair floats around my head, appearing aqua in the soft light coming in through the cutout in the wall next to the mirror. My eyes, the same color as my cerulean tail, look wider, more anxious than I remember. My skin shimmers with a pearlescent glow, like someone dabbed my skin with a makeup highlighter, and it's smooth and hairless apart from my eyebrows and head.

Luna holds out a thick strip of woven sea grass, wrapping it around my back before criss-crossing it over my chest to tie the loose strands around my neck. She shifts on her tail, leaning toward the shelf on the wall, and grabs a few seashells and stones.

She carefully uses her nails to string small loops through the woven grass before tying a few dozen blue stones into my top. It sparkles in the light, matching perfectly with my tail. She takes a braided strand of sea grass and ties it at the bottom part of my new top, using another few pieces of grass to tie it to the woven band. It creates a triangular cutout on the center of my chest where my spark glows brightly from my heart. Only Carter can see it, and I'm pretty sure she chose this style just for him. Scooping a few seashells from the shelf, she picks out a scallop shell. She pokes a hole in it with her nail and ties it to a strand of grass before attaching it to the band of woven grass so it dangles in the cutout.

Surprisingly, the top is more beautiful than I could've imagined. It's nothing like the one Starla wore. Hers was made from wrapped seaweed and didn't have any of the decorations. This is the type of top I'd expect to find on a mermaid. I'm kind of excited to show it off. I bet Giselle would love it.

Trailing my fingers over the halter strap, I grin at myself in the mirror. "This is amazing, Luna. Thank you."

She grins. "You're welcome. If you'd like, I can make you a few more. I love having a variety."

I nod. "I'd love that."

She rests her hands on my shoulders, hovering behind me, and studies me for a moment before running her fingers through my hair. Taking a few pieces of bright purple coral, she braids it into my hair, creating a crown along my hairline. She leaves the rest of it loose, but it's pulled back enough to keep it out of my face.

I can't even believe my reflection. It's like Luna waved a wand, turning me into a fairytale mermaid, the kind you find on pretty trinkets in one of the many souvenir shops of Azure Waters.

Luna claps her hands when she's finished. "Beautiful! All the mermen will be jealous of your mate for having found you."

I smirk. "They should be grateful. I tend to cause a lot of trouble."

She laughs, her eyes nearly closing as bubbles release from her mouth. "You're so funny, Ava. I bet Carter doesn't think you're trouble at all. You know, I've seen you both in passing, and I couldn't believe how in love you both look yet you refused to officially couple. So many mermaids would've loved to have been chosen by that boy."

I never thought of the possibility of Carter choosing some-one else as a mate. I had always known he'd given up his one chance to transform a human on me, but I didn't realize it also meant he'd never get to choose even a mermaid. If I had denied his love, he'd have lived a lonely life. It's why humans aren't transformed on a whim.

I push the thought away. I can't stand the thought of Carter being lonely.

"Can you not choose your own mates?" I ask.

She shrugs. "It's more common for a merman to pursue a mermaid."

Kind of like the human world, though my girl friends are bolder than most. Sapphire, Giselle's cousin, had asked her boy-friend Matty out first. She loves telling the story of how awk-ward and shy he was the first time they hung out.

God, I miss my friends.

"I guess Carter did ask me out first." I'll never forget that day since it was the day I drowned, but it was more than that now. It was our one and only date with me as a human before the sea changed things forever.

"So, you knew him before he transformed you?" she asks. "I bet it came as such a surprise."

No one's really asked me how it all happened. I had as-sumed Starla had told everyone I was a klutz who fell overboard of the yacht Carter worked on during our first date and drowned moments before he could save me.

I think about that day more, remembering how nervous Carter was when he asked me out, and how I teased him because he had made it sound like hanging out with him wouldn't be as fun as hanging out with my friends. I remember how he gave me his hoodie to wear, like he knew I didn't pack for the cool night, and how he had prepared a tray of desserts, which I now know is his favorite food.

I don't remember Carter jumping off the boat after I fell overboard or drowning, but I do carry his memory of the events with me. The only memory I know is truly my own after falling under is the spark in the water, his life essence, and how it called to me. How it chose me.

"He worked on the yacht I was vacationing on and thought my fear of the ocean was interesting," I say. It feels so normal having such an odd conversation. I didn't realize how much I craved a friendship outside of Carter here. Luna seems nice enough.

"Oh, my Ocean. Afraid of the sea?" She giggles into my mind. "I couldn't imagine."

It wasn't so funny before my first transformation, but now, it does seem kind of ridiculous. I had good reason for my fear. I don't mention it to Luna, though. The thought of Bailey still flourishes a deep ache in my heart—because I was the lucky one.

Silence falls between us after a moment. Right on cue, Tide pops through the hole that leads to the tunnel that'll take us back to the grand room. Luna quickly runs her fingers through the loose hair cascading from my braided crown once more before hooking her arm through mine to pull me toward the hole.

Tide lets us enter first and follows behind as we leave the dressing chamber. When I exit the tunnel and swim into the grand room, King Attilonious and Carter wait near the old ship bow. A warm blush moves up my chest to flourish on my neck, and I meet Carter's gaze. Loving emotions cross his face. He smiles the smile he saves for me, dimples flashing and a strong intensity to his gaze that makes me feel incredibly beautiful.

Carter doesn't even give me a moment to swim closer before he closes the distance between us and wraps his arms around my waist to spin me around. With the adoration and desire he holds for me in his eyes, I can almost forget I didn't actually agree to the coupling ceremony. I can believe that maybe King Attilonious was right—Starla, too. Making my life official with Carter is the best thing to do...except, with it, I feel like I'm losing a part of myself I've been clinging desperately to. The human side of me that thought this was crazy for someone my age.

"You look absolutely stunning, Ava," he whispers into my mind, brushing his lips against mine. "I can't wait to show you off to the colony."

King Attilonious' shadow casts over us as he swims closer. Carter pulls away but doesn't take his hand off my waist. The king tilts his head slightly, gazing at me for a moment, but not in a creepy way. It's more like he's appreciating a piece of artwork.

"Like a shining pearl in the night-darkened ocean," he says after a moment. "You really do belong to the sea."

Except I don't. I might look the part of a mermaid, but my humanity begs to break free.

I don't have a chance to dwell on it, because the king motions us to follow him to the wide balcony that overlooks the colony. He unhooks his golden staff from the wall and swims to face his merpeople. Carter twines his fingers through mine and practically drags me to the king's side.

The sea of smiling faces greets us, and dozens of voices echo into my mind at once. The sudden cacophony of chattering voices causes me to swim back. Everything has been so silent until now. It's like I'm hearing the world for the first time, and it's scary and loud and all-consuming. The rush comes so quickly, I can't even distinguish one person from another.

The only thing stopping me from clutching my ears is that Carter's voice echoes the loudest in my mind, drawing my attention away from the merpeople in the crowd all here to see me.

"Shut them off, Ava. You don't have to listen to them," Carter says, raising his voice loud enough for me to hear. "Just listen to me."

I close my eyes, concentrating on isolating his voice and how warm and loving it feels compared to the intruding strangers all begging for my attention.

"That's it, Aves." Carter's words turn into soft humming to the melody of a song I recognize. It's enough to calm my heartbeat and get me to focus on what's happening.

The voices dissipate, and my mind no longer feels crowded as the king raises his staff into the air. The light from the surface sparkles in the giant diamond at the top of it, sending rainbow colors through the water. He then holds his hand toward me and Carter, and Carter swims us to the spot at the king's side.

"Today is a spectacular day, merpeople of Pearlestria. I'm here to announce the official coupling ceremony of Carter, son of Mateo and Starla, to Ava, the newest mermaid of our very own Pearlestria colony, which will be held here at the palace during the full moon. It is officially a royal affair as the sea has given Ava the greatest gift of all—a home among us. We shall celebrate her new life as mermaid as well as another love that'll last all eternity."

The king lowers his staff, smacking it on the stone, sending a cloud of bubbles toward the surface. Carter bows, and I follow suit, and then all the merpeople below also bow before their king. A moment later, loud cheers burst in my mind, nearly scaring me out of my skin. I bend forward, clutching my temples, my head feeling as if it'll explode.

A million emotions rush through me. Fear, surprise, love, anger, sadness, hope—it's too much to handle as I realize how real this is—how I'm giving myself not only to Carter forever, but also to the sea. This is something I should do with my family. They should be the ones excited and cheering, but they'll never be a part of my life like this ever again. I'll always be a voice over the line, a million miles away.

Panic seizes me, the voices pushing away even my own thoughts. My head swims with the foreign thoughts about me. Some mers congratulate me and send their approval while other's stand in disbelief because of the sudden unhappiness they see cross my face. I try the best I can to push them all away, but it's hopeless. Carter's voice can't even reach me.

Shadows darken my vision, and I flick my tail to escape. Propelling back into the palace wall instead of through the cutout, I hit my head and back hard on the rock, shooting pain through me. The last thing I see is the pretty ocean blue color of Carter's eyes before darkness consumes my very being.

•10•

FATE AS A MERMAID

"AVA, GIRL. CAN YOU HEAR me?" The familiar feminine voice echoes through my mind, breaking the barrier I put up to protect myself from the intruding voices that tried to rip my mind apart. "Ava?"

Light flickers in my vision against my fluttering eyelids. The tiny bit of light shoots agonizing pain through my skull, radiating from a spot on the back of my head. I haven't felt this bad since the time I drank too much champagne for Giselle's eighteenth birthday months ago.

"Do you have any aspirin?" I ask without opening my eyes

completely. I'm not sure I even projected the question to Grandmer.

A cool hand settles on my forehead, half covering my eyes to shade them from the light. The gentle touch helps ease some of the pain. "There's no aspirin down here unfortunately."

I squeeze my eyes shut, trying to remember what happened. All I can remember is the horrible disharmony of too many voices in my mind. And the king.

"Where am I?" I stretch my arms up, my fingers knocking into a warm, solid body.

"Oh, God. You don't think she's forgotten who she is?" Carter's concern enters my mind, and a smile creeps across my face.

I lock my fingers around his waist. "I know who I am, Carter."

Soft lips brush against mine. "I was worried you might've forgotten you were a mermaid."

I flick my tail, squinting into the hazy water. "The tail would never let me forget." I shimmy against the sand until Carter pulls me onto his lap. "What happened anyway? Where did you come from, Grandmer?"

"You hit your head at your coupling ceremony announcement," she says, wrapping her cool fingers around my right hand.

Oh, that. I was hoping that might've been a dream...or nightmare. The whole day's events rush back to me in a hot wave. How the king took away my ability to make decisions in regards to my relationship, how he's forced me to lie to Carter so he thinks it's all my idea, how the king took a normal future with my family away and tossed it to the unforgiving sea. How he broke me to shape me into who he wants me to be under his so-called kind and generous rule.

"You do remember you agreed to make things official, right?" If Carter didn't sound so worried, I would consider lying to him once again and telling him I had no idea what he was talking about. But, I can't do that to him. Not now. I already hurt him once before. The king wouldn't be happy either. I just wish it really was all a dream.

"How could I forget?" I try to sound happy about it, but it comes out more like a whine.

It's enough to make Carter frown. "What's wrong, Ava?"

"My head is killing me." I know that's not the answer he wants to hear, but it's the best I have to offer. Hopefully he'll buy it, since I can't hide the sinking feeling that sends my heart into my stomach. I can never tell Carter that his king isn't exactly who everyone portrayed him to be.

"Are you sure everything else is okay?" He helps me sit up by lifting me from under my arms. I sprawl my tail over his, relaxing in his comforting embrace.

My only response to his question is to lean my head back and rest it on his shoulder while closing my eyes again. Avoidance is my best bet.

Grandmer's figure shadows the light filtering in through the cutout of our home. I didn't even realize I was here until this second. The old mermaid uses her fingers to pry open one of my eyes completely, sending a shooting pain to my brain.

"Ava, did you hear Carter?" she asks, sending her voice into my mind.

I blink my eyes open to get her to stop trying to look into my closed eyelids. "What?"

Carter and his grandma look at each other, concern crossing both their faces. I don't speak up though. All I want to do is close my eyes and feel Carter's body against mine, holding me together when the ocean tugs at my very essence, threatening to rip me apart.

Guilt nudges at me for making them worry, but I'm afraid that if I try to lie now, I'll break down into a confusing mess. I need to be strong if I want to hold onto even a small semblance of my human life.

"Ava?" Grandmer asks again.

I scrunch my face, knowing neither will leave me alone if I keep avoiding answering their questions. "I'm fine. It's just a headache."

"I'm not so sure, dear. You seem disoriented. I'd like to take you back to the palace for another opinion," she says.

My eyes widen. "No! Please, no."

Thrashing away from Carter, I swim across the room. I slide to the sandy floor against the wall, flicking my tail out when Carter tries to get near me. He flies back a few feet at the sudden current too strong to have been created with just my tail, especially with his powerful swim.

It's like what happened with the swirling sand of the king's pool.

"I'm fine," I say, pushing the thought from my mind. Carter looks too concerned with my attitude to think anything about it to me either. And Grandmer remains utterly silent. I can't even look at her.

"Ava," Carter says, swimming a foot closer. "Are you sure?"

I nod without saying anything. I refuse to go back to the castle. I refuse to be in the presence of the king. And I know Carter would take me back to the palace because he's worried about me. But I can't even fake being normal when the ocean feels wrong. I feel wrong and out of control. If I wasn't bound to the sea, I'd probably trigger a transformation.

And I hate everything about this now. The king stole from me the one person I talk to by commanding me to lie to Carter. He didn't tell me what would happen if I told Carter, but I'm sure it'd have something to do with cutting me off from my family, and I can't risk it. I'd rather push Carter away even with how much it hurts me, physically makes me ill, than see him freaking out over me.

I cover my face with my hands so I don't have to look at him. All I want is to get away from here to clear my mind—to think things through.

"Ava, you're scaring me." Carter's worried voice nearly breaks my heart.

"You can't make me go back to the palace. I just—I need to swim. If I swim, things will be better." I direct my thoughts only to Carter, peeking at his expression through my eyelashes. My reaction is enough to stop him from dragging me to him by my caudal fin. I can refuse to tell him all I want, but I know he's going to want to know why I won't go. And I'll have to lie again.

If I thought I could get away with it—if my world wasn't on the line—I'd dart back to the castle and give King Attilonious a piece of my wrath. I've never hated someone so much in this moment, not even Starla. I think even Carter can feel my heat in the suddenly swirling water from an odd current that snakes around the room, circling me, moving my hair out of my face when all I want to do is hide behind it.

Carter turns to his grandma. "I think I need some alone time with Ava, Grandmer. Can you come back later to check on her?"

Grandmer frowns but doesn't argue. "She could be really hurt, Carter."

He shakes his head. "I know Ava, and this is something else."

They have another silent conversation before Grandmer turns her sad gaze to me. She swims forward, touches the end of my caudal fin, and then swims through the window cutout instead of heading through the house to the front door.

Carter cautiously swims closer, waiting for me to lash out at him again, but I don't move. He eases to the floor next to me and wraps his arms around my shoulders. I still don't react. I can't let him see me break again. He doesn't need to share my stress. This is supposed to be the happiest time of his life, and I refuse to ruin it because of the king's demands. It wouldn't have been so bad if he didn't turn the situation into something devastating. I know I could've gotten over the fact that I'm being rushed into the coupling ceremony. I'm merely mad I don't have a choice in the matter, and I have to lie to Carter. What really threatens to damage my very essence is that my human life is in jeopardy.

"Still want to swim?" Carter asks after a moment instead of asking me what's wrong again for the millionth time. He's never one to pry or ask questions. For the first time, I'm thankful for that.

Nodding, I slide my hands over his shoulders and around his neck until I'm riding on his back like the dozens of times before. Carter reaches up his hand to caress my cheek once before he takes off, swimming through the window cutout. He circles the house around back and bolts toward the colony wall a few hundred feet in the distance.

His speed pushes my hair out of my face, and I let the current wash away all the thoughts on my mind. When it's just me and Carter swimming in the vast ocean, everything else doesn't seem to matter. I can almost lose myself to the sea.

A pod of dolphins swims near the surface, drawing my attention to the fading light of the sky above. They jump out of the water as they swim, peacefully and happily enjoying the freedom they find among the rippling ocean. I wish I could bottle up their enjoyment to hold onto it for later.

Carter swims upward, just below the dolphins, and two of them dive down to greet us. A smile crosses my face when one swims right next to me, close enough to touch. It nudges Carter as it swims, and I reach out and glide my hand over its smooth skin.

Diving down a moment later, Carter takes us away from the pod before they start to play games. I grin into Carter's shoulder blade, wishing I could go back to when we first met. I wouldn't take so much for granted.

A familiar landscape appears in front of us, and Carter slows down. He navigates the bottom of the ocean through a kelp forest, and I know that if I head south-east, I'd end up on the beach in front of my Victorian mansion in Azure Waters.

"I thought bringing you somewhere familiar might make you feel better," Carter says, coming to a stop.

He grabs me and flips me over his shoulders to hold me in his arms. Hovering an inch away, he gazes into my eyes, trying his best to see what's going on in my mind. But I've closed it off from him.

"Thank you," I say, spinning around to watch a seal dart past us toward the shallows. Carter watches me expectantly, waiting for me to say more. "This helps a lot."

"Do I have to swim you through all the oceans of the world, or will you tell me what has gotten into you? As of right now, I'm fearing the worst." He reaches out and cups my face in his hand. "The only thing I can think about is how you met with King Attilonious alone and came out with a whole new attitude. Did he hurt you, Ava?"

I blink a few times. "No. He just wasn't what I expected." The king didn't physically hurt me. If Carter thinks he did, I'm afraid of what he'd do. I'm sure he'd be hurt or worse if he tried to go after the king.

"And what was that?"

"Nice," I say simply.

"But he's hosting our coupling ceremony—you seemed so happy..." His thoughts cut off as he thinks to himself.

I wish he wouldn't push this, because with him I'm a terrible liar. He'll see right through me if he doesn't already. I just want the next few days to fly by so I can get the ceremony over with, accept my status in Pearlestria, and have my first visit out of the sea.

I force myself to smile. "And for that I'm grateful. It's just that he's decided my fate as a mermaid." The king never mentioned that I couldn't divulge to Carter what he's decided about my life on land. I just hope Carter doesn't put the two things together.

His blue-green eyes darken as the silhouette of a boat crosses over our heads. "I don't understand. He gives everyone a choice."

"He has limited mine." Instead of telling him every detail, I kiss him and send the memory of my conversation with the king to him, leaving out his demands about the coupling ceremony. I'm not risking Carter finding out that. He'd never agree to go through with it, and I'll be left in pieces because all I want is to return to shore.

After the memory ends, Carter pulls away with a frown on his face. "I'm so sorry, Ava. I had no idea he'd do that."

"There's no way I can keep up this charade. My parents will become suspicious. What if they hire someone to look into my life and find out that I'm lying? What if they dig too deep and discover what I am? They'll be killed. King Attilonious would probably murder them himself." I close my eyes for a second to push the thought away. "It's over, Carter. My human life as Ava Adair is officially over. I have to cut ties."

He shifts his eyes to gaze around the kelp forest like he might find the answer in its tangled depths. "Don't give up so easily, Aves. We can manage a year. I know it."

It's not just the year—it's forever. "I need to see Giselle," I finally say after a moment. In a time where my world feels like it's sinking under, Giselle has always been the person I turned to, even as kids. She stuck by my side through everything that happened with my sister. She's protected me all this time, always by my side without pushing me. And now, I need her more than anyone in the world. She'll help me figure this out. It involves her life, too.

"Wait here. I'll see what I can do." He kisses me once before bolting away, leaving me alone in the kelp forest where it feels like I'll soon lose my human life—I'll soon lose a part of me.

The water is nearly completely dark before I sense Carter again.

The sun has long since set, leaving me in the glowing depths of the lively kelp bed. A few boats have crossed overhead, but most have gone back to shore until an hour or two before dawn when the fish will surely bite. Unfortunately for them, I've been extremely bored. For every fish they snagged on the line, I've unhooked it, letting it swim free. It's kept boats from lingering long. They probably assume one of the playful seals have stolen their catch.

"Ava, can you swim near the harbor?" Carter's voice enters my mind though I don't see him anywhere.

Just as I start to follow his voice, it suddenly disappears. Emptiness settles through me at his absence, and despair crosses my mind thinking about how horrible the ocean would be if he never returned to me. While we're officially not coupled in the eyes of the king, I know in this moment that it doesn't matter. I'm as attached to him as he is to me, and our souls are already coupled. The thought ignites the pull of his spark, drawing me to him through the water even though I know he isn't a merman now.

It's enough to know that I'd go crazy alone in these waters. How he'd go crazy if he ever resorted to giving me his ring, something he'd do if the king decided to never release me from the ocean's depths. It's in this moment that I know I would never go through with it. I'd never abandon Carter to the sea for a life on land with everything I love. I'll remain in hopeless despair forever to save him from that kind of fate.

Weaving through the busy kelp forest, I avoid a few large

bat rays and a leopard shark as I stick near the bottom of the ocean floor, following the sand as it inclines toward the shore.

As the purpling sky fades to black above, I flick my tail and propel myself toward the surface to get a better view. I can't swim all the way here without at least sneaking a glimpse of the shore. Peeking only my eyes above the water, I peer around the open air, cool with the ocean breeze. Light flickers from the mansions lining the shore, and it only takes a second to find my beautiful renovated Victorian that had once belonged to my grandfather.

A figure moves on the other side of the doors that leads to the beach. Like I've been granted a miracle, I gaze at my mom stepping outside. She crosses her arms over her chest, glancing at the dark waves of the night. She wouldn't be able to see me from here, and I can barely see her, but I'd know her anywhere.

I'd give anything to transform into my human self so I could swim to shore and throw my arms around her and explain the mess I got myself into. I'd apologize for ever leading her to believe I was fine, and I'd tell her the truth about being a mer- maid. I imagine she'd understand it isn't safe for her to contin- ue seeing me, but she'd accept I have a new life. That as long as I'm away, everyone would be safe.

But those dreams could never happen. She can never know. She'll have to spend the rest of her life wondering where she went wrong to push me so far away that I only see her once a year—if that would even be possible.

Shaking the grief from my head, I dip back underwater and

head north toward the harbor, following the pull from my spark, guiding my way. It takes me twice as long as it would with Carter, and when I get there, I don't see him at all. I remain off shore, quite a ways away from where dozens of boats and huge vessels remain at the docks for the night. I float underwater, bobbing around the current, and wait for what feels like forever until I decide to break the surface.

Spitting out water, I inhale a deep breath of salty air, letting it settle into my soul to remember later when I'm hidden in the protected depths of Pearlestria. The lighthouse near the cove shines its bright light over a long trail of rocks that disappear into the ocean. It's where I had gone to transform when Giselle had taken off my ring before she knew what I was. For only being a mermaid for a short period of time while I was trying to keep my human life, I have a lot of memories I'd do anything to relive again.

A dull light from a small motorized boat shines across the water, startling me. I dip under, afraid that the night fisherman might've spotted me in the water. The last thing I need is to have them start the rumor of the mermaid of Azure Waters. I can just imagine the king locking me away somewhere in his palace for the rest of my long mermaid life.

The boat crosses right over my head, sending a trail of bubbles behind it. The dull light from the boat shines into the water and blinks a few times. I shift my eyes, looking around. That's not something a normal fisherman would do, but I have no idea if I should risk breaking the surface.

"Carter?" I ask, sensing him nearby. His voice remains silent still.

Then the light flashes again.

Instead of popping up next to the boat, I swim a dozen feet away and ascend to the surface without spitting out water to gasp for breath. The light turns from the water and shines in my eyes as the boater directs it at me.

"Ava!" Giselle calls. "It's us!"

I flick my tail, sending my head and chest out of the water completely. I clear my lungs to suck in a breath and use my arms to swim me toward the boat. Carter cuts off the flashlight he's holding and sits down on the cracked leather seat next to Giselle, who has taken the driver's position behind the wheel.

"You stole Logan's boat?" I ask, pulling myself onto the side to dangle my arms near her legs. The boat rocks a few times, but it's not going anywhere.

"Borrowed," she corrects. "It did take a lot of convincing. He wanted to come."

Of course he did. Logan loves adventures, even if it was just a boat ride after dark. "How'd you convince him otherwise?"

She reaches down and dangles a paper bag from her fingertips. "Tacos." She hands the bag to Carter so he can open it. "Your boyfriend said you could use some comfort food, and I know they're one of your favorites and easier to eat than enchiladas. I brought you a cupcake for dessert, too."

Tears burst from my eyes. The hot saltiness of them startles me, and I hiccup. It's been so long since the ocean hasn't automatically washed them away before they had a chance to brand warm streaks down my cheeks.

Covering my mouth with my hand, I muffle another sob. Giselle stares at me with wide, watery eyes, watching me break down. Carter leans over and squeezes my shoulder. I wish he'd just jump in to hug me.

But he doesn't have to. Giselle pulls off her sundress and flips herself over the side of the boat, splashing me. She treads in the water next to me, hugging me to her. The flick of my tail keeps us both above water, and I cry into her shoulder as she rubs her hand up my short dorsal fin.

She cries right along with me even though I haven't even told her anything. Just knowing how upset I am is enough to set her off, and I can't help the ridiculous laugh that bubbles from my throat.

"Why are you crying?" I ask, choking back a half-laugh, half-sob.

She swipes a hand across her cheeks. "Because it hurts me to see you like this. Carter mentioned that things have changed. He didn't tell me what, though."

I suck in a deep breath, refusing to let go of Giselle. "It has. I'm so sorry, Giselle. I'm not going to be able to ever come home to live as a human. The king has forbidden it."

She covers her hand with her mouth. "But college!" Her dreams of us sharing a house together while attending UCSD get lost in the current around us.

"I can't go."

"And what about your parents?"

"The king says I can call once a month and visit once a year."

"What the hell? That's totally not going to work," she says.

I throw my arms into the air, and Giselle dunks under before popping back up. I grip her arm to keep her above water. "That's what I said."

She turns her attention to Carter. "There has to be something you can do."

He turns his gaze to the star-speckled sky. "I wish there was."

"I'll figure something out, Aves. I swear. I won't let those stupid rules ruin our life together. We're going to be best friends forever. No stupid ocean or king is going to ruin this. This isn't over, okay?"

I nod my head, wishing I could gather the hope she clings on to. But in this moment, all feels lost to the black waters.

•11•

THE KING'S DAUGHTER

"WHOA, AVES. HERE, TAKE MY last taco," Giselle says, handing me the carne asada taco she cradles on her lap.

I take it from her despite the embarrassment burning my cheeks. I've eaten both mine and Carter's tacos, and now half of Giselle's. But I can't help it. I'm starving, and tacos really are my favorite. Tasting the spicy salsa and hearty meat is like heaven. Not a single bite has the salty taste of the ocean, and I wish there were a dozen more to eat.

I consume the taco in four bites. "God, I love you both. And these tacos. The world doesn't seem so bad as long as I know that there will be more of this in my future."

Giselle laughs. "If you can sneak away tomorrow, I'll bring Chinese."

My mouth waters at the thought, and I shift my gaze to Carter. "You have to make that happen."

He smiles softly, but then shakes his head. "Tomorrow's not good."

Giselle huffs. "Why not?"

"Tell her, Ava," Carter says.

"Huh?" And then I remember the coupling ceremony and its obligations. "Oh, that."

He frowns. "Yes, that." I'd be upset for wanting to ditch our ceremony for Chinese food, too.

Giselle throws her hands up. "Tell me already!"

For Carter's sake, I beam my brightest smile at my best friend. If I say it any other way, Carter will doubt that I agreed by my own freewill. He'll piece it together.

"Well, Carter and I are coupling on the upcoming full moon, and we'll be spending the next few days getting ready," I say.

She raises an eyebrow. "What does that even mean and should I be excited?"

"It's like the equivalent to getting married on land," I say quietly.

"What! You're getting married? But you're only eighteen. And what about me? What mermaid is going to be your maid of honor?" Giselle rocks the boat, reaching down to me and shakes my shoulders. "This is crazy and—" Her words cut off when I hold her gaze for a long moment, begging for her to reel it in. "Congratulations! How so freaking exciting! You guys are totally meant for each other."

Carter flashes his sexy dimples, meeting my gaze. My fake smile turns genuine as Giselle's confusion and doubt shift to joy, even if she doesn't mean it. She has the same feelings I do. She doesn't have to tell me to know.

Keeping her back to Carter, she narrows her eyes at me in a way that says she wishes she could talk to me alone. "I swear! If this is legit in the ocean, you better not skip out on an actual marriage on land."

I laugh. "That's not happening any time soon."

Carter's head tilts to the side, thinking about what I've just said. We've never talked about a formal human marriage ever. It's the last thing on my mind, but I guess he assumed we'd make it official across both the sea and land.

"I want to wait until I have my legs full time," I add. Because it's true. But maybe when I'm like twenty-five.

"That makes perfect sense," Giselle says before Carter can say anything. "You'll have to make sure your one day in Azure Waters is during the summer. It's the best time of year here for a wedding, you know."

I smirk while shaking my head. "Why don't we get through this whole thing first before making those kinds of plans?"

She rolls her eyes. "You're right. Because one thing's for sure, I'm not waiting a year to see you. Carter better tell me where you're going to be when you get to call, and I'll figure out how to get to you. I don't care where."

I smile. "You know I owe you my life, right?"

She hugs me. "You don't owe me anything."

Tilting my head back, I dip my dry hair under the cool water. It muffles the sound of Carter's voice as he says something to Giselle, but I can't hear him over the sudden pounding in my head.

And then I hear it.

"Ava? Carter?" The masculine voice wraps me in familiar anguish, but only because I know where Mateo is, Starla will soon follow.

Panic seizes my chest. "Carter, your dad is calling us. We have to go!"

Giselle shifts in her seat. "Oh, crap."

Carter tugs his T-shirt over his head. "Ava, go find him. Keep him occupied. I'll be there as soon as I get Giselle back to the harbor." He starts the small engine of the boat, and it hums to life.

I meet my best friend's startled gaze. "Thanks for everything, Gi. I'll see you again as soon as I can. Please, be safe."

She hugs me once more before the boat takes off, leaving me in the bubbling water. Bobbing underwater, I spin around and peer through the glowing ocean, afraid that I'll spot Mateo watching me descend from the surface. But he's not there.

Diving deeper, I dart along the shore and away from the harbor back toward the familiar beach in front of my house.

"Ava? Carter?" Mateo's voice swirls through my mind again.

I swim as fast as I can. "Over here," I say, sending my voice to Carter's dad.

It doesn't take long for the muscular merman to find me among the kelp forest, holding onto the strands of the green plant in my hands. The sudden shift of water pushes me back, and I drift a few feet on the current created by Mateo.

I haven't seen Carter's father since my first night in Pearlestria when he kissed his wife goodbye so he could return to take care of their business on land. His bronze skin, darker than Carter's, glimmers a faint gold in the water instead of the pearl shimmer both mine and Carter's contains, and his almost black, shoulder length hair floats around his head. When he draws his gaze to mine, I see my own reflection in his dark irises, like I'm looking into two black pools.

Without a word, he wraps me into a strong hug, rocking me back and forth in the water. It's the same way he greeted me on land before he discovered that Carter had given me his spark to transform me into a mermaid. Pulling away, he kisses both my cheeks and gives me a smile that reminds me of the one I fell in love with on his son.

"My beautiful daughter," he says, giving me the once over like he hasn't seen me in my mermaid form before. "What are you doing so far from Pearlestria and so close to your home? And where's my son?"

A million lies tumble through my mind, but none of them

sound good enough to believe.

"To celebrate, Dad," Carter says, his voice wrapping me in comfort. "You know how much Ava loves the waters of her home. She made me the happiest merman today, so I thought I'd make her even happier tonight." He lies so easily that I almost believe the words he says.

Carter swims up behind me and hooks his fingers on my hips before leaning in to kiss my cheek. Mateo looks between us with a smile that takes up half his face. I didn't even know someone could smile so big.

Mateo closes the distance and flings his arms around the both of us, squishing me in a merman sandwich. "I wish I had been here for the announcement. Couldn't get away from the shop until closing though."

"It wasn't that great," I mutter, bringing my hand to the back of my head even though it doesn't hurt any longer. My mermaid blood heals me faster than if I were human.

Carter squeezes my hand when Mateo frowns like I've said the rudest thing in the world. "Don't mind Ava, Dad. She's a little embarrassed about knocking herself out cold in front of the entire colony."

A wave of heat flourishes up my neck and in my cheeks. I hadn't even thought about that. All this time I was worried about what the king said and how it affected my life that I didn't even think about how merpeople must be talking about how I injured myself during a royal announcement. God, can't I ever catch a break?

Mateo reaches out and squeezes my shoulder. "I'm sure it's fine, Ava. When everyone comes to celebrate your big day, they won't even remember that stuff."

I can only hope so.

"Thanks, Mateo," I say, puffing out my bottom lip, thinking the words to him.

"Call me Dad, Ava. You're my daughter now. I've been waiting forever for one, you know. Did Mom ever tell you I had hoped Carter was a girl?" He laughs, looking at his son.

"You don't have to call him Dad," Carter says to me. "I know it's kind of weird."

"Well, I'm glad you didn't get your wish, *Dad*," I say, the words feeling incredibly wrong coming from my mind. My dad is probably overlooking his patients at the hospital right now. "Because then I'd have never met Carter."

"You're right, Ava-girl." Mateo holds out his hand. "How about we head back? Your mom's waiting on us. She's completely thrilled."

I swallow back the anger I still hold toward Starla. "Sure."

Without even letting me prepare myself, Mateo yanks me forward, taking off, speeding in the water even faster than Carter.

Carter laces his fingers through my free hand and balances me out so I'm not strung along like a rag doll. I don't even bother flicking my tail as the two mermen swim me along through the vast ocean. In this moment, things don't feel so bad. As the surroundings rush by, I feel like I'm flying on the current.

If the protective walls of Pearlestria didn't sneak up so quickly, I could imagine being free. But the moment we enter the walls, it's like a door closes on my underwater prison cell.

This time of night, the colony is empty as merpeople hang out inside their houses. The palace glows with a strange white light, like the king has somehow managed to install electricity underwater, but I'm sure it's just another magical thing I'll never understand.

If it weren't for my mermaid vision, the colony would appear pitch black. Strange sea creatures swim through the sand channels this time of night, exploring without getting shooed away by the merpeople.

Carter points out the freakiest looking shark I've ever seen. Its long, pointed nose makes it look like Pinocchio when he tells too many lies, and its weird mouth looks like it escapes its head as it gobbles up a nearby fish. It's the type of creature I'd love to take a photo of to show to Giselle. Something she'll never get to see in person.

"That's a goblin shark," Carter says into my mind. "Some of the mers call it the nosey night guard."

Carter always uses the human words for all the sea creatures like he doesn't want to forget that part of him. The language of the merpeople is different, mostly told in images through thoughts, but my brain translates it for me. Everyone's distinct thoughts come through in a particular voice, but Carter says most sound identical to what they would sound like if they were using their vocal chords.

"It's so ugly it's cute," I say, watching the shark swim by.

Mateo laughs, bubbles erupting in the water. The faint sound of his voice drifts to my ears, though the water muffles it. It's one of the only times that I've heard a sound that wasn't the ocean, except for the times I've made Carter laugh out loud, and it feels weird.

Carter smirks at me. "My dad has trouble adjusting back to the ocean. He rarely comes here."

Mateo shrugs, now laughing into my mind. "I'm sure Ava understands, son."

More than anyone.

When we reach our small house, Starla waits for us on our front sands with her arms crossed. I frown, wondering why she hasn't gone inside, but then I remember that it isn't her house, and it's probably just as rude to barge in here as it is on land— or maybe she doesn't because she's used to the land.

She greets Carter with a huge smile but doesn't bring her eyes to mine. They share a silent conversation, and Carter bobs his head before he glances at me in his peripheral vision.

I'm getting pretty annoyed that so many people have been having private conversations with Carter lately. I have a feeling Starla is required to be here for the coupling ceremony, but she knows we're still mad at her. It hasn't been long since she left.

I turn to go inside, but Carter reaches out and grabs my hand. "Is it all right if my parents stay the night with us? It's kind of crowded at Grandmer's."

I twist my lips to the side. "Of course they can stay. They're your parents, Carter. What kind of person do you think I am?"

He narrows his eyes for a minute. "I think you're the most amazing person in the universe. I was asking because this is our house. The decision is for both of us to make."

Instead of arguing, I wave my arm toward the door, smiling. If I fake it long enough, I'll start to believe myself. Maybe that's what the king was hoping. "Why don't you two stay with us tonight," I say way sweeter than I normally think. "We're so happy you could join us."

Mateo hugs my shoulders, nudging me inside and peers around our bare living room. After seeing the palace, I think about all the things I could do to make it feel more like a home. Maybe Carter can find a shipwreck to salvage something cool from, or even ask Giselle to go shopping.

"I see you got rid of your bikini top," Starla says, directing her attention to me. "You look even lovelier."

I glance down at my grass woven top. Giselle thought it was the most amazing piece of clothing and asked me to bring her one. "Thanks, Starla. One of the king's servants made it for me. Luna was her name."

Starla's eyes widen. "Princess Luna is not a servant."

I close my eyes for a quick second. Neither Luna nor the king mentioned she was his daughter and the princess of all merpeople. Thank God I didn't say something crazy in front of her. Things could've ended badly. How embarrassing.

"Oh, I didn't know," I say.

"Of course you didn't. I wasn't here to tell you."

Oh, great. Not this. I'm too exhausted to deal with her. So instead of telling her off like I want to, I say, "Make yourselves at home. But if you don't mind, I'm going to get some rest. It's been a long day."

Carter slides his arms around my neck. "I'm going to let Grandmer know you're okay and visit with my dad for a bit if that's okay."

I nod. "Have fun."

Starla and Mateo watch me swim to the room. I don't lie down on my kelp woven blanket in the sand though. I don't think I could sleep even if I tried.

Gazing out the cutout window, I decide to swim through it and around the house to the long stretch of sand that will take me to the spot I go to when I want to get away. It's the first time I've gone at night, but I can't think of a better thing to do to clear my head.

But unfortunately, when I arrive at my little underwater grass meadow, someone is already there, sprawled out in the grass bed.

"Ava?" a feminine voice asks. "Is that you?"

I swim forward and face the girl I just found out was actually the king's daughter. I never expected her to be outside of the palace alone, especially at night. But I guess this isn't the human world, and she has nothing to be afraid of.

"Oh, hi Luna," I say. "I didn't expect anyone to be out

here. I come to this place to think."

She smiles, patting the grass next to her. "Me, too. The king has been anxious all afternoon since your coupling ceremony announcement."

"You mean your father." I only say it because I want her to confirm that she's actually the princess.

She brushes her black hair from her face. "You know."

"I wish you would've said something, princess. I wouldn't have complained so much," I say.

"Don't start with those annoying titles. My name is Luna. Plus, I didn't think you complained much. It was nice being around someone not from around here. I've always dreamed of going to land."

My mouth drops open. "You've never been? Why not?"

"The king doesn't think it's a good idea. Unfortunately, what he says goes for me."

I frown. "Same."

"Sorry about that. I overheard him consulting with one of his advisors. I couldn't imagine not being able to see my father all the time. He might be difficult sometimes, but I love him." Luna stretches out her tail in front of her.

I don't respond. There's no way I'm saying anything she could report back to the king. The last thing I need is to have someone telling him my every move. It'd probably be best if I just made an excuse to leave, because I shouldn't even be here, but it's been so long since I've had any socialization in the colony besides Carter and his family.

After a long moment of contemplation, I say, "I understand. Even people on land have problems with their families." Though, I don't. Not with my parents. When you lose someone close to you, like how we lost Bailey, things change.

"Will you tell me more about it?" she asks.

"The land?"

She nods.

"Yeah, I'd like that."

Instead of worrying about what I say about my feelings toward the king, I take the opportunity to reminisce about everything I love about my home—about the land. It's the first time someone has really asked. Most of the merpeople, including Carter, think reminding me is only going to make my adjustment harder.

I tell Luna about the things I loved to do, like baking and hanging out with my friends. I tell her about my favorite music and try to explain TV to her. She listens with wide eyes as I describe everything the best I can.

"This is so amazing. No wonder you didn't want to leave," she says.

"I'm going back as soon as I can," I say. "Your father promised me one trip a month."

She sits up, smiling. "Think I could come?"

I frown. The last thing I want to do is bring along the king's daughter on my one chance to enjoy the land, but something about her excitement gets to me. I feel bad. It's easy to put myself in her position, and I wonder which of us is worse off—me, because I had the chance to grow up and experience the human world, to enjoy it, rely on it, find solace in it, but also had it all stolen away from me. Or is Luna worse off, not ever getting to experience it at all? It's hard to decide. She can't miss it like I do, but she can always have that nagging what-if wonder.

"Um, I thought your dad doesn't let you," I say.

She shrugs. "I have access to his collection of sea stone rings. He'd never have to know."

Hearing her talk about the rings sends excitement through me. What if she could sneak one to me? I could run away with Carter, and this time, no one would be able to stop us. I'd figure out how to get away and never come back. I could convince my parents to move away from Azure Waters.

I think about it for a long moment. It all sounds so easy, but it also sounds too good to be true. This could all be a test. "I don't know, Luna."

"You don't trust me because I'm the king's daughter," she says, reading my mind though I don't share those thoughts with her.

I shrug. "Not completely, but don't you think the king would come down on me instead of you if we were caught? I have a lot at stake."

She digs her fingers into the sand. "We won't get caught. Please, Ava. Just once. Maybe just to the beach. It's something I can't do alone. No one ever goes to the surface around here."

Except Carter. I don't say it though. "I'll have to talk to

Carter."

She flings her arms around me. "Thank you! I never even hoped of getting to experience land, and now I might get to. You won't regret it."

Her excitement rubs off on me, pushing away the nagging doubt of what happens if this plan fails. But how can I not even consider it an option, a way out? If I can convince her to get me a ring in exchange for taking her to the shore, I could figure my way out of all of this. It's the first time in weeks that I have a fighting chance to make my future the way I want it. Because as of now, the king is forcing me to remain in the sea. Monthly visits ashore isn't enough. He didn't guarantee my permanent return to land, but getting a ring back might do just that. This has been what we've been waiting for.

With Luna, I might actually get my freedom back, and she doesn't even have a clue.

Maybe she'd want to join me.

If the king wants to steal my happiness away, maybe I can take his and show him just how it feels. Maybe it's all I need to get my life back.

12

ACCIDENTAL LOVE STORY

IT'S NOT UNTIL LIGHT BREAKS through the surface that I realize I've been lying back in the sea grass with Luna all night, and Carter hasn't checked on me once. I sit up on my elbows and peer around the quiet waters. The colony will be arising soon.

Luna braids another few pieces of sea grass together before tying it around my wrist. We each wear a dozen, all adorned with the tiny shells we've dug from the sand. After talking to Luna for hours, I've realized a few things about the king's daughter. For one, we have more in common than I realized.

She's desperate for a life she controls, one of her making. And two, she's starved for a friend. As starved as I am for someone to talk to apart from Carter. Someone who won't give me everything I want. Someone who'll tell me when I'm acting insane.

"So, will you come with me?" Luna asks, twirling her hands in the air, pointing to the surface. She's asked me to surface with her to watch the night sky turn to day. It's as close as she's made it to the human world, breaking through to take a peek at the ocean from a different perspective.

"I don't know. Carter will probably be looking for me soon." I haven't seen a sunrise above the water in weeks, but I feel like this is something I have to talk to Carter about. Only he's taken me to the surface. I'm not sure if I'm forbidden from doing so—not by him but the king. There have been unspoken rules set upon me. Like leaving the colony alone.

"So," she says. "If he wants to find you, he will. You don't need to ask his permission. He's your mate not your ruler."

She's right. I've never felt like he controlled me or what he says goes, but he might question my judgment. So many things could go wrong following the princess to the surface. What if King Attilonious discovers us? I'd seriously be testing my luck.

"I know, but your dad—"

She rolls her eyes in a very Giselle fashion, making me miss my best friend already. "It isn't forbidden. Look around, there are no boats. I've done this a million times."

"Okay," I say, only because I love the idea of breaking the surface. To feel air fill my lungs instead of water is as close to transforming into a human as I can get. "But just for a few minutes."

Taking my hand, Luna pulls me from the spot next to her and nearly drags me up to the surface. I glance below at the sleepy colony, still absent of life as the merpeople remain in their rock houses. From here, it looks like I'm gazing down at some magical place meant for storybooks. It doesn't feel real. It feels like it's all just a dream I'll wake up from when I gasp for breath.

We swim side-by-side, holding hands to keep pace with each other. Luna's golden tail shines like tiny mirrors encrust each scale, and her hair cascades behind us like a black waterfall. She beams a smile bright enough to outshine the rising sun, and I wonder if I could ever look so happy.

"Get ready," Luna says as we near the rippling surface.

"For what?" I ask.

She spins to swim facing me while taking both my hands in hers. It isn't until we're mere feet away from the air that I realize we're not going to stop to cautiously break through. We're going to breach.

Luna flicks her tail, launching us out of the water and into the cool morning air. We both spit out water, flipping in the air to dive back under in a graceful arc. When we pop back up, Luna spits water in my face all while laughing. Her black hair hangs in her eyes before she tosses it back, creating a wave on the top of her head.

I suck in a deep breath and tilt my head back to stare up at the clear sky. Soft yellow light sets my golden hair ablaze as the sun peeks up from the horizon in the east. The wide ocean surrounds us with no sign of land or boats or even birds to let me know that humans might be nearby. Here, treading water above Pearlestria, it's like we're alone in the world. I never thought I'd be hanging out with a mermaid princess, but here I am, living my childhood dream before the day the ocean took my sister.

"Isn't this amazing?" she asks. She laughs, her voice musical over the hush of the swells that lift us closer to the sky before dropping us back down. "Sweet Blue Ocean, my voice. I forgot I sound like this. I've never broken the surface with someone to talk to before."

"It's pretty. I didn't even think you could talk, especially in my human language." I giggle, watching her float on top of the water, smacking her tail on the surface.

She splashes water in my face. "How do you think we've been communicating telepathically? Plenty of merpeople can speak many languages of the human world, especially those who want to explore the shores. It's easy to learn things from each other. My mom was fascinated with the land and showed me as a merbabe. Hasn't your mate showed you? I've seen you kiss."

"Oh," is all I can say. I haven't heard anything about Luna's mom before, who would be the queen, but I don't want to ruin the mood by asking now. I let the thought drop.

"Yeah." It gets another musical laugh from her, and I think about what she says for a minute about the way merpeople learn, the thought making perfect sense. It's how Carter showed me his entire life in a day. He shows me stuff all the time. I guess I never really put things together.

Mirroring Luna, I lie back and stare up at the crystalline sky. We're surrounded in a world of blue—one that seems less complicated than it did last night. "I'm glad I came," I say, changing the subject. I don't want to think about the merpeople while the salty air dries tendrils of hair around my face.

"Me too. I wasn't sure if you would."

"Why?" The one thing that really pushed me into coming to the surface was I didn't really want to go back home.

She slightly turns her head to glance at me. "Most mermaids don't like to leave their mates. It's one of the reasons I haven't chosen one, though the king occasionally brings someone he thinks is worthy enough for me to meet."

"Maybe your mate awaits for you on land," I say instead of responding to her comment about not wanting to be away from my mate, since she's clearly curious and surprised by my actions. I also don't want to admit that I'm not like most mermaids. My only thoughts of Carter over the last few hours have been how he'll probably freak out when he realizes I'm not asleep in our room.

Luna splashes her tail. "Then I'll probably be lonely forever."

I grimace at the thought. Relationships are obviously the most important thing within the colonies. It makes me sad to think that Luna might never get to meet someone she likes if she's not given the opportunity to widen her search. Maybe the king fears she'll fight to remain on land. How would that look if a mermaid princess chose to give up the sea?

"That's what friends are for," I say, splashing her with my tail.

A smile lights her face before it flickers away. "But you'll leave me one day, too. Carter has already chosen the land, and so have you."

Which is true and will happen hopefully sooner if she gives me a ring. Because at this point, the king will only approve once a month visits. He might never approve more than that. Not with me, at least.

I don't tell her what I'm thinking, though. "You don't have other friends?" I ask.

She shrugs. "No one important."

I thought my life was bad. I couldn't imagine being in her place. "No wonder you want to come to land with me."

She's quiet for a long moment. "You know, we don't have to wait until my father gives you permission to leave after your ceremony. He has the whole ocean to watch over. It takes the focus off me."

If she had suggested it last night, I wouldn't have considered it at all. I'd have shot her down and swam away. But now, after spending all night getting to know her, I realize she doesn't approve of the king's rules. She isn't trying to test me or set me up. Like me, she wants to break free of her limitations, to make her own decisions. She wants the life I'm desperate to get back.

But fear of the unknown has kept her back.

Going on land alone has never been an option. She doesn't know the human ways. She's been sheltered into the perfect mermaid princess.

"Carter would never agree to take us now. He won't put his own ability to go on land at risk. It's too important in maintaining my human life as much as possible," I say. I don't want him to risk it either, but I can't imagine going alone. *What are you talking about? Yes, you could.*

"Does he have to come? We can sneak away late tonight. No one will ever know." It's like she can read my mind.

The sinking feeling in my stomach says not to agree. It's too risky. But, what do I have to lose now that my human world is already slipping through my fingers the way the waves steal the sand from the shore. I've lost my legs. Now, I have the chance to get them back. It's not the same as running away, but it gives me the option if I wanted to.

I open my mouth to tell her it's a bad idea, but instead say, "That's true. It might just work."

We smile at each other as our plan sinks in. It's really happening.

Another swell lifts us higher into the air, but instead of falling back down, hands grip my waist, holding me above the water. A wave splashes over Luna, causing her to laugh, and I flip backward to dive under only to meet Carter's curious gaze.

I knew he'd discover I was missing sooner or later. I'm surprised it wasn't sooner.

I flick my tail to propel us to the surface where Luna remains. "Apparently Carter started to miss me," I say.

Carter slides his hands over my shoulders. "I figured I should get you before my parents realized you stayed out all night when you claimed to be too tired to visit with them."

I cringe. "You knew?"

He chuckles and kisses my cheek. "I saw you leave."

Luna raises her eyebrows. "Okay, you two are the strangest mers in the ocean. First you wait forever to couple, and then it doesn't bother you to be apart. Maybe I need to hang out closer to shore to see if I can save a human of my own."

The thought bothers me more than it should. It's different than finding a human and giving them the choice to immerse in this world. While I might've eventually chosen this life to be with Carter, I wouldn't have done so on a whim. I'd have done things a lot differently. Carter knows this.

A flicker of sadness darkens his eyes. "It wasn't that simple. I got extremely lucky. She might not have fallen in love with me," Carter says.

Luna raises her brows. "How could she not?"

A rosy blush blooms across Carter's tan face, but he doesn't say anything.

"Right?" I ask. "There was never a doubt in my mind I wouldn't love the boy who changed my world. We were both lucky." I hope my words make him feel better. Every time he sees me unhappy, I know he blames himself. And even though I'm miserable at times, I'm thankful he saved me, a girl he had only known a short time.

He spins me around to kiss my lips. "You changed mine, too."

Luna releases a long sigh as she smiles at us. It's enough to make me laugh and pull away from Carter. Giselle would probably make a face and tell us to get a room if she were here. That's how different merpeople and humans are. Luna has probably spent her whole life thinking about finding her mate—Carter, too. But me? No. Dating was the last thing on my mind. I never imagined my life would turn into an accidental love story.

And I refuse to believe that's what my life will always be about.

Carter turns his gaze to the princess. "Well, Luna. Thank you for keeping Ava company through the night."

"I had fun," she says to me.

She dips under the water, and I follow suit to grab her hand to stop her from leaving.

"Hey, want to have breakfast with us? We have some plans to make, remember?"

She grins, releasing a breath of bubbles. "I'd love to."

I haven't looked forward to something as much as I do in this moment. And for once, my plans don't revolve around Carter. If only I didn't feel bad about it.

"Say it again, Ava," Starla says, swimming around my room.

I pop the last piece of the seaweed wrapped tuna Carter spent nearly an hour fishing and preparing for me into my mouth. Luna smirks at me from the spot near my window where a butterfly fish floats over her shoulder, hiding in her black tresses.

"I hereby promise to share the very essence of my being with the merman who—" The words fade from my thought. The coupling ceremony is a lot of memorizing, and I usually use note cards for this kind of thing.

"Promised his life to me to live as part of the great sea," Luna says only to me.

I repeat what she says so Starla can hear. "I promise to cherish the gift of life with love, loyalty, respect, and thankfulness," I add, remembering what I'm promising to Carter. I kind of hate that none of these are my own words.

Leaning back, I thump my tail against the sand. Luna grins at me while Starla glares. She places her hands on her hips and would probably wag her finger at me if she thought she could get away with scolding me like a child.

"You need to try harder and say it like you mean it," Starla says.

I roll my eyes. I can't help it. "Well, I don't mean them when I have to say it to you."

Luna gasps in my mind, hiding her smiling face with her hands. She slinks toward the window cutout, preparing to exit if things grow even more uncomfortable.

"Are you going to hold everything against me forever?" Starla asks, sinking into the sand. "I thought you might've changed your mind since you agreed to go through with this."

It's no different than when I did it to get her off my back. I don't say it, though.

I direct my attention to only her to tell her that of course I'm going to hold a grudge against her forever—that she doesn't deserve anything less for stealing the ring Carter gave me right off my finger. For pressuring me and belittling me and making me feel like my emotions don't matter.

But Carter swims into the room, cutting off my thought. He wears a ridiculous sea grass bow around his neck, looking like the sea version of a shirtless male dancer my mom and her friends laughed over when they went to Vegas last year.

"What're you wearing?" I ask only to Carter. "Please, tell me you're planning to give me a private dance later."

I've never seen him turn so red in the face. Ever. Nothing usually fazes him, but I guess he thinks the bow-tie is as stupid as I think it is with his bare chest and aqua tail.

He rips the bow-tie off and tosses it at me. It drifts through the water on the current created by his tail, and I snatch it from the water and twirl it between my fingers, smiling at him as he composes himself.

"I knew that thing was a horrible idea," he says only to me. "But my dad—"

"Oh, my God. It's part of the coupling ceremony, isn't it?" I slap my palms on my tail and laugh through the water, bubbles escaping my mouth. "How on earth am I expected to hold a straight face?"

He rubs the back of his neck. "I could wear it until it stops being funny."

"Only if it comes with a dance."

He grins, swimming toward me to wrap his arms around me. "I think I can work something out."

Luna and Starla watch us without a word as we share our private conversation. They probably thought the bow-tie was cute. After a moment, Starla excuses herself to talk to Mateo in the living room.

"I take it you hate the coupling bow," Luna says with a smile.

Carter steals it from me and tears it in two. "You'd understand if you ever lived on land."

"Maybe I could come up with something different," I say. "Does it have to be a bow-tie? What about a necklace or a cord?"

Luna claps her hands. "I could help! Would you mind if Ava came to the palace with me? I planned to create something for her as well."

Carter leans back on his elbows. "Even if I did have a problem, which I don't, Ava could go if she wanted to."

While I don't want to go to the palace, I know I must agree because in a few short hours, Luna will be stealing two sea stones that'll allow us to return to shore in human form. All through the afternoon, we've been discussing ways to get away without people noticing. And going to the castle to work on my coupling ceremony top seemed like the best excuse—one no one could deny me.

"That'd be great, Luna," I say like it's the first time I've heard the suggestion.

"Then it's settled." She pushes off the floor to take my hand. "Let's go."

With a quick kiss to Carter, I let Luna drag me through the window cutout so we don't have to face Carter's parents, since Starla might ask to join us. Instead, we dart through the colony, all smiles, thinking about the open air, the crashing waves of the shore, and the beautiful legs that'll soon take me home.

•13•

BREAKING THE SURFACE

"Good evening, your majesty," I say.

Luna guides me from what she likes to call her workroom and into the grand hall of the palace. She spends a lot of time in her little space creating different tops, because she always dreamed of going to the land.

"What a nice surprise, Ava. I hope you're feeling better after yesterday," the king says, swimming closer. He acts like he didn't just threaten to ruin my life yesterday, but it's not like I can give him the attitude he deserves.

My cheeks warm, fighting between embarrassment and anger. "Much better." The less I say the better.

"Ava and I were just working on some pieces for her big day," Luna says, cutting in. "So, if you don't mind, there are some things we need to collect if that's okay, Dad. I thought some sea glass jewelry would look amazing." Luna holds up a grass woven bag, which contains everything we need to go to land.

He grins without looking at its contents. "I don't mind at all. Will Carter be escorting you two?"

Luna nods for me. "He's just finishing up some family obligations and will meet us soon."

She lies so easily that I almost think Carter will show up at any moment to guide us over the walls and into the vast, darkening sea. In reality, he has no idea we're even leaving. If he did, we'd definitely not be heading toward shore.

"Then have fun, you two." The king responds like any normal dad would, and I'm kind of taken aback that he doesn't insist on seeing Carter first. All he does is smile once more before turning and swimming away to his living quarters, leaving Luna and me in the grand room.

Luna watches the archway to her father's living quarters for a moment before she motions for me to follow her. Heading toward a small tunnel below the balcony, she waves me forward and then enters first with me right on her tail. We enter a windowless room with a shocking amount of glittering jewels scattered about. Different jewelry pieces, including several crowns and tiaras rest on small shelf cutouts. My eyes immediately fall on a gold box, like a small treasure chest, but it isn't locked. The lid is open and within it are hundreds of silver rings just like the one Carter had given me.

"It's rare for someone to request one, but they're always here to show people they can make a choice," Luna says.

"I'm surprised the king allows anyone to leave at all," I say.

"He does because all merpeople eventually return to the ocean. Living among humans also brings knowledge to the seas. He has his own reasons, but those are the two I know for sure." Luna scoops up two rings and hands one to me.

"Have you ever transformed before?" I ask as I slide the ring on my finger.

She shakes her head. "I'm nervous. I don't even know how it works."

I tilt my head to the side wondering if I should stop her from putting the ring on. I let her do it anyway. "I think I can help you. We'll wait until we're swimming distance to the shore though before I explain. The last thing I want is for you to accidentally try and do it right here. I once transformed when I was way below the surface, and I could've drowned."

She slides the ring off her finger and sticks it into the bag across her chest. "That sounds awful."

I shrug. "It was but not the worst thing to happen to me." Actually drowning is probably number one followed by my sister getting swept away to sea.

Luna peers around once more. "This was, wasn't it?"

I shake my head. "This is just the low point of a swell.

You're about to make things a million times better. I just don't know how I'll ever repay you."

She smirks. "You don't owe me anything. This is enough for me." She sounds like Giselle. I wonder how she would react if I introduced her to my best friend. Giselle would die of excitement if she knew she met a mermaid princess. *Too dangerous, Aves.*

I twist the sea stone ring on my finger. This one feels differently than the one Carter gave me—this one is simply the key to transforming into a human and not the ring that held a promise of eternity.

"I think we have everything we need," Luna says. "Ready?"

I smile. "More ready than ever."

Luna holds my hand as we swim through the glowing water. She's not nearly as fast as Carter, and I'm able to keep up with her pretty easily. We don't talk much, racing through the current, swerving around schools of fish, the occasional shark, a jellyfish bloom, and even a squad of squids.

The more I swim toward home, the more familiar the sea is to navigate. When we reach the familiar kelp forest, I slow down. In a few short minutes, we'll be on the shore of Azure Waters, and I'll have my legs.

"We need to get as close to the shore as possible," I think to Luna. "It's dark, so the beach should be empty near my house."

"I can't believe I get to see where you lived as a human,"

she says, spinning excitedly in the water, tangling her arm in kelp.

With a quick slice of my nail, I cut her free. "If you like it enough, maybe we can come back and actually explore a little. But we'd need to prepare more. People wear actual clothes."

She bobs her head. "I can't wait!"

Taking her hand, I pull us forward, weaving our way along the bottom of the kelp forest. Only one boat floats along the surface, and I let it be instead of cutting the hook from the empty line that floats through the current.

The water lightens as we enter the shallows that will lead to the beach. The almost full moon hangs in the sky, casting a luminous glow on the rippling surface. With a wave of my hand, I motion for Luna to wait for me while I ascend to the surface. Slowly popping my head out, I peer around the black sea. Whitecaps crest in the close distance, lighting the shore just for us, welcoming me home.

A few lights glow from the beach mansions, but the sand looks abandoned from here. I dive back under and wave for Luna to follow behind me, and I head close enough to graze my tail along the sandy floor when I float upright.

"Go ahead and put the ring on. All you have to do is want to go to the land with all your heart. Your body will do the rest. Don't be afraid when you feel the pain. It happens pretty fast," I say, cringing when she frowns. "It's only like mild cramps. Don't worry."

I close my eyes when she closes hers. I imagine what it was

like the first time I changed back to my human form. How Carter held my hand, talking me through it. How my body felt like a thousand pinpricks were tickling my skin. How it felt to kick my legs.

The familiar cramps start from my caudal fin, trailing up my tail to my stomach. My muscles seize, causing me to bend forward and grip my tail as my slippery scales smooth to human skin.

"Whoa, Ava," Luna says in my mind.

I don't open my eyes until the temperature of the water changes. I stare through the blurry water, Luna in front of me still in her mermaid form. If she's thinking anything, I can no longer hear it, and if I don't break the surface soon, I'll drown because my new lungs beg me to release the saltwater to take in air.

Fear doesn't even have a chance to take hold. Luna arches her back and then bends forward, transforming right before my eyes. The shimmer of her golden skin fades into a deep tan. I watch in awe as her gold tail smoothes and browns right before it splits apart and transforms into two human legs.

Her eyes snap open a moment later, fear lining her deep blue eyes, and she reaches out to me. Together, we head toward the surface and expel the ocean from our lungs.

Luna struggles in the water. She tries to kick her legs, but they're unfamiliar to her like the first time I got my tail. Carter had to teach me how to use it. Slinging one arm around her, I kick toward the shore for the both of us.

Luna watches how my arm cuts through the water and how I use all my limbs to help us along unlike how we usually swim with our tails. After a moment, she doggie paddles with both her hands until a cresting wave propels us toward the shore.

My knees hit the sand, and another wave washes over us. Luna coughs and spits next to me, not used to relying on air, and I push her forward into the sand. I drag her by her wrists until we're both out of the crashing waves, and then I fall over next to her and laugh, staring at the glittering night sky.

"I did it!" Luna yells out, her sweet voice echoing through the air. She sounds child-like with the excitement, and it makes me smile even more.

I fling my hand out and cover her mouth. "Shhh! People live like twenty feet behind us." I didn't exactly pick the most secluded place to return to shore, but I don't care. About a half a mile away lies my house.

"Who cares? We have *legs*." She lifts her foot into the air and runs her fingers over her knee, admiring herself.

"Yeah, but we're half *naked*. Where's your bag? It's not normal to find girls half naked in the water. It'll be bad enough if they see us wearing sea plants."

Luna pulls the sea grass woven bag from across her chest and pulls out the two skirts we spent all afternoon weaving together. They're only about seven inches long, but we didn't have a lot of time to make something more appropriate.

It doesn't matter though. I don't plan on bumping into anyone.

Luna hands me the grass skirt, and I tie it around my hips. It's just long enough that I'm covered, but if I bend over, my butt would show for the whole empty beach to see. It takes me a moment to compose myself, and when I do, I find the energy to stand. Surprisingly, my legs don't wobble. Even though I've been without them for weeks, I still haven't forgotten how to use them. The almost eighteen years of walking has helped.

Luna claps her hands like I've just performed the most amazing trick. I laugh, brushing back my wet hair. Kneeling next to her, I help her with her own skirt. Her black hair clings to her damp skin, and we're covered in sand, but that doesn't stop us from enjoying every minute we have of breathing in the cool ocean air.

The goosebumps don't even bother me. I enjoy the chill that causes me to shiver.

"I'm going to need some help," Luna says, holding out her arms to me.

I grab her hands and pull her to her feet, but she stumbles and falls back to the sand in a fit of laughter. I sit down next to her, tapping her new legs. They're longer than mine and so smooth and unblemished. Brand new.

"So, you have to make sure to bend your knees. Take it slow." I get back to my feet and help her up again.

This time, she just stands in place like a wobbling newborn giraffe. Her legs shake, supporting her weight, but she doesn't fall over.

"This is amazing, Ava. Thank you." She hugs me as she

holds onto me.

"I should be thanking you, Luna. You don't even know how much this means to me. If Carter weren't back in the water, I'd suggest we stay and never go back." I shift her weight against me and take a small step forward.

"I wish. I just want to see everything!" She studies how I move my feet through the sand and takes her first step without stumbling.

I continue to shuffle, one step at a time, slowly showing her how to use her new legs. After twenty minutes, Luna manages to take a step without leaning all her weight on me. She'll be walking in no time, adapting easily to her new form.

Gaining more confidence, Luna lets go of me and stumbles a few feet forward without falling. She holds her arms out wide for balance and glances over her shoulder at me with a brilliant smile on her face.

"Did you see that?" she asks.

"You walked!" I clap my hands. "Soon you'll be running."

She takes a few more steps before she falls to her knees. "I'll walk the entire beach if I have to. I'll get these legs working."

I move forward and help her back to her feet. "Maybe in the other direction. That's my house." Raising my hand, I point at the beautiful sea green Victorian mansion looming a few houses away. No lights glow within, and I guess tonight must be a Friday night, because it's one of the few days my parents go out.

"It looks empty," Luna says, gazing to where I'm pointing.

"My parents go out sometimes."

"We should check it out."

I turn to stare into Luna's smiling face. My mind screams that her suggestion is a terrible idea, that I could get caught and will have to explain how I made it back from Washington so soon and without Carter.

But it's my home, and I miss it. My heart wants nothing more than to take a quick peek.

I don't say anything for a minute. I've already made the decision, but I can't find the will to force my legs to do the moving. So Luna does it for me. She grabs my hand and yanks me along, making me fall over as she tries to walk too fast on her wobbling knees.

When we're standing mere feet from my back patio, I stop in place and peer around at my neighbors. Mr. Johnson's bedroom light is on, but the rest of his house is dark. And like my parents, the Franks are out enjoying their Friday.

"Wait here," I say to Luna. "I'm going to go around front and let myself in. I'll open the door for you."

She grins as I motion her to sit on the patio chair. She kicks her legs up on the table and stares at her toes while I walk through the side gate that'll take me to the stairs leading up to the guest apartment.

I punch in the code to the key box and let myself into the guest apartment. Only the nightlight in the hallway illuminates the place. I stop in front of my bedroom, peering in, seeing it exactly how I left it, though all the clothes I left behind on the floor have been put away.

I jog down the stairs and head to the game room to open the back door for Luna. Reaching out my hand, I pull her from the chair and help her climb the small step into my house. The more she walks, the steadier she gets on her feet.

Using a towel from the storage bench, I dust the sand off her as to not leave behind traces that we were ever here. She peers around my dark house with a smile on her face and shuffles toward the wall of pictures my mom has had hanging in this room since I was a child.

"You have a sister," Luna says, pointing to a picture of me and Bailey on the beach right outside this house.

"She died," I say. I'd love to just simply answer yes, but then Luna would have more questions for me.

A frown crosses her face. "I'm sorry."

I shrug. "It was a long time ago."

Sliding my hands over her shoulders, I guide her to my favorite place in the house—the kitchen. Her eyes widen, and we step into the wood and marble room with gleaming stainless steel kitchen appliances.

She perches on a barstool, running her fingers over everything she can at the bar that looks out the window near our pool. I immediately head to the fridge and open the door. There's no way I'm going to let her go back to Pearlestria without trying human food.

On the top shelf in a plastic container is a half eaten cheesecake. I frown as I stare at it, but what was I to expect? My parents love dessert and their baker is supposedly traveling the coast. I just wish it didn't feel like they were cheating on me with the Azure Waters Cake Boutique.

Luna watches me pout into the fridge, and I force myself to grin as I pull out the cheesecake. Taking out two paper plates and two plastic forks from the bottom cupboard of to-go stuff, I serve us two small pieces of the cheesecake using a butter knife. I rinse it off and stick it in the dishwasher with the rest of the dirty dishes.

I hold out Luna's fork. "Try this. Carter tells me that he'd give up his tail completely if it meant he could eat dessert for all of eternity."

She doesn't hesitate before she sticks the fork in her mouth, much braver than me when it comes to trying new foods. She'd probably taste anything I gave her. Closing her eyes, she moans, savoring the piece of cheesecake.

"Mmm," she says, shoveling the rest of the small piece in her mouth, barely chewing it. "I could get used to this. Way better than fish."

"Right?" I eat my piece of cheesecake just as quickly.

When we're done, I bury the evidence deep in the trash before I guide Luna through the house. I turn on and off the TV, blast the radio for a minute, and then I grab the house phone from its receiver.

"I'm going to call my friend real quick. Then we can go," I say.

She pouts but doesn't argue. "It's weird that you can't just send her your thoughts."

"Telepathy only works when we're mermaids. In human form, we use telephones, which is pretty close. I just dial a number, and she'll pick up and talk to me without actually being here." I dial Giselle's number, one of the only ones I have memorized, and wait for her to answer.

"Hello," she says after the third ring.

"Hey, Gi," I say. "I don't have a lot of time, but I just wanted to call you and say hi."

"Oh, my God! You're *home!* Does this mean—"

"Yes and no. I'll tell you later, okay? I wanted to see if you wanted to meet again. I need to borrow some *things.*"

"You're not alone." She picks up on my need to keep things simple.

"No."

"What about tomorrow? I can leave a bag on the rocks for you."

I open my mouth to say yes, but a door slams, causing me to drop the phone to the wooden floor. It clatters away, leaving me no choice to forget about it. I can't risk getting caught. Instead, I grab Luna's hand and spin to look in the direction of loud footsteps.

14

BAD IDEA

"AVA! PRINCESS! WHAT THE HELL are you two think-ing?" Carter's angry voice echoes through the hallway leading to the game room.

Luna steps in front of me like she can somehow lessen the blow of being discovered. Neither of us answers as we meet his narrowed gaze. He's completely naked, dripping saltwater on the wooden floor, and I just stare at him in all his humanness. He came straight from the sea, following the spark that guarantees we can always find each other no matter the form we take.

"Well?" he asks, placing his hands on his hips. I wish he'd

at least try to cover up in front of Luna, but he's so mad that he doesn't even care. I'd die if my parents came home this second to discover the three of us in the house.

Luna clears her throat. "This was all my idea."

I slide past her to face my mate. It wasn't Luna's entire idea. I did agree to come here. "Please, let's talk about this outside. I have to clean up before my parents get home." It might also give Carter a minute to cool off.

He finally realizes he's dripping sandy water on the floor while giving us both a show, though Luna keeps her eyes trained on Carter's face and not the rest of his muscular body. Pushing him toward the back door, I gently press my fingers into his shoulders hoping my touch will calm him down. He's never been this angry at me, and I hate it more than I thought I would. I don't think he should be angry at all. He should be happy I had the chance to transform into my human body.

I scoop up the towel I used to dry Luna off with and hand it to him so he can cover up. I steal another towel from the cupboard and do my best to clean up the floor while Carter and Luna wait for me on the sand a few yards from my back patio. I flick off the light, lock the back door, and jog toward the others.

"They won't miss the towels," I say, wringing the one I used to clean the floor between my hands. "We have dozens."

Carter turns to face the ocean without responding. I half expect him to grab my hand to pull me back into the waves with him, but he doesn't. He just stares at the almost full moon reflecting on the black waters.

"I'm sorry, okay?" I say, his silence screaming at me louder than his voice ever could. "I didn't think you'd freak out so much. We're just having fun. Luna wanted to see the land, and she has access to sea stones, so we figured why not? No one will know."

His spins around. "You think this is a game? You *stole* from the king and went against his wishes. You put the princess in jeopardy. This is serious, Ava. Why would you risk our futures for a trip to shore?"

"What future? The king stole *my* future!" I don't mean to scream. My loud voice is bound to wake the entire neighborhood. "I knew you wouldn't understand. This is why I didn't tell you. You're so concerned about yourself and your access to the land that I'm pretty sure it wouldn't even matter to you if I never transformed into a human again."

Carter jerks back like I slapped him.

Luna steps a few feet away, and I wish she didn't stand there and listen as I basically stoop as low as I possibly can because I'm so upset that Carter doesn't understand me at all. I've been dying to come to land, to get my legs back. Instead of humoring me and letting me enjoy this moment, he's made me feel like a criminal—like I'll be the reason we don't have a future.

I can't bring my eyes to Carter. He stands in front of me, his shock and hurt flooding through me in waves. I know I'm not being fair by putting words in his mouth, but nothing is fair in my life.

We all stand in silence for a long while. Luna shifts on her feet, probably wishing to head back to the ocean. Carter doesn't do anything but stare at me like I'm some stranger standing before him. Maybe I am. Now that I have legs and remember everything I've been deprived of, I can't help thinking that going along with things like a good little mermaid is the wrong way to go. I should fight harder for what I want. If the king thinks he can push me around, he will. *But he can push you around...*

I swallow the lump in my throat. "Say something, Carter."

He kicks at the sand. "I don't know even know how to respond, Ava. How can you even think that? If it makes you feel that badly about me returning to land, then I won't." He tugs his ring off his finger and tosses it onto the sand, throwing the one thing that keeps him in his human form to the ground.

My eyes widen, and I jerk down to swipe it from the sand before the surf carries it away. I grip the ring in my hand, watching Carter slowly back away from me. I can't believe he did that.

"Carter, take it back," I say.

He shakes his head. "No. I want you to understand, Ava. I don't care about the land or the sea. I don't give a damn where we end up. All I care about is you. I chose you."

With those words, he dives into the ocean, leaving me and Luna on the sand. I step forward into the water to go after him, but I'm not so sure I can face him after all this. All I want to do is run back to my house and crawl into my bed. I want to pretend like I didn't just shatter the heart of the boy who'd die for me.

Instead of doing either, I fall to my knees in the sand and sob. Salty tears blend with the ocean water splashing my face. Even though I'm sucking in huge gulps of air, I still can't breathe.

Tonight was supposed to be the best night ever. It was supposed to be fun as I showed Luna what my world was like before turning into a mermaid. But now, my human life doesn't seem so important anymore. Legs mean nothing if I can't run into the arms of the boy I love.

I sniffle, wiping my cheeks with the backs of my hands. "I'm sorry you had to see that. I ruined everything."

Luna kneels next to me, sliding her arm around my shoulders. "He'll forgive you, Ava."

I press my lips together, staring at the dark sea. "He shouldn't."

"Why? We made a mistake."

"Because I still don't feel like it was a mistake, Luna. And I want to come back again." I shift my gaze to watch her reaction.

She smirks. "So do I. I don't even want to leave."

I don't want to either. But I have to. Because my heart hurts too much to even think about leaving things as they are when I know I need to suck it up and make things right with Carter. I'm supposed to spend the rest of my life with him. The coupling ceremony is in two days. Unless I don't show up. *How can you even think that? Don't lash out at Carter for something the king did.*

"But we have to," I say, pushing myself from the sand.

Luna stands next to me. "I know."

We peer around us once more. Luna removes the sea stone ring from her finger and drops it into her grass woven bag. I slide Carter's ring onto my finger on top of mine for safe keeping, though his is too big. As much as I know I should have Luna return my ring to the king, I can't find the nerve to give it back to her. I want to have the option to return to land if I ever need it.

Luna holds out her hand for me to take, and we walk into the waves together. I help her swim far enough away from shore, and we transform back into our mermaid forms without a problem. It's easier to control than I remember, and Luna doesn't have a choice since she's not wearing her ring.

A soft light glows in the distance like a beacon calling my name. I know it's Carter without even having to see him up close. He might be angry, but he wouldn't abandon me to find my own way back. Just knowing he still cares enough to watch out for me makes me feel a tiny bit better. Luna was right about him forgiving me for tonight, but I can't help wondering if he could forgive me for my unofficial plans to return in the future. At what point will he stop forgiving me?

I hope I never find out.

Without saying a word, Luna and I swim in Carter's direction. He doesn't greet me with a smile, but he doesn't pull away when I twine my fingers through his. As long as we're swimming, I can forget about all my troubling feelings. I can pretend the world doesn't keep spinning and time doesn't keep ticking. I can pretend I didn't hurt the boy I'm about to vow my life to.

But pretending won't change things. Only I can do that.

After dropping off Luna with a promise to meet with her tomorrow, I follow Carter back to our house where I hear half a dozen unique voices echo through my head as Mateo and Starla visit with their friends much too late for me to deal with. All I want to do is sink into bed and hope that sleep can erase at least some of the hurt in Carter's eyes.

By the frown puckering his bottom lip, I can see he had the same idea as me. But it'd be rude to ask the others to leave. It's part of merpeople customs for guests to treat the home like it's their own. It's why I didn't know our house didn't belong to Starla.

Before Carter can swim through the door, I pull him to a stop. His shoulders sag, and I take both his hands in mine, studying his face for the first time since the beach. His blue-green eyes shadow with a sadness comparable to the day Starla stole my ring right off my finger, condemning me to the ocean, and I hate that this time the sadness isn't for me but because of me.

I pull both rings from my finger and hold them out to him. "I want you to hold my new ring for safe keeping. This way you'll know when I choose to go back to shore."

He rubs his hand over the back of his neck. "You're going to let me hold the ring even though you know I don't want you going back? How do you know I'll give it back to you?"

I puff a bubble through my lips. "Because I trust you, Carter. And I don't want to have to lie to you about it anymore." I already have a heavy heart from the lie I'll probably take to my grave.

He puts the rings on the chain around his neck and swims closer until our noses almost touch, but he doesn't kiss me. Instead, he rests his forehead against mine. "I wish you didn't lie to me in the first place. I know you were desperate and the opportunity arose with Princess Luna, but what if the king was using her to set you up? What if this was all a big test and you failed?"

As quickly as the fear arises, it fades, because I don't think the king would do that—or Luna for that matter. Why go through the trouble to test me when the king already holds my world in his hands? And as for Luna, she wanted it more than I did. I could see it in her eyes. She wasn't lying to me.

"She doesn't like to be called princess, and I know it wasn't a test. Luna doesn't agree with her father." A million other reasons storm through my mind, but I don't share them with Carter.

"I hope you're right," he says.

"I *am*. Trust me."

Carter closes the inch of distance between us and kisses me like our lips can erase everything that has happened tonight. He holds me against him, our hearts beating against each other in perfect sync. Sliding his hands down my sides, he explores the curve of my hips before scooping me into his arms, holding me from the backside of my tail.

"I do trust you, Ava," Carter says, projecting his voice into my mind. "I'm just worried. The king could change his mind about anything at any moment if you give him a reason to."

"I'm aware of that. He made it crystal clear," I say.

"He threatened you." He doesn't have to ask. He already knows. I'm not great at hiding the emotions that cross my face.

"He's the king. He's looking out for his kingdom." It's all I can say to stop myself from pouring my heart out to Carter about everything.

"And I'm your mate. I'm looking out for you."

"Then you understand. I'm looking out for you too, Carter." Cupping his face in my hands, I peer into his eyes, hoping he sees the truth in my words. "I know I'm selfish, and I can be a pain most days, but I just want you to know that I want you to be happy, too. I want to keep you safe and protect your heart. I am really sorry for how things unfolded on the shore. I said those awful things because I was hurting."

"I'm sorry, too. Sorry because you were partially right. I don't want to lose my access to the land. I hate that I feel this way; it's why I gave you my ring. Because you were right, and I shouldn't think like that." His eyebrows knit together as he speaks the words in my mind. "But you do matter to me. I would care if you could never transform again. I'd risk stealing a ring myself, and if that didn't work, I'd give you mine."

I hold the two rings around his neck between my fingers.

"But now you don't have to. Luna won't tell, you know. She's keeping hers, too."

A smirk crosses his face. "So you're willing to take the risk to go to land?"

"The king has already stolen my chance to choose everything in my life. I'm only stealing back the one choice that was supposed to be mine to begin with," I say. "And admit it, even though you were mad at me, you loved every second we were together on the shore."

He sucks in his bottom lip. "So, so much."

"Then let's go back. Just me and you. No one will miss us."

He hesitates. "This is a bad idea."

I kiss him, sharing with him a memory of me with legs he won't be able to resist. "But a good one, too."

He shudders before breaking away to swim in circles around me a few times. "Ava." His voice sounds barely above a whisper in my mind. "You make it incredibly hard to say no."

"You're saying no?" It wasn't exactly the answer I had expected. My bottom lip pouts, but there's not much I can say or do.

He swims around me a few more times before stopping for another kiss where he projects the same image I shared with him back to me, like he can't get it off his mind. "I said you make it hard to say no, not that I was saying no."

I pull his bottom lip between my teeth. "Really?"

Without answering, he hooks his arms around my waist, and we take off into the dark ocean.

15

BACK TO REALITY

THE EARLY MORNING SUN WARMS my skin. I stir in Carter's arms, water lapping over our legs. We lie together on the secluded beach of an uninhabited island somewhere in the Pacific Ocean. It was the only place he agreed to come with me far from humans.

When I shift to sit up, Carter moans before pulling me back down next to him. Sand clings to his tan skin, his chest rising and falling as he breathes in the crisp sea air. The roar of the waves hums in my ears, and I can't stop myself from curling against him.

The night couldn't have been more perfect—exactly how I imagine it's supposed to be—just me and him, enjoying both the land and ocean with no one to worry about. Another wave crashes the shore, rolling over us, and it's enough to pull Carter back to reality. The one I've wanted to avoid—the one where I have no control.

Carter's blue-green eyes shine bright in the sun. I had almost forgotten how pretty they were in the light. He tucks my sandy hair behind my ear before kissing my jaw only to work his way to my lips. He smiles against my mouth, inhaling a deep breath of the sea-perfumed air around us.

"I don't want to go back," he says after a moment. "It could take them a while to find us if we stay right here."

I close my eyes, just imagining what it'd be like to make this beautifully desolate island our home, but it's no different than the sea. My family and friends aren't here. It's probably the type of life the king would expect us to have, far from human civilization.

"Not with the full moon tomorrow," I say. We can only stay out of the ocean for so long before it forces us back. And with the full moon comes our coupling ceremony. I couldn't run to shore to escape it even if I wanted to.

"And our ceremony," Carter adds, thinking the same thought as me except he says it almost dreamily.

"Yeah, that." The words come out flat.

He takes my hands in his. "Why do I get the feeling you're less than thrilled about it? I thought this was what you wanted."

"It's you I want. The ceremony—" I snap my mouth shut. "I'm nervous is all." Better than saying the king made the decision for me.

"I am, too." He tilts his head to the brilliant blue sky. His words make me feel slightly better. "But we'll be together. I'll make sure it's everything you hoped for."

Except I haven't hoped for anything. All I hope is to get through it without puking from nerves or making a fool of myself. At this point, I just want it to be over with so I don't have the expectation hanging over my head. And it sucks that I feel this way.

"I need to be honest with you, Carter," I say.

I don't know if it's because we're cuddling on a beach in our human bodies or if it's the fact that the king is far away and can't intimidate me here—either way, I can't stop thinking about how I'm lying to Carter. It makes it even harder to swallow the idea of the coupling ceremony if we start our new lives together with me being dishonest. The king was crazy to think I could never tell Carter. I have to. Even if it risks losing the hope of remaining in contact with my family, however far-fetched that is under the king's new rules for me.

He sits up straighter, digging his bare feet into the sand. "You don't want to go through with the ceremony." Rubbing his hands over his face, he groans while shaking his head, like he knew it was coming, though it's not what I'm about to say.

"It's not that, Carter." I suck in a deep, shaky breath to help me get through this. "It's just—well—" Why can't I spit the words out? *Because you don't want to hurt him.*

Continuing with the lie will hurt more if he ever found out.

"Ava," Carter says, "you can tell me anything."

Doesn't make it any easier. "The coupling ceremony wasn't my idea," I finally say. "King Attilonious didn't give me a choice. He thinks by not agreeing to officially couple with you that I'm turning my back on the sea. He thinks the only way to accept who I am is if I accept my position as your mate. But Carter, please, you can't tell him. He told me I couldn't let you know." Telling the truth has never felt so good and awful all at once.

His expression morphs to anger, and he shoves his hands into the sand. "Damn him. He had no right. And to demand that you lie to me?"

I'd love nothing more than to watch Carter swim home and stand up to the king, but that can only end badly. I wrap my arms around his tense shoulders. "This doesn't change any-thing, Carter. We're going through with the ceremony."

"But you don't want to," he says.

I rest my cheek on his shoulder. "I didn't say that. I said the king didn't give me a choice. Tomorrow, we're making this official in the sea, and then we can focus on the rest of our lives, okay?"

"I don't know, Ava." He shifts in the sand to reach up and run his fingers down my cheek as he looks into my eyes.

"What don't you know? I thought you wanted to do this?"

"When I knew you were in it for us, without a single doubt in your mind."

It is the only reason I'm doing it—for us. To help us while we're under the king's fin. Leaning forward, I brush my lips against his, hoping he can sense I'm not saying my next words only to make him feel better. "This is for us, Carter. Don't you see? Everything I agree to do is for us. I love you, and even if it's not how I imagined things turning out, it doesn't mean I don't like how they're going. I realize that now more than ever. So, will you go back with me and make things official? Or should I prepare to be stood up?"

He's quiet for a long moment. "I'd never stand you up, Aves. But after tomorrow, I'm not going to sit back and hope for the best. I'm getting us out of Pearlestria and away from the king."

"How?"

He shrugs. "I'll figure it out."

We sneak in through the window cutout like I would if I were coming in late at home in Azure Waters. It's silly, but the last thing we need is to be bombarded with questions while his parents are here, living in our house for a few days like they own the place.

Carter stores my new ring in the metal chest where we keep all my other human possessions—at least the ones he managed to bring me from the shore—before we settle onto our blanket in the sand. I smack my tail against the ground a few times, still adjusting to the lack of legs I had quickly grown used to having.

Carter rests on his side, leaning on his elbow, tracing circles on my stomach, occasionally pinching the ridge that separates my skin from the scales of my tail between his thumb and index finger.

Even though he doesn't send his thoughts to me, I can see he has a lot on his mind. I hate that he knows I'm only doing the ceremony willingly to make things easier. He says he'll get us away from here, but I know it doesn't mean escaping to land. We're in Pearlestria for a reason. The king wants to keep an eye on me.

We don't have a moment to discuss it though, because Mateo's voice rings through our minds, asking if we're awake yet.

Neither of us answers right away. We lie quietly next to each other like if we don't move, Carter's dad will just go away.

"Son? You have a visitor," Mateo says, hovering in the archway. Carter's father's dark hair flows around him like a curtain, and he smiles at us as he pushes it from his face. "It's King Attilonious and Princess Luna"

I stiffen in Carter's arms. The last merperson in the ocean I want to see is now in our house. A million fearful thoughts rush through my mind. What if he found out I took Luna to the shore? Or that I told Carter the truth? So much could be so wrong.

Carter side glances me, but his face remains expressionless. He pushes from the sandy floor, tugging me along with him by my waist. He knows I won't move unless he makes me. I'd rather hide in here until he finds out what the king's visit is about. It must be important if he didn't send a messenger to summon us.

"Oh, God. He knows. You were right." I direct the thought only to Carter as we slide past Mateo.

"Calm down, Ava. Our ceremony is tomorrow. It could be nothing," he answers.

I grip his fingers. "It could be the end."

"Ava!" Luna swims across the room when she sees us and thrusts her arms around me in a hug comparable to one Giselle would give me. Who knew a friendship could blossom so quickly, but things are much more intense in the sea than they are on land. "I can't wait to show you the finished pieces for tomorrow."

I stand still in her arms a moment. She projects her voice to everyone in the room. A moment later, I realize I'm frozen solid, and I bring my hands up to hug the mermaid back. "I'm so excited!" I send my own voice to everyone. "I don't even know how to thank you."

She brings her gaze to mine, directing a thought to only me. "You already have. Everything's fine. Relax before my dad thinks something is wrong."

I release a bubble through my lips and turn to the king with a bow. "Welcome to our home, my king."

Carter bows as well. "It is an honor, your majesty." The thought is as relaxed as he is, and I wish I could learn to compose myself at all times.

"If I'd known Ava's company would bring my daughter such happiness, I'd have summoned you both sooner," King Attilonious says. Except I might not have enjoyed her company if I were forced so quickly into things in Pearlestria. I don't mention it, though.

Carter bows to Luna. "Princess Luna has made quite the impression on my mate as well, your majesty. A friend apart from me was exactly what Ava needed. You know how the human world works. Relationships with friends can run as deep as family."

"Is that true?" Luna asks only me.

I nod my head. "I love my friends dearly. Just as fiercely as I love Carter. You know, Luna. You remind me of my best friend on land. I'd love it if you could meet her. I think you'd get along."

"You want me to meet your human friend? Oh, Ocean. I'd love that. I think I understand what Carter meant about different relationships. I can already feel a bond to you." She smiles shyly.

"Same," I say. And I mean it. There's something that draws me to Luna, and I trust her.

"Ava? Did you hear King Attilonious? He asked if it would be all right if you and Luna spent the day together so the rest of us can get things prepared for tomorrow. She can help you with everything you'll need to do." Carter asks, breaking my attention away from Luna.

With heated cheeks, I turn my attention to the king. "I'd love that, my king. But are you sure I'm not needed?"

Luna grabs my hand. "Why would you be? It's Carter's job to prepare everything, not yours."

Hmm. Well, that's different. I thought everything would fall to me, like most things fall on the bride in the human world. All I know is I have to memorize the vows I don't really want to say. I always imagined writing my own. Maybe I can still say some of my own things.

Starla places her hands on her hips, drawing attention to herself for the first time. If she'd have stayed against the wall, I could have pretended she didn't exist. "Things are different here, Ava. Carter chose you, so it's our responsibility to plan the ceremony. All you need to do is show up. I've even agreed to stand with you."

My brows furrow. "What?"

Carter swims up behind me, twining his fingers with mine. "It's like the maid of honor position. She'll make sure things run smoothly and help you if you forget."

My frown deepens as disdain crosses my face. "Can't your dad or grandma stand up with me?"

Carter keeps his face straight as the others watch us have our obviously private conversation. The king leans on his golden scepter with an expression I can't read—like he's waiting for me to just accept whatever everyone says.

"No, Ava. My dad is standing up for me. Grandmer won't get in my mom's way. It'd be rude," he says.

I shift my gaze across the room until I meet Starla's confident eyes. She's daring me to have an outburst in front of the king.

But what she doesn't know is that I don't give a damn about what the king thinks of me at this point. "I don't want her to stand up with me, Carter."

Carter's jaw tenses as he clenches his teeth. "I know, but what am I supposed to do?"

I pull away from him and stand to face Starla. "I'm sorry, Starla. No one consulted me about you standing up with me. If I had known, I wouldn't have asked Luna."

Luna's surprised expression nearly gives my lie away. It's the only thing I could think to do to make it look like I'm not still holding onto my eternal grudge against my future mother-in-law. I can't help it. I know she means well, but she could've left us alone. I refuse to have her by my side.

"Oh," Starla says. "I didn't think that you—"

"That I what?" I ask.

She shakes her head. "Never mind. What an honor to have the princess stand up with you."

If she agrees. Luna still looks like she's in utter shock. After a minute, a smile finally crosses her face as she brings her eyes to mine. "It's my honor to do it. I never thought I'd get the opportunity."

If Carter wasn't still holding my hand, I'd sink to the floor in relief. He smirks at me, flashing his dimples at my quick thinking, probably relieved he doesn't have to stress about me being miserable at our coupling ceremony.

"What a wonderful ceremony this will be," King Attilonious says. "It'll be one remembered for ages."

All because I'm the girl who was transformed on a whim.

"We can only hope," Carter says with a small smile. He turns to me and kisses me softly on the lips. "You have fun with Luna, okay? You know what to do if you need me."

Luna swims up next to me, and I take her hand when she offers it out. Instead of heading out the front cutout, I pull her toward my bedroom first. I need to make a stop, because there's no way I'm wasting another opportunity if the king will be busy.

Luna has the same idea as me, because she jiggles a small woven bag in front of me. "We'll have until dusk."

I grin. That's so much time. Closing my eyes, I send a private thought to Carter. "We're going back to shore."

"Ava," Carter says. I expect him to rush into the room to stop us. I expect him to argue with me. But he doesn't do either. All he says is, "Be careful."

I smile though he can't see me. "I will. Promise." Turning to Luna, I ask, "Ready?"

She swims through the window cutout and waits for me on the other side. "More ready than ever."

•16•

MERMAID OUT OF WATER

"WAIT HERE," I TELL LUNA as we reach the rocks where I hope Giselle left a bag of clothes for me.

Luna remains near the sandy floor while I peek my head above the churning water. A gray bag rests on the rocks exactly where Giselle sat the first time I saw her after I was allowed to leave the colony. I swim closer and use my tail to propel me up and out of the ocean.

Opening the bag, I smile at the four different bikinis and three sundresses. She thought I might want options, and I'm glad for her thoughtfulness. I won't have to figure out how to get Luna something to wear. The dresses might be on the shorter side, but we're about the same size otherwise.

I pull two of the bikinis out of the bag before closing it up so the water doesn't soak the rest of the stuff. Dipping back underwater, I wave the bikinis at Luna, who stares at me with wide eyes.

"Carter brought these here late last night," I say to answer her silent question. There's no way I'd let Luna know that a human knows our secret. We might have a budding friendship, but when it comes to life or death for Giselle, I'd do anything to protect her.

Luna rocks back and forth in the water, taking the black bikini from me. "I told you he'd forgive you."

I nod. "He's not happy about it, but he understands."

She doesn't think about it much longer because the shore calls to us.

Swimming closer to land, we bob in the waves just deep enough that our tails touch the bottom. The transformation takes hold of me immediately, and the cramps last merely seconds before I'm kicking to the surface. It's the fastest I've ever transformed, and I can't help but think that maybe Starla had been right about how living in the ocean would help me gain better control. I'd never admit that to her, though.

It takes Luna a few minutes but not nearly as long as it took me to transform in the beginning. She's lived in the ocean her whole life and has dreamed about the land. I doubt she'll be out of control like me. I'm almost jealous of how easy it is for her.

She spits out a mouthful of water and smiles at me, kicking her legs to stay afloat. I stop her from sinking under, and we trade our sea grass tops for the swimsuits. I help Luna swim toward the shore, staying near the rocks where the closest beachgoer is far enough away not to notice us emerge from the water.

When we tumble through the waves and into the sand, Luna laughs loudly. Her voice echoes through the air in a musical sound fit for a siren. She flips on her back, chest heaving, and stares at the sun shining overhead. I fall next to her, not caring that the sand sticks to every inch of me.

"I can get used to this," she says, digging her feet into the sand to kick it into the air. It rains down on us in a soft shower.

"Right?" I sit up and pull her up with me.

I manage to help her to her feet without as much trouble as last night. She wobbles for a moment, but then steadies herself. We trudge through the sand together to the public beach in the opposite direction of my house. After a quick rinse off in the outside shower, we let the cool breeze dry our skin before I pull the dresses from the bag.

It's not until then that I realize there's a phone in the bottom of the bag along with a couple of twenties. Giselle is totally the best person in existence. I'd give anything to have her in both my worlds as long as it didn't mean she had to give up everything, too.

"What's that?" Luna asks, pointing to the stuff in my hand.

"The cell phone is so I can call my best friend. The money

is if we need to buy anything," I say.

"Like what?"

"Food, clothes, transportation—you have to pay for everything on land," I say.

Her eyes widen. "Really?"

"Yeah."

"That's so weird."

I shrug. "It's probably why not many merpeople venture on land."

"It's not going to stop me, though."

I smile. "Good. It shouldn't."

I send Giselle a text message instead of calling her so I can secretly explain I'm bringing a new friend with me. Giselle offers to pick us up where we are, and I immediately agree. I'm not worried about the consequences. I just want to spend some much needed time with my BFF on land.

Ten minutes later, I guide Luna to the parking lot where Giselle pulls up in her dark blue convertible Mustang. She rarely has the top up because she usually sticks her surf board on the backseat, but she left it at home today. Idling the car, she hops out to throw her arms around me. She bounces in my arms, laughing, and it takes her a long moment to pull away.

"I've missed you *so* much!" She shakes me by my shoulders.

I blink my tears away. It hasn't been more than two days since I've seen her, but it feels like forever since I was stuck in the water last time. "I've missed you, too." I hug her once more before turning toward Luna. "Giselle, I want you to meet Luna.

She's a friend of Carter's. Carter's visiting with his family, so I invited Luna to come hang out here for the day."

Giselle offers Luna a wide smile before hugging her like she would any of our friends. "I'm so glad you could come. How do you girls feel about grabbing some lunch and then checking out our—my—new house?"

Luna looks to me to respond. Everything is so new and exciting to her that she doesn't even question why Giselle isn't suspicious of my story.

"That would be great! Are you okay with that, Luna?"

She furiously nods her head with a huge smile. "Yeah, totally."

"Perfect," Giselle says, heading back to the car. "Then let's go."

I had expected Luna to hesitate before getting in the car, but she didn't. She didn't even need help with the seatbelt. She caught on by watching me, mimicking my every move. No one would ever know she's never really been into the human world before. I'm super proud of her ability to adapt. The king is totally wrong for keeping her away from a life she clearly belongs to—like me.

When Giselle parks in front of The Taco Palace, I hop out of the car and am bombarded by a giant hug from Logan, followed by Daisy. I haven't seen my friends since the night I accidentally transformed in front of Giselle on the balcony at the gala. I didn't even tell them goodbye.

I expected them to be a lot angrier, but they surprise me by showing me just as much love as they would've had they known I was leaving.

"Sapphire and Matty went to pick up Chloe," Logan says. He turns to Luna. "This isn't Carter. What'd you do? Get bored and find a new travel companion?"

I playfully slap his arm. "Luna's my new friend. I met her through Carter. He's spending time with his family."

"That's too bad. I thought he could go surfing with us later."

I roll my eyes. "And I thought you'd want to spend the day with me. That hurts, Lo." Fake sarcasm lines my words, but it does sort of annoy me that he would rather spend time surfing with my boyfriend rather than hanging out with me on land.

He chuckles with a shrug.

"Whoa, wait. So, you're not staying long?" Daisy says, pouting. "You just got back after a spontaneous friend-abandonment vacation, if I might add. No invite to join the fun. No video chats or pictures of you. Just lame texts and boring scenic photos." There's the anger I was expecting. The guys have always been more forgiving, but only because it's not like I've spent hours talking on the phone with them to just stop talking to them altogether. And now I have to pretend like it's my choice.

I blink away oncoming tears. "I'm sorry, Daisy. I'll try harder, I swear. But I really can't stay. I promised Carter I'd be his date to this wedding tomorrow." I don't know why I say it, but it's like if I can put the words into the universe, it'll be like my friends could be with me. We've always been together through all the big milestones—I thought we would always be. But mermaid coupling ceremonies weren't exactly on the list.

Before Daisy can respond, Matty yells, "Ava-babe!" from the parking lot. Sapphire hangs on his arm, her tank top sparkling in the sunlight with tiny beads. She tugs him forward, and they hug me together.

Chloe waits her turn before holding me by the shoulders. "You're lucky I don't slap you for abandoning us for the hottie. I can't believe he quit the Ocean Jewel to basically run away with you. You guys are nuts. If I didn't know any better, I'd think he knocked you up, and you don't want to be the talk of the town."

"Logan bet me you eloped," Matty says, smiling. "Tell us who won."

Oh, my God. My friends. Of course they'd come up with this sort of thing. It's bad enough they're basically right about the marriage. I refuse to even think about the other thing.

I glare at Logan. "You think I'd get married and not invite you guys? Where's the fun in that? Plus, my bet's on that Matty and Sapphire head to the altar first."

Logan holds out his hand. "I'll take that bet."

We shake on it and laugh. Things haven't changed one bit even though I haven't been around. It feels so good. I was worried my human life would be in shambles—irreparable—but as it turns out, I have a lot of people who wouldn't give up on me no matter the distance.

Sapphire rolls her eyes. "Great, now my five year plan is going to get messed up because of a bet."

Matty kisses his girlfriend. "You know I love when Logan loses."

Luna steps up next to me, drawing attention to herself. She's been super quiet this whole time, standing next to Giselle, who has been equally quiet—both for the same reason they have no idea they share.

Matty looks between us. "Carter got a lot hotter."

I only laugh to humor him because he thinks he's so funny. "This is Luna." I turn to Luna. "Luna, meet Matty, Sapphire, Logan, Daisy, and Chloe." I point out each of my friends. "Now that everyone has met, can we please go inside? I'm starving. You can't get tacos like this anywhere else."

I hook my arm through Luna's. She stares at the dozen Mexican food posters hung up in the windows of my favorite taco shop. Giselle strolls on my other side, falling into step with me, and we find a big, red leather round booth to sit at in the corner of the shop. Logan and Matty head to the counter to order for us, which will end up being way too much food as always. Too bad tacos won't stay good in the ocean for long.

Sapphire taps my leg with her foot under the table. "Giselle says you've lost your fear of the ocean."

"That's still so strange to me," Luna says.

Chloe leans forward. "She wouldn't go in for like all the time I've known her."

"Why is that, anyway?" Luna asks.

I rub my hands over my cheeks. "I still prefer the land."I don't answer Luna. The last thing I want to do is talk about Bailey and why I'm the one mermaid who hated the ocean before I was forced into it.

"I hate to say it, but Carter's been good for you, Aves," Daisy says, drawing attention away from the fact that I didn't respond to Luna. "I'm a little jealous it was him who helped with your crippling fear and not us. How did he even manage to do that?"

I shrug. "It's hard to explain."

"Do you like the water, Luna?" Sapphire asks, being the good friend and changing the topic I'm clearly uncomfortable talking about.

"I live in it," Luna answers, like it's the most normal thing on the planet.

The others frown. Not because of Luna's answer but because she says it in such a way that would make anyone question whether or not she's being literal. She really is a mermaid out of water.

"Her dad owns one of those vacation resorts where you can rent a room underwater," I say.

Sapphire's face lights up. "That's so cool!"

"It's really exclusive. You basically have to be royalty to even stay there." Which is partially true. You'd also need a tail.

Luna blinks as I create a new life for her—one that is actually pretty fitting for a princess. The boys return to the table with four trays of food just in time to halt any further questions directed at Luna.

I understand what Carter goes through, how he always speaks on my behalf in the colony. I'll be doing that a lot for Luna as well. I feel like I should've better prepared her before dragging her in front of my friends. They'd never in a million years expect we were mermaids—because that's not the first thing someone thinks about—but they might become suspicious if things don't add up. We won't be here long enough to do so, though.

My friends laugh and talk, telling Luna all the same stories they've shared with Carter before. It feels so normal. I can't help wishing that I didn't ever have to go.

Luna and I eat way too many tacos, more than even Matty, and we laugh with each other when Matty nods his approval when we all reach for the last soft taco on the tray.

"Jeez, Ava-babe. When was the last time you two ate?"

"Yesterday," Luna and I say at the same time.

He holds his hands up. "It's all yours."

I tear the taco in half, laughing out of nervousness, because my friends probably think I'm not getting enough to eat on the road though they know my parents are footing the bill for my travels.

"You had better have let them have that last taco," Giselle says. "You owe Ava forever."

No one has to say why—Matty was the one who knocked me overboard on the Ocean Jewel, and I'm absolutely positive

Giselle holds it against him. If he hadn't been acting recklessly, I'd have never drowned. Carter and I could've had a normal relationship on land. Things would be a lot less intense. If the situation were different, I might not have even been in love with him yet.

I can't imagine not loving Carter, though. That's a different life altogether.

"Why does he owe you?" Luna whispers between bites of her half of the taco.

"He knocked me overboard while we were all on vacation," I say.

"And if Carter hadn't dove after her, she'd be dead. He saved her life," Giselle says with such certainty, because she knows I did die.

"That's super romantic," Luna says. "I'd love to find my mate that way."

It barely sounds normal enough for my friends not to comment on her word choice. I've grown so used to Carter being referred to as my mate that it takes me a minute to realize what she said might stand out.

"It is now that we know Ava's fine," Giselle says. She pushes her bronze hair from her forehead, meeting my eyes with a look of sadness—the same expression I saw on her when I told her I had to leave after she found out the truth.

The door chimes, drawing my attention away from my friends. My mouth falls open when I see Carter standing in the doorway, his hair dripping water onto his shirt. Luna tenses next to me, and it takes everyone a minute to realize who it is, which is about to blow up my lie in my face.

"Carter? What are you doing here?" I ask, sliding out of the booth. "Is everything all right?" Panic grips my chest. I won't be able to explain to my friends why I need to suddenly leave.

"Carter, man!" Logan says, waving his arms over his head. "You swim here or something?"

"Or something," Carter says with an easy smile.

Before he can come closer, I close the distance, pushing him back out of the taco shop. Luna remains frozen in place, and all my friends watch us through the window. Giselle looks ready to jump up to chase me if she thinks we're about to run.

"I told them you were visiting with your family. They're going to know I lied. What are you even doing here?" I poke him in his hard chest with my finger.

Carter's smile only widens. He looks me up and down, taking in the clothes Giselle gave me. "How was I supposed to know you were planning on hanging out with all of your friends? Where did you even get the dresses—never mind. I know exactly where you got them." Carter raises his hand and waves at Giselle through the window.

She smirks while twitching her fingers. I try to read the lips of my friends as they have an obvious conversation about us. Luna shakes her head a few times and shrugs. Hopefully she's acting as clueless as I was.

"All that doesn't even matter. What are *you* doing here?" He takes my hands in his before I can poke him again.

"I was able to get away from the palace for a bit," he says.

I pull my hands away and place them on my hips. "You're checking up on me."

He sighs. "Well, yeah."

"You didn't have to. It's not like I'm planning to run away with Luna."

"You sure about that?" I know he's joking, but I can't help the grimace that slips onto my face.

"Positive. The only person I'd run away with is you."

Carter closes the distance between us, tugging me to him by my waist. He leans down, brushing his lips against mine, and I sink into him. He softly moans into my lips as he reluctantly pulls away.

"Are you going to send me away?" he asks in nearly a whisper.

I shake my head. "I'm not giving my friends more to talk about. Come on. They've all been asking about you."

17

TRUST

MATTY GIVES CARTER A FIST bump as we stand in front of the taco shop. "You have to reel it in, dude. You're making me and Logan look bad."

Carter chuckles, tipping his head back slightly so the sun sets his brown hair aglow. "Sorry, man. I can give you some pointers if you'd like."

Sapphire laughs from next to her boyfriend. "Hopefully about how not to drive me crazy when we move in together next week."

"Already?" I ask. Summer is flying by faster than I want it

to. Soon I'll have to figure out how to tell my parents I'm not coming home or going to college in the fall—that is if I can even manage to find the words. It'll also be when I have to figure out what to tell them about my inability to be around. I'm not sure there's any excuse in the universe that will make this right with them. I can't even fake it like I'm going to college on the other side of the country.

"You guys should come check it out sometime. Add it to your itinerary," Matty says.

Carter nods. "Definitely."

Giselle honks her horn from the parking lot, drawing our attention away from the rest of my friends. Luna sits beside her in the front seat, and I quickly give the others a hug. They're heading to the beach while Giselle is supposed to take us to her new condo—the one that was supposed to be ours.

Carter rests his hand on my lower back, and we stroll through the crowded lot to climb into the back of Giselle's Mustang. The AC blasts through the vents though the top is down, and she plays one of our favorite bands, *Nightmare Madness*, on her stereo.

"I love your friends, Ava," Luna says, twisting in the seat to look at us. "Giselle invited us to stay at her house whenever. She said it's on the beach like yours."

I suck in a long breath through my nose. "That would be great. You know, it was supposed to be my house, too."

"It still can be," Giselle says, wagging her eyebrows.

Luna crinkles her nose. "No, it can't. Ava lives with

Carter."

I lightly tap her shoulder, giving her a look that says to watch her mouth. Even though Giselle knows, Luna can't know she knows. She can't slip up either. That'd put Giselle at risk even more.

"We don't live anywhere together yet," Carter says, correcting Luna. "Unless you count hotel rooms."

She covers her mouth for a second, figuring out what she did. "I forgot."

Giselle flicks on her blinker and changes lanes. "I assumed Ava would be moving in with Carter anyway. Can't you see how in love they are? It sucks for me, but I'm happy for my BFF."

"I'm happy for her, too," Luna says, leaning her head on the headrest while looking up at the blue sky.

I smile at my two friends while resting my head on Carter's shoulder. He twines his fingers with mine before bringing my hand to his mouth to kiss the top of it. He smiles, kissing the ring on my finger, and I close my eyes to soak in the sun beaming down while feeling the sea breeze blow through my hair.

When Giselle stops at a stoplight, Carter leans forward in the seat. "Hey, Luna. Can you let me out?"

All three of us look at him. I'm the first one to speak up. "Where are you going?"

"I have some errands to run," he says as Luna rushes to let him out. Carter leans over the side of the car and kisses the top of my head. "You two be careful. I'll come pick you up before sundown." He turns to Giselle. "Sorry I can't hang out longer, Gi. Tomorrow's a big day."

Giselle's eyes widen, remembering what day it is. "Good luck, Carter. I'll catch you around."

With that, Carter jogs from the car and disappears in between two buildings that'll take him to the main stretch of road into the small downtown area of Azure Waters. Luna glances at me from over her shoulder, but she doesn't say anything.

Giselle accelerates through the green light and enters the freeway that'll take us to La Tortuga Point, where the condo is.

Thirty minutes later, Giselle hits the garage opener and pulls her Mustang into the garage attached to a condo at the end of a small complex. We hop out and enter the spacious place. It's a dream—my dream—and my heart hurts seeing all my best friend's stuff.

A new sectional couch rests in the corner of the living room, facing a wall with a flat screen mounted on an entertainment stand. The dark wood floors gleam in the light coming in through the sliding glass door that leads directly to the beach. She has a small folding chair on the concrete slab, but nothing else yet. A collection of surfboards lean on the wall, ready for Giselle to just grab one and go.

She doesn't have a dining room table yet, but two barstools are pushed directly in front of the bar that faces a small white-cupboard and gray granite countertop kitchen. Framed photos, mostly of the two of us, decorate the side table next to the couch, but she hasn't done any more decorating.

"This place is amazing!" I exclaim, spinning around the living room.

And then I start bawling my eyes out. I can't help it. This place was supposed to be mine, too. This was supposed to be my life, living with my best friend in the entire world, having get-togethers with our friends, having the ocean as a backdrop, living life without much to care about except passing classes and making sure I didn't oversleep.

But now, I feel like my life is pointless. I have nothing more to look forward to. And I hate it. How can I love Carter so much but hate everything else around us? This blows.

Giselle sinks onto the floor next to me, cradling me in her arms. She brushes my hair away from my wet cheeks and just comforts me as I sob. Luna takes a quiet seat next to me, touching my knee. Both want to say things, but neither do so.

After a minute, Giselle says, "You know what? I can't pretend anymore." Fire laces her voice, a mixture of fury and protectiveness clinging to her. She's the kind of person to stand up for me even if it puts her in danger. If she had the capability, I'm sure she'd make her way to Pearlestria and give the king a piece of her mind.

I jerk my watery gaze toward her. "Giselle, no." With Luna here, she doesn't really have to. I have no idea what she wants to say next, but it can't be good. It screams danger, and I want nothing more than to hop to my feet, drag Luna away from my best friend, and disappear.

She shifts to look at Luna. "Can I trust you? If I tell you a secret, will you die before sharing it? Because I can die if I tell you."

Luna's brows pucker, considering Giselle's words. She slowly nods her head. "Yes, I can keep your secret."

My heart races, and I feel like I'm about to throw up. Luna is the king's daughter. Even if she's nice to me now, I've only known her for days. Her life isn't the one hanging in the balance. That would be Giselle's.

I turn to Giselle, considering jumping on her to slap my hand over her mouth. "Giselle. Don't do this."

Giselle huffs a huge breath, ignoring me. "I know, Luna. I know about Ava and Carter...and you. I know you're all merpeople, and that Ava is coupling with Carter tomorrow."

Luna gasps, jumping back in surprise. "What?" She glances at me. "You *told* her?"

I shake my head, my hair hitting my cheeks. "I wasn't so good at controlling the transformation in the beginning. I accidentally did it right in front of her. She's my best friend, though, and I trust her with my life. I hope we can trust you too, Luna. Because if you tell anyone, you know what the consequences are."

"They'll kill her," Luna says quietly, the words more real coming from the princess' mouth.

"It was all an accident, and I've never been more terrified in my life. You have to swear you won't say anything." A dozen threats cross my mind. I never knew I'd be capable of even thinking about hurting someone, but I'd do it to save Giselle.

I'd fight and die for her. She's not just my best friend. She's my family.

Luna swallows, wetting her lips. "Of course I won't say anything. You're my friend, Ava, and I don't want you to lose yours. I'd hate for something bad to happen."

Giselle releases a breath. "That makes two of us."

I hug my arms around the both of them, the sudden revelation enough to distract me from breaking down over my ruined life. We're all silent for a long moment as we process the new knowledge we share.

"Is this why you were crying?" Luna asks after another minute.

I shrug. "It's part of it. This was supposed to be my house all before Carter changed me into a mermaid. I was set to go to college and not basically get married. I'm only eighteen." My voice rises through the room. "But I can't back out of it because of your father, Luna. He's made sure that I won't. And at this point, I don't even care. After tomorrow, we're leaving the colony. I can't stay there."

Giselle pets my arm without saying anything. She just embraces me in quiet comfort.

Luna, on the other hand, sits up straighter with a million thoughts crossing her dark blue eyes. "Oh, Ocean! I can't believe my dad. Does Carter know everything?"

I nod. "I just told him. It was his idea to leave. We're going to go to the colony near Australia." If they allow us to.

"Reefaria is beautiful," Luna says. "But I hate that you're

leaving."

Giselle clears her throat. "I guess that means I won't be see-ing you as often."

More tears prickle my eyes. "We'll manage. Carter can get us back here in a couple days swim."

"My dad's not going to like this," Luna says.

"He doesn't have a say anymore. I'm doing everything he's asked of me."

She rubs the sea stone on her ring. "That's not why. He's going to be upset because I'm coming with you."

The sun hangs low on the horizon, and I've spent the last few hours thinking about what's to come. I know I should try to talk Luna out of leaving Pearlestria—tell her she's being rash—but I don't even know what to say. Maybe it'll take the heat off me and Carter, but it could also make things worse. But who am I to decide what's best for Luna? I already hate that the king thinks he knows what's best for me.

"I want to see you tomorrow, Gi. I'm afraid it might be a while before I get back here, and I need my best friend to give me a pep-talk before everything's official with Carter." I twist the hem of my sundress between my fingers. I've gone all day without thinking of the ocean, and I'm relieved by my control over my transformation.

"I'll wait right here all day," Giselle says. "I just wish I could be there for you."

Luna touches Giselle's shoulder. "I know it's not the same,

but I'll be standing in what I guess would be your place if this were to take place on land. I'll make sure everything is perfect for Ava."

Giselle smiles. "Since it can't be me, I'm glad Ava has a princess to watch over her. It's a total fairytale."

One of the old ones with the not so happily ever after endings.

"A what?" Luna asks. Then she smiles. "I'm just kidding. We have stories under the sea, too. Mostly about humans and stuff. I'm sure Ava will be a story everyone tells their merbabes one day."

"Then we better get going, or else it might not have a happy ending," I say.

Giselle frowns with tears in her eyes before she throws her arms around me. This goodbye—with me on my legs—seems ten times worse than the one the other night on the side of the boat. Because now, the temptation to stay is real. We could get in her car and drive to the middle of the continent far away from the ocean and just pray a saltwater bath would suffice come the full moon. *The call of the sea would kill you...*

Pulling away from my best friend, I turn toward the ocean, spotting Carter's head popping up through the waves. Fortunately for us, the beach is empty as most of the condos haven't been bought yet, and the nearest public access is a mile away. It's the only reason I dare to run to the ocean in our sea grass outfits—which are now coming apart from being dry for too long. It doesn't matter though. What matters is I don't have to run completely naked into the sea, since I can't return with Giselle's bikini. Neither can Luna.

Luna dives into the waves before me, sinking under before she disappears into the sun-tinted water. The orange glow makes the ocean look like it's been set ablaze, though the coolness causes my human body to shiver.

Turning around toward the shore, I wave my arms at Giselle before I flip backward into a wave and let it pull me out to sea. I don't even have a chance to get past neck-deep water to transform before warm hands slide around me. Carter hugs me against him, running his fingers along my thighs and down my legs. I kiss his jaw right above his gills, wrapping my legs around his strong tail as he dives us deeper under. I don't even care that my lungs burn from the lack of air. All I care about is letting him hold me in the form I love the most.

He slides his hands up my sides and over my arms until he reaches for my fingers. Gently, he slips my sea stone ring off to trigger the transformation so we won't have to break the surface for me to breathe.

If I were the girl before, I'd panic this deep underwater with no chance to find air, but Carter doesn't let go of me, his intense gaze blurry through the water I haven't adapted to yet. He leans over, kissing me, and cramps seize my legs as I transform. I suck in a deep gulp of seawater, my gills letting me breathe, and I smile against Carter's mouth.

"Luna knows about Giselle," he says into my mind, not really asking, just pointing it out.

"Yeah."

I expect his anger to rush over me, but it doesn't. He just hugs me instead like he knows I need it.

We don't move for a long moment, just holding each other like we're the only two in the ocean. The seconds after my transformation are always the most intense, like I'm feeling everything again for the first time. The hug of the water around me, the strength of my fin, the warmth as my spark glows in my chest just for Carter. But then reality sinks in and reminds me I'm a mermaid, and this is my life now—a life that just feels like living without a purpose.

"I wish I could be enough for you, Aves," Carter says, thinking into my mind. "But I understand I'm not. And it's okay. I shouldn't be what your life is about."

I didn't realize I was projecting my thoughts out to all who could listen. And I feel absolutely terrible about it. But I was born human—I still think like a human—I can't help it.

"I want it to be enough, too. More than anything. I want to be satisfied to be a mermaid, but I want more from life. More from us. I want to make it count, you know?" I run my fingers along his scruffy jaw line. "I think that's why I was so hesitant to go through with the ceremony in the first place. I'm not just stubborn, I swear."

He laughs out loud, sending a stream of bubbles toward the surface. "I know that, and I love that about you. I wouldn't want you to accept anything less. You're not Ava, Carter Stevens' mate—you're Ava, the fiercely protective and loyal girl, who is smart and kind-hearted. Who might be a little stubborn but only because you know what you want. Not to mention that after everything, you still return my love though I probably don't deserve it. Just because I stole you back from death doesn't mean you owe me anything."

If I could melt, I'd dissolve into the ocean never to be seen again. Carter could rub in the fact that had he not given me this life, I'd be dead. Most people would be grateful—and I am—but being grateful and my happiness don't always coincide. But he doesn't. He still carries the guilt of not giving me the option. Nothing I say or do will ever change that. It's my actions that have to speak volumes. I have to show him he made the right decision, even if it sometimes doesn't feel that way.

I smile, floating in what feels like a bubble of his love. I was dreading the coupling ceremony—dreading the commitment because I thought I was losing a part of myself. Dreading it because the king didn't give me the choice to wait until I felt like I've done something with my life. I was dreading it because it meant I was accepting I belong to the ocean.

But now, I see it's much more. I'm not losing anything else. Nothing is changing either, because I've already unofficially promised my life to Carter, and by doing so, he's promised his life to me. And together, we're going to do more than live. I know it. We're going to discover whatever else is out there.

I linger an inch away from his face, stopping short of kissing him. Looking into his eyes, I project my thoughts to him. The thoughts I know he deserves. "I don't want you to go into tomorrow thinking I'm unhappy, that I'm only going through with it because I have to. I do want to. I'd do it right now without all the fuss of everything, because I love you. I love you more than the land and the sea. You've been incredible to me. More than I could imagine. And I'm ready to move forward. Right now, even after everything—I'm happy. I'm happy to be alive, to be with you. I'm happy that tomorrow, I'll be your mate for the rest of our lives and even longer."

He closes the distance, kissing me deeply, wrapping me in his warmth against the cool water. He sends me dozens of images, like a slideshow from every moment we've been together. All of his love and memories given to me in a single kiss, one that'll linger with me for a lifetime.

"Ava?" Luna's voice trickles into my mind. I had forgotten that she was here as she left Carter and me to our private moment. "The king is calling. Want me to keep him busy?"

Pulling away from Carter, I turn toward the princess who swims far enough away that I wouldn't have seen her if I wasn't looking. "No, we're ready to go back."

"You sure?" she asks.

I lace my fingers through Carter's, and we swim in her direction. "Absolutely certain. It's our last night in Pearlestria. Might as well try to enjoy it."

•18•

OUT OF CONTROL

CARTER'S FAMILY GREETS US AT the palace when we return from Azure Waters. It's customary to have a formal dinner—as formal as you can get in the ocean—before the coupling ceremony.

My stomach rolls at the sight of the dozen fish that are intended to be our meal. They swim around the room without a clue that they're about to become dinner. Carter notices my reaction and gives me an apologetic look. It's a good thing I'm stuffed with enough tacos to last me days. I don't want to seem difficult to the strangers that will now be my merfamily.

"Ava, Carter!" Starla gushes as we enter behind Luna.

Luna swims across the room to the king's side, but no one looks at the two royals. All eyes are on me. Carter's family is a lot larger than I expected. I thought I had already met everyone, but I was wrong. He rarely talks about anyone outside of his parents and Grandmer. I only met his uncle by chance, and it didn't go over so well. I haven't seen him since.

Mateo swims forward and pulls me away from Carter. "Daughter, come say hello to your family. Everyone's so excited to finally meet you."

I force myself to smile though my heart is about to jump from my chest at any moment. Meeting humans has never been a problem for me, but meeting other merpeople—it's tough. It might be because these merpeople are supposed to be my new family. What if they don't like me?

Carter hooks his fingers on my waist even though Mateo grips my hand in his, nearly dragging me to the closest couple. I'm regretting the tacos now, feeling the sudden urge to throw up.

"You're shaking, Aves," Carter whispers into my mind.

I press my lips together, wishing I could look at him. "I'm going to puke."

"You can't puke."

"It sure feels like it."

He swims closer tread rests his chin on my shoulder. "They're just my fam—"

"Ava, I want you to meet your Grandmer Oceana and

Pops. They're my parents from the Caribbean colony," Mateo says, nearly thrusting me forward.

The woman, slightly more weathered than Carter's other grandma, opens her arms to scoop me into them. She kisses my forehead, petting my blond hair, a contrast to her dark hair with the same blue streaks as Carter's other grandma. Her eyes are the same as Mateo's, so brown they look black. But her tail is the prettiest magenta color I've ever seen.

"My girl," Oceana says into my mind. "I'm so pleased to have a granddaughter, and a worldly one at that. Your Pops and I enjoy the island life occasionally. It's not a wonder that my son and grandson enjoy the land, too."

A smile pulls at my lips. "I'd love to visit sometime."

Pops beams a smile and pulls me to him next. "We'd love that!"

Before the two grandparents can hog me, Mateo guides me forward to meet the rest of the merpeople. Carter stays by my side, proud and protectively, as Mateo introduces me to the rest of his family, who I can only remember the name of his sister, Maka, and then he hands me off to Starla to reintroduce me to her brother, Tobias, and his mate, Sailor, whose parents lived on the land until they passed away, choosing to never return to the water. Carter's the oldest of all his cousins, and I hug the six younger cousins before scooping the tiniest merman I've ever seen into my arms.

He wraps his little fingers in my hair, smiling with half of mouth full of baby teeth, while sending me a dozen random images of fish into my mind instead of the normal verbal thoughts I've grown used to.

I rub my nose against his with a smile, wishing I could just play with the merboy all night instead of answer the dozens of questions I'm sure will head my way.

"This is Reef," Carter says, ruffling the baby's downy hair. "Maka and Flynn's son. He's just over a year."

I swim in a circle with him in my arms. "He's so sweet."

After a moment, Reef wiggles free before swimming back to his mom. Everyone stares at me with smiling eyes, and I can't stop the blush from heating my cheeks.

"A merbabe in your arms suits you, daughter. I can't wait for you and Carter to have a child," Mateo says, wrapping his arms around both our shoulders.

My mouth falls open in surprise. I don't know why I didn't expect that sort of comment—a coupling is equivalent to marriage—but the thought of children never even touched my radar. Just the thought gives me the urge to swim away as fast as I can.

Carter shakes his head with a smile. "You'll be waiting a while, Dad. Ava and I have big plans that involve only us for a while."

"Plans?" For the first time this evening, the king decides to speak up.

Carter stiffens next to me, and I lace my fingers through his, because I'm afraid of where this is heading. "Yes, your majesty. It's a great ocean out there. We'd like to see it all."

Surprisingly, the king smiles. "You won't be disappointed. But Ava, if you choose to travel, you must return here for your ring if you still care for our agreement."

"But that's unfair, my king." I don't know why I say it. I now have my own ring that Luna gave me. It's the sentiment of it all. "What if I choose to spend my few hours somewhere else? You never mentioned I would be limited to here."

The room falls silent, everyone keeping their thoughts to themselves. Starla gives me a don't-you-dare look while Carter pulls me even closer to him.

The king taps his golden staff into the hard rock floor, sending a noise loud enough to make the water quiver around us. "I offered those few hours a month on land to help you maintain your human life enough to keep you satisfied, not to pretend you're the same girl you were before the ocean chose you. It's a privilege, not a right, and if you're unhappy with my decision, then I'm sorry."

"Don't argue, Ava," Carter says to only me. "It's not worth it."

He's right, but I can't stand how much control the king thinks he has over me. I want him to know what it feels like when something happens out of his control. To give him a taste of his own awful medicine.

I close my eyes to get up the nerve to respond without anger in my voice. He can't know how much he got to me, because then leaving here won't be as easy. It'll already be hard enough with—

"Dad, we all get it," Luna says, interrupting not only my response but my thought. "You control everything. The ocean, the merpeople, even Ava's decision to go through with the coupling ceremony. Instead of demonstrating your power, why don't you just let Ava enjoy her night?"

I smile widely at Luna. I can't help it. Everyone else is afraid to stand up to the king but not his daughter. She has nothing to lose. She already doesn't get the choice to live on land. She has never been far from Pearlestria on her own, either, because she's always by the king's side.

The king makes an expression, all brooding eyes and angry lips, but not at Luna. It's directed at me. It's enough to make me swim a few feet backward. "You told Luna about the coupling arrangement," he says only to me. "I warned you."

"You told me I couldn't tell Carter. You didn't mention anyone else, your *majesty*." Anger emanates from me. "How was I supposed to know?"

He fists his hands. He knows I'm right. "That's beside the point. You have a duty to fulfill as a mermaid and as a mate. You put that in jeopardy."

I release Carter's hand to face the king. I don't care that he towers over me or looks like he could send me across the Pacific Ocean with the flick of his tail. I've done nothing wrong...that he knows of. I shouldn't have to feel like my life and wants and needs don't matter. Because they do. "I've put nothing in jeopardy, because I've decided I actually *want* to go through with this and not because you said so. You know, everyone told me what a fair and kind king you are, but they're wrong. You want nothing more than for me to be some compliant little mermaid whose only meaning in life is sitting quietly and doing nothing."

"That is the meaning of your life," the king roars, unable to keep his thoughts directed only to me.

The king's eyes widen as he realizes I got under his skin enough for him to lose his composure. And he's pissed. I swear the water gets hotter around me. He could boil me to death if he wanted to, and there would be nothing anyone could do about it.

Raising his large hand over his head, he aims it at me. The only thing I can do is close my eyes and brace myself for the impact.

Strong hands lock around my waist and yank me back, and I hit the wall behind me with a soft thump. Carter uses his body to shield me, blocking me from the king. Panic grips at my chest, because even Carter can't protect me. The king reaches out and pulls him away, flinging him through the water from me.

Luna steps in next, grabbing onto the king. Towering over me, he shakes her off with the flip of his tail, and she screams for me to swim, but I'm frozen in place. The king hits his staff on the floor again, sending the water churning, making it impossible for anyone to come to my rescue. A whirlpool, strong enough to catch the fish intended for dinner in its current, circles around us like an impenetrable wall.

My gaze flicks to Carter. He presses against the strong current, fear and despair crossing his face. Even Starla looks panicked, something I never thought I'd see in regards to me. I lie helplessly on the rock floor below the king in all his raging glory.

"How dare you disrespect me in front of my merpeople!" The king's sapphire eyes blaze brightly, like they're being lit from behind.

I squirm, the water continuing to warm with his projected anger. It takes everything in me not to start screaming in pain. I'm sure that would please him, hurting me, and I won't give him that kind of sadistic satisfaction. I refuse to break and show Carter just how bad it is. My pain will surely be his undoing. All I can think about is how horrible everyone must feel watching the king lash out at me for something they have no idea about. He'd murder me on the spot if he knew Luna and I went ashore.

"Please," I whisper. My whole body burns. The hot water filling my lungs makes it hard for my gills to work. "You're hurting me."

But he doesn't stop. He aims his staff at the spark in my chest, sending terror to my very soul. "Let me make myself clear, because you can't get it into your mind that you belong to the ocean, and the ocean—it belongs to me."

I nod my head, my vision growing fuzzy. "I understand. I'm sorry."

"I'm not finished." He pokes me once in the chest with his

staff, and pain bursts through my body. "I have given you plenty of chances to figure things out on your own. I've been kind enough to give you the opportunity to do something that no human-turned-mer has had the chance to do, and you have the nerve to call me unkind? You're ungratefulness clearly shows me you don't deserve that chance. You don't deserve the gift of life the ocean restored in you."

I close my eyes. I guess he's going to kill me after all and right here in front of Carter—in front of Carter's family and Luna—all because I stood up to him and called him out for what he is.

Maybe I am ungrateful. Maybe I don't deserve this life I've been given.

But that doesn't mean I should die.

Someone brave would stand up and try to fight. Someone brave wouldn't let the king push them around. But right now, I'm terrified. I'm not against groveling.

I latch my fingers around his caudal fin. "Please, your majesty. I get it now, and I'm sorry. I know you're a kind and generous king. I know this life is good for me. I'll do anything."

The water cools as his face softens. "Will you give up your human life?"

I nod even though my heart rips to pieces at the thought. "Yes," I whisper.

"The safety of the mers is the most important thing to me, and I can't stop thinking you'll jeopardize it all. Your human infatuation will not only get you hurt or worse, but it'll hurt your mate—and with my daughter's growing fascination with you—you might hurt her, too. I can't allow it. This is for the best," he says.

But I know it's not.

Because he doesn't know what's best for me. He'll never know. All he cares about is controlling his kingdom and everything in it. If he cared about me or what was best, he wouldn't have ruined tonight.

The current separating us from the others dissipates, and Carter swims to my side and pulls me from the floor. His blue-green eyes shift wildly as he peers around the room, and I know he's looking for the quickest escape route.

The king bumps his staff on the floor, sending another jolt through the water. "I apologize for losing my temper. Everything was a misunderstanding. Right, Ava?"

I force my head to bob up and down. "Right."

"You all know how important everyone's safety is to me, and I'd hate for something to jeopardize the safety of our colonies. I'm afraid that as a human-born, Ava did not understand the risk. She still has a lot to learn. It's why she's agreed to give up the land and all her human ties, just like it should've been from the start." The king motions to Carter. "And now that your mate has chosen the ocean, you'll no longer need your sea stone ring."

"What?" Carter says, folding his arms over his chest. "I know Ava wouldn't agree to give up the land."

"Just give him the ring, Carter," I whisper.

He turns his gaze to me. "No. He might rule the sea, but we have a choice."

The king holds out his hand. "The ring, Carter."

Carter shakes his head. "It's my right."

"Not if your mate chooses the ocean," the king says, glancing toward me. "Which she has done."

"You manipulated her." Carter's not going to back down. He's going to get himself hurt or worse if I don't say anything.

"Carter, please. Do as he asks. I have chosen the ocean. I want to live here now." The words come out nearly a whisper in my thoughts, but I project them to the entire room, the other merpeople tense with worry.

He swims back. "I'm not giving up my ring. I know you, Ava. I can tell you're lying."

"This is your last chance, Carter. Give me the ring before I take it from you. You heard your mate. She chooses the ocean." The king's voice shakes the ground as it travels through the water and into our thoughts.

"She's not officially my mate," Carter says. "And if this is how it will be, then I'm not going through with the ceremony." Despair crosses his face when he looks at me. "I'm sorry, Ava."

With a quick hand, the king raises his staff at Carter. The world slows, and I watch in horror as a blur of gold cuts through the current and heads straight for the boy who'd die for me.

Darting forward, I swim between Carter and the king, holding my hands out to block Carter from the king's wrath.

The staff slows down, like the water has turned to jelly, and I scream out.

"No!" My voice rings out through the water instead of from my mind, and a large pulse erupts from me as I direct my fear and anger toward the king.

He jerks back, like I've physically pushed him. His eyes grow wide, and he stares at me with a startled gaze. Whatever just happened was enough to stop the king in his tracks. And now he's wary of me.

Before we can figure out what has happened, Carter grips me by my arm and pulls me through the nearest tunnel that leads to the grand room. Clinging to his back, I press myself against him, swimming faster than ever before.

"I can't believe you did that," I say to Carter, holding on tightly to his shoulders. "You could've been hurt."

He smiles over his shoulder, the special one that's just for me. "But you saved me."

"So that was me?" I ask. "What was that even?"

"Our last hope."

With those words, we dart into the dark, open sea.

19

TROUBLE

CARTER BANGS ON THE BACK door of Giselle's condo. He's completely naked, dripping wet, and covered in sand. I'm no better, with my sea grass top and my backside showing for the world to see. Thank God it's dark out.

The back patio light flicks on, and Giselle thrusts the blinds open before flicking the lock up to allow us in. She rushes to the bathroom and throws us both towels to cover up with before sliding and locking the door behind us.

"We're in trouble, Gi," I say.

She waves her hands in her face. "Oh, God. What happened? Did they find out about me? Do I need to pack?"

I grip her shoulders. "No, but I did something bad. I stood up to the king, and something happened. I think I can control the sea. It stunned him before he could hurt Carter."

Grandmer mentioned mermaids had gifts, and she thought I might have a connection to animals, but I'm starting to think it's much more. Now that I think about it, this wasn't the first time I've done something to shift the current. I can recall a few times I did it to Starla when she annoyed me. Also, the first day I met the king, I disrupted his black sand pool—something we both noticed. I remember how he looked at me. But it didn't make sense at the time. I didn't know what I did wasn't normal. And then later, I controlled the current with Carter when I thought he was going to make me go back to the palace after the king forced me to agree to the coupling ceremony. I had no idea until this second it was the water reacting to my emotions—that it was allowing me to control it like the king.

Pushing the thought away, I rehash every detail from the moment we arrived for what was supposed to be a celebration dinner that turned into a nightmare fight. I only hope the king doesn't take things out on Carter's family.

I'm a little freaked out about my family on land, but Carter swears the king won't pursue them. They know nothing about me, and it'd only put the king at risk, because I'm sure my parents would fight like crazy. Outside of the sea, he doesn't have the same power. It's not worth it. At least I hope.

Giselle brushes her hair out of her eyes. A moment later,

she playfully slaps Carter's arm. "I can't believe you called off your mermaid wedding." Only Giselle would say something like this to lighten the mood.

It's enough to calm my heart. I poke Carter in his bare chest. "Yeah. That's twice now."

He scratches the back of his neck, smiling, though worry lingers in his eyes. "The real one will be worth the wait. Promise."

Giselle makes a strange cooing sound as she glances between us. "Are all mermen like you? Because I might change my mind about the whole thing if you have a cousin."

I kiss Carter's cheek. "He's one of a kind."

Giselle heaves a giant, fake sigh. "Figures. I don't want to live in the ocean anyway. I prefer riding the waves of the shore not swimming beneath them."

I smile at my best friend. The world could be ending, but with her around, things don't seem as dire as I thought they'd be. It's almost like none of tonight happened. Like we're not on the run from the king.

I hug her. "Me, too. This whole thing is crazy. I don't even know what we're going to do. The full moon will force us back into the water tomorrow, and then we'll have nowhere to hide."

"You can't just sit in the bathtub with a gallon of salt?" she asks.

"If only it were that simple," Carter says.

"What if I bought a giant aquarium?" She twists her lips to the side, touching her finger against her chin. The thought of sitting inside a glass tank only makes the fear running through me worse.

"You'd need a swimming pool sized tank," I say. "Carter's nearly eight feet long as a merman."

"Then we'll find a saltwater swimming pool," Giselle says.

I pout my lip. "I wish it were possible, but the sea calls to us like a gravitational pull. You could have the perfect setup, but it doesn't guarantee anything. I'm too new to resist. I'd be in agony."

She places her hands on her hips. "What's a half a day of agony when some evil king merman wants you dead now?"

She has a point.

Carter slides his arms over my shoulders, embracing me from behind. "We'd have a better chance in the sea. The pull of the moon could possibly kill Ava. It's only her third full moon."

I puff air through my lips. "We're screwed. We can't fight against the king, Carter. Death isn't worth the land. Maybe we should just go back and beg for forgiveness."

"And then endure a lifetime of misery?" Carter asks. "The king can't be everywhere at once. We can do this, Ava. Just like we planned before. The king might control the ocean, but he doesn't control us. I'm not going back. I'm not letting you either."

"Then we need to leave. We can't stay here," I say.

Carter rests his head on my shoulder. "I don't trust you to safely fly yet, Ava. Not this close to the full moon. Anything can trigger the transformation early."

"Then we head north," I say.

"Where my parents will surely be looking?"

I shrug away from him to spin and face him. "Then what, Carter? My passport is in my parents' safe at home. Do you even have one? Going south isn't an option unless we swim."

"Then we'll hide. I've swam this area a million times. I know of some caves near the La Tortuga Cliffs. They're like the one you stayed in when you found me in Orange County after the dress fiasco." He's talking about when Giselle accidently took my ring off before the gala. It seems so far away now. A different life altogether.

Giselle claps her hands. "That's it! I can have the car ready and waiting as soon as the moon sets. Your parents won't be able to find you if we're in a car, so we can easily drive through San Francisco. Maybe we can go to Alaska or something. You'd be far enough to swim, right? I could fly."

"We?" She's crazy if she thinks she's going with us anywhere.

"Yes, *we*. Having a human around will make sure the merpeople don't try anything crazy if they find us." Giselle taps her foot on the floor. "I'm already standing on the edge. Might as well dive in."

I open my mouth to argue, but Carter squeezes my arm. "She's right, Ava. As much as I hate the idea of putting her in danger, she can help us. At least until we have a better plan."

"Then it's settled," Giselle says. "I'll start packing."

"Sleep, Ava," Carter whispers into my ear.

I turn in his arms to face him, my nose touching his. His lips brush against mine in the softest of kisses, helping relax the nerves bunching in my back. I've been staring at the sliding glass door for hours in fear of naked people emerging from the sea to take us away.

As unlikely as that is, I can't shake the feeling. I know other merpeople can't find us on land like they can find someone who was their mate, but it isn't entirely impossible to track us. They've done it before. Carter's uncle knows how. And then I have to also worry about Luna. She knows where this place is. What if she gives us away? I know she wanted to come with us, and we had to abandon her.

"I'll sleep later," I say, pulling away. "Right now, I need to think about everything that could possibly go wrong."

"Why not everything that'll go right?" He kisses me again, trailing his lips to my jaw before kissing my neck. "This might not be the way we wanted things to go, but we're together, and we're going to live on the road like we wanted. We could get a boat and travel the world."

Until the king finds us and causes us to shipwreck. I don't say the words out loud, though. Unlike me, Carter carries enough hope for the both of us. He thinks things will go in our favor. He thinks our love can get us through anything. Why do I have to be so cynical? Love only saves the world in fairytales. This is my life. Our love could very well be our end—our undoing.

"I'd love that," I say instead of what's really on my mind. "Who knows? Maybe the king will give up when he realizes I'm not a threat to the mers entire existence."

He chuckles against my lips. "That was overly dramatic, right? The fall of an entire species would not be your fault."

He's right. I'd never put us in that sort of danger. All I want out of life is to live it how I want to, and that doesn't involve revealing myself to the world. That wouldn't accomplish anything except get me stuck in a tank or in some lab—or at least that's what every mermaid I've ever watched on TV was afraid of. I think there are enough good people in the world—people like my best friend—that would stop that from ever happening. Plus, humans love the ocean. They wouldn't want to risk it turning against them completely.

I suck Carter's bottom lip between mine, needing to take my mind off things outside of us. His hands run over my sides and to my back, and he trails them lower to pull my hips against his. He kisses me deeper, his tongue grazing against mine, tasting like the mint chocolate ice cream we had for dinner since neither of us had an appetite for much else.

Carter makes it easy to lose myself in his kisses, in his arms, in his very essence. As his fingers explore every inch of me, I listen to his deep breathing, something I don't get to hear in the ocean, and to the sound of our beating hearts as they thump-thump, thump-thump in sync.

A quiet knock on the back door causes me to startle in Carter's embrace. His arms tighten around me, like if we lie here quietly, whoever is on the other side of the slider will go away. But another knock sounds out, slightly louder.

Giselle yawns, coming into the room. She doesn't look like she's gotten any sleep either. She saunters past us and to the kitchen where she pulls a kitchen knife from its holder on the counter. I highly doubt it's an intruder—they don't usually knock—but Giselle looks like she's willing to stab anyone who might come to threaten us.

The knocking continues, quick taps that mirror the rapid beating of my heart.

Giselle looks at us frozen on the couch. "I'm going to answer it."

Carter shakes his head. "You shouldn't."

"I'll be fine. You two should go hide. If you have to, pop off my window screen and leave that way." She tiptoes up to her slider with the knife clutched in her hand like whoever is on the other side of the glass will shatter it at any second.

Carter pulls me from the couch bed and guides me down the short hallway to the master suite. I linger outside the door, shrugging him away when he tries to pull me in. I'm not leaving Giselle to answer the door alone. What if it's the king?

"Luna?" Giselle asks out loud. "What are you doing here? Is something wrong? Is Ava okay?" She's a much better actress than I ever could be.

The door lock clicks, and I tense. Giselle shouldn't open the door for anyone. Especially the daughter of King Attilonious.

"I know Ava and Carter are here," Luna says. Her soft voice trickles down the hallway, sending a wave of uneasiness over me. She shouldn't be here. Coming to Giselle's puts everyone at risk. The king could be following her. This is bad.

"I don't know what you're talking about," Giselle says. "It's just me. What happened to Ava?"

"Giselle, please. My father has the entire colony searching the seas for them. They think they're hiding near Azure Waters or San Francisco. No one knows Ava has a ring, but they think Carter would give her his to escape the ocean. Even if they're not here, I know you'd know how to find them. Please, no one knows I'm here. I've come to run with them. What my father did—I just—please, Giselle. I want to help. I know my father and the ocean better than anyone."

Taking a deep breath, I step from the hallway. Luna could very well make a good ally, and she has no reason to lie. Carter comes up behind me protectively. When I meet Luna's worried gaze, I know immediately she speaks the truth. She's alone and scared, and probably took the one chance she had to leave home, risking the wrath of her father if he were to find out.

Luna rushes forward and wraps her arms around me. "I was so scared, Ava!"

I rub her back. "Your father's crazy."

She hugs me against her. "You've done something no one has ever done before. You put fear into his heart."

"Good," I mutter. I don't know what else to say. I hope the king is shaking in his skin.

"You don't understand," she says. "You've showed an affinity for the ocean. Only my dad has that. It's why he's king."

She confirms my newfound suspicion that I can somehow control the sea. But I don't know how to do that. Creating a current is no match against the merman who can create whirlpools, heat the water to unbearable temperatures, even create the magic stones allowing us to walk on land.

"So, he's going to kill me because I'm suddenly his competition?" I ask. I purse my lips. It wouldn't be the first time someone wanted to eliminate a potential threat to keep a firm hold on power.

"Maybe," she says, sucking in her top lip. "But I don't know. The last mermaid gifted with an affinity for the ocean was my mom. They ruled together until she abandoned us. And the ocean chose you for a reason. No one knows why it does what it does. Only my father could answer a question like that."

I stand frozen, her words sinking in. All merpeople talk about the ocean like it's a living, breathing person, like it's a goddess or something. But the ocean has never felt that way to me. It's always just felt uncontrollable, unforgiving. The ocean and I were never really on good terms. Not even now.

I hug myself. "You're wrong. The ocean didn't pick me. The ocean tried to destroy me. Carter picked me. Carter saved me. Maybe this is why all this is happening. Maybe it's upset it lost me again and again."

Luna's eyes widen, and she covers her hand with her mouth. Shaking her head, she says, "That's not true. Tell her

Carter."

"She's right, Ava," he says from behind me. "You wouldn't have been gifted like this if you weren't meant for this."

"Well, I don't want it. I don't want anything to do with this. All I care about is staying far, far away from the ocean."

Carter pulls me away from Luna. "And we will for as long as we can. I'm not putting you in danger of facing the king again."

We all silently stare at each other, and I glance from Carter to Luna and then to Giselle still standing near the door with a knife in her hand.

"So what now?" I ask, not really expecting a plan, but I figure it wouldn't hurt to put out the question to the universe. If only the universe would respond. If only the ocean would. Because as of now, we don't have a choice but to return. And then, I have no idea.

"We sleep," Carter says. "We all need to rest and let our bodies prepare."

"Does this mean I can come with you?" Luna asks.

Carter and I share a long, quiet look. If only I could read his mind while in my human body.

"I'll do whatever I can to help. I just—I can't stay at the palace anymore. Not after tonight. My loyalty lies with you two," she says with a small bow. "I know it's what the ocean wants."

I frown. "Of course you can. I had already promised you."

Carter tilts his head to the side but doesn't say anything.

He had no idea of the plans I set with Luna. I never got the chance to tell him. Luckily, he doesn't care. It never hurts to have a princess on our side.

Giselle clears her throat, drawing attention to herself for the first time since Luna walked in. "Come on, Luna. Let me get you something to wear. You can sleep in my room with me. And tomorrow, we'll get everything settled. We still have all day to figure things out."

If only it were enough time.

20

A THREAT

CARTER SLEEPS PEACEFULLY NEXT TO me, his chest rising and falling under my fingers with every deep breath. I have no idea what time it is or how long I've slept, but it couldn't have been more than a few hours since the sun rose.

Streaks of light cut across the wood floor from the blinds of the sliding glass door, and I sneak from the couch bed and tiptoe across the living room to peek outside.

The bluish-green ocean rushes the shore in rolling whitecaps. Puffy clouds float in the endless blue sky like giant cotton balls while the sand is so light, it almost looks white in the sun.

La Tortuga Point is as beautiful as Azure Waters, if not more breathtaking.

Tears prickle in the corners of my eyes, thinking about the life I was supposed to have. Waking up here every day with a new take on life was what I wanted. Without the fear of the ocean crippling my life, I could've enjoyed the beauty of it. And whenever I wanted, I could dance among these waves, familiarizing myself with every inch of the beach that was supposed to be my home while I went to college.

But now, I have to stay out of the ocean completely, only following the pull of the full moon as it tries to drag me back into the ocean's depths where my enemies await—the merpeople who'd rather see me suffer than happy.

Anger washes over me, and I glare at the unforgiving sea. It's enough for me to unlock the door and slide it open. I step into the warm summer air, inhaling a delicious breath of the sea's breeze. It sends chills down my back as I'm repelled by the idea of even an ounce of the ocean getting into my lungs.

Peering around, I step forward into the sand. My foot grazes a smooth rock, and I bend over to pick it up. It's hot from the sun beaming down, but I don't drop it. I want to feel the sensation of it in my palm, because I'm afraid that after tonight, I'll never feel the heat of the sun on my skin again. I have to prepare myself for the worst. I have to prepare for the ocean to lure me in to never release me.

I trudge through the sand and toward the crashing waves, staying just out of their reach. Swinging my arm back before jerking it forward, I chuck the rock as far as I can into the waves.

"I'm not letting you take me," I say out loud, more to myself than anyone. "You've already stolen enough from me. You can't have me again."

I'm not sure if I'm talking to the ocean or to King Attilonious, wherever he may be. Squatting down, I scoop up a handful of sand and throw it at the water, too. It disappears in the wind, and I watch the ocean pull another wave back out to sea.

Seagulls caw from overhead, drawing my attention to the sky. They circle around, looking for their next meal. One lands nearby, squawking as it waddles near. Seagulls here aren't afraid of people, but this bird is especially fearless, because when I wave my hand to shoo it away, it flies up and lands on my arm.

"Get off me, you stupid bird!" Thrashing, I spin around, sending it flying before I fall to the sand.

A shadow stands over me, blocking the sun, and Carter grins down at me.

"Even the birds are out to get me," I say.

Plopping down in the sand, he pulls me into his lap to hold me. "Seagulls are worse than dolphins and seals combined. They'll only befriend you to steal whatever you have that they want."

I rest my head against his firm chest, feeling the rise and fall of it as he breathes. His muscular arms lock around me, holding me to him, even though I want to jump back to my feet to find something else to throw at the water. It's the only thing making me feel slightly better about the situation.

I inhale a long breath and release it. "Do you think we'll be on the run forever?"

Carter leans back, pulling me with him. We lie together in the sand, looking up at the sky. His turquoise eyes glow against his tan skin. Cream-colored sand speckles his dark hair, and I comb my fingers through it to dust it out.

"I hope not, Ava. I want to settle down one day, maybe have a place like this," he says, digging his fingers into the sand.

"And what if we can't?"

Carter kisses my temple. "We will. The king will see you're not a threat. He'll back off."

"That's if we get the chance."

"Aves? Do you think it's a good idea to be lying so close to the ocean? I had a nightmare last night that naked people dragged you under like before." Giselle stands on her patio. The beach around us is empty apart from a man who jogs along the shore in the distance.

I tilt my head back to get an upside down view of my best friend. "We'll be in soon."

She pouts her bottom lip but doesn't say anything as she turns around and goes back inside. I wish I could say something to comfort her, but she should be as prepared as I am for the inevitable if they find us.

"She's going to be okay, you know. Giselle's tough," Carter says.

I smile. "I know. I just hate I put her through all this."

He bobs his head. "I know what you mean. You don't know how often I go back to the night you went overboard to try to think of another way I could've saved you."

I cup his face in my hand. "It wouldn't have changed any-thing, Carter. Don't you see? Luna was right. The sea chose me. It's been after me since I was a kid. I think this was fate."

"While I won't argue with the ocean wanting you, I don't believe in fate. We control what we do and how we deal with all this."

"Even though no matter how hard we try, we always end up there?" I point at the blue horizon.

"Even then, Ava. Because as much as the waves pull you in, they always spit you out. We can always swim—even in the roughest water. The ocean, it's no match against you. You al-ways win."

I smile. I never thought about it like that. I guess I have al-ways won. Somehow, I still manage to make it back to shore. And now, it's just another fight to stay above water.

For the first time since last night, I have hope. I have hope, because I know how to swim through the storm.

Giselle hugs me near the edge of the cliff top. The only way to avoid swimming to the caves is to jump, so it's what Carter, Luna, and I are going to do. I'm slightly nervous, but it can't be worse than diving from the balcony of the Grand Le Mer Hotel.

"Everything's ready, and I'll be waiting as soon as the

moon sets," Giselle says. "Nothing bad will happen, okay? I'll make sure of it." We took out all the money from both our bank accounts and left it with my car where Giselle's been storing it at a storage facility. She packed as much of her stuff as she could to help us as well. I don't know what I'd do without her.

I force myself to smile. "You better not be planning anything crazy if it does."

She shrugs. "Not at all."

Before I can argue, I feel the pull of the ocean, demanding me to return home. I can't see the moon yet, but I know it's rising in the sky. Neither Carter nor Luna react, but they have better control than I do. The ocean can't pull them away so suddenly. Not like me. If the ocean beckons, I have to go.

My toes tingle, sending prickles up my legs. I push the feeling away the best I can. I'm not ready to say goodbye to my best friend. I don't want to go yet. It isn't fair.

The wind knocks from my chest as I convulse, the moon fighting with the magic of the sea stone ring. It won't be much longer before I lose my legs and gain my tail.

A groan escapes my lips. "It's happening. We need to go."

Falling to my knees, another shudder rolls over me, cramps rushing through my every muscle. My legs are too weak to stand. I couldn't even jump if I wanted to.

"Hurry, Carter," Giselle says. "She's in pain."

Lifting me from the ground, Carter cradles me in his arms. The pull is stronger than ever, ripping through me, causing more pain than I've ever felt during a transformation. I know it's because I'm resisting, but I can't help it.

Tears burst from my eyes, a sob grabbing hold of me. The wind whips around us as Carter stands at the edge of the cliff overlooking the roaring ocean. He holds me tighter the louder I sob, and in one quick motion, he leaps forward, far from the rocks.

My stomach rises into my throat, the world zooming around us, and then suddenly, the ocean embraces us in its cool waters. Carter yanks my bikini bottoms off the second before my legs fuse together into a tail. He pushes me away from him and toward a small cave that hides half under the treacherous waves.

Both Carter and Luna catch up to me before I even make it to the entrance. Carter lifts me up first, followed by Luna, and then he grips the rocks and pulls his tail over the edge. The shallow water causes us to drag ourselves through the cave. A deep pool in the back waits for us as the waves that hit the cave stream in to create a waterfall.

Carter swims in a few quick circles around me, spinning me into his arms. My tail throbs from the crawl, and there are tiny patches of raw skin where my scales rubbed off on the rocks, but other than that, I'm okay.

"This is so strange," Luna says, swimming around the perimeter of the pool. It's just deep enough that we can hover upright, but the space is pretty tight with all three of us. "I never really believed in the call of the ocean until now. It's different when you're in human form."

I blow bubbles through my mouth. "I hate it."

"I kinda do, too," she says.

Carter anxiously circles me again. It's probably because he prefers to swim at ridiculous speeds through the open water when the full moon rises. Here, we're basically trapped in a tank. It sucks, but I'd go through this every month if it means I get to spend the rest of the time as my human self.

"So, what now?" Luna asks, bobbing up and down with the rise and fall of the pool.

Carter stops swimming around me to focus on the princess. "We hope no one finds us."

"And if they do?" she asks.

"We fight."

Our minds fall silent as we think to ourselves. I'm not much of a fighter. I can throw a mean punch if I want to—I took kickboxing for a few summers in high school—but that doesn't do me any good in the water. The force isn't nearly strong enough to outmatch a merperson who's been swimming in the water for years.

"Let's hope it doesn't come to that," I say. "I don't want them to have reason to hurt us."

Carter flares his nostrils for a second. "Then we'll try to flee."

As the night drags on, we spend the time making small talk. Luna tells me about her life as a princess, and for the second time since we've met, she tells me about her mom. King Attilonious doesn't like to talk about his queen, because she always dreamed of the land like Luna. The king wouldn't let his queen make the choice either, and then one day she just disappeared. No one knows how, but the queen died somewhere in the sea. King Attilonious could never find his mate.

I'd think after that, the king would have more pity for me—even for Luna. But maybe he blames the land for the demise of his mate. I'll never know.

"I'm sorry, Luna. That must've been hard," I say, reaching out to hold her hand.

She lifts and drops her shoulders. "I don't even remember her all that well."

"Is that why you stood up for me to your father?" I ask.

She smiles. "Among other things. I never knew a friendship like yours was possible. I always assumed I'd only find one in my mate. The world feels much bigger to me now."

"It's endless, really," I say.

Carter rests his chin on the nape of my neck. Every few minutes he swims around the perimeter of the pool, but he's mostly settled down now that the night is halfway over. "And I can't wait to show you, Aves," Carter whispers into my mind, sending the thought only to me.

I tilt my head back, enjoying the feel of Carter against me. Through the bubbling surface of the pool, a strange light flickers through the cave, sending fear through me. I nudge Carter with my elbow, pointing up, and he flicks his tail, sending us both to the surface.

The hum of the waves rushes my ears, but through the

white noise, I can hear the sound of a boat engine nearby. And then the cave is set aglow again by the flickering light.

The light fades away with the sound of the boat.

"They couldn't have gone far. Have you searched the shoreline?" A familiar voice rings through my mind as a merman projects his voice through the sea.

"Starla is cutting through the waves now. I just hope to the ocean we find them first." Grandmer's voice sounds through my mind next.

"Carter, Ava, if you can hear me, please. You have to come back," Grandmer says.

The strange light I saw wasn't random. It was a warning. The boat, while it could've been random, doesn't feel like it. Giselle is somewhere nearby. The merpeople don't know that she can see them in the water because she knows our secret.

And her plan was pretty perfect—reckless—but perfect. No merperson would risk popping their head through the water if a human was nearby. It gives us a better chance of remaining hidden since the cave isn't completely submerged. I just wish she had told me.

Carter pulls me back under and motions me to swim next to Luna. He slinks down next to us, draping his tail across mine like he can protect me from whoever lurks nearby. The voices are clear enough to hear, but it's hard to judge the distance. Hopefully they just pass by.

"Mateo, I've combed the shallows. I say we keep heading south," Starla says. "Maybe we should call for them again?"

"Carter, son? Are you out there? We need to talk. Running away will make things worse. The king believes Princess Luna is with you. He's willing to forgive you if you bring the princess and Ava back to Pearlestria. We can work things out." Mateo's voice sounds out with a sense of urgency. "Please, son. We don't want you getting hurt. We love you and Ava."

Luna clutches my tail. "Tell my father I'm not going back. Tell him I'm my mother's daughter, and I won't stand by him any longer."

The sound of Luna's voice projecting through the sea sends a stream of fear down my back.

Carter rubs his hand down his face but doesn't say anything. Neither of us can stop her from talking.

"Princess Luna, you need to be reasonable. If you refuse to come back, it puts my son and daughter at risk. The king protects you like he does our ocean. Do you want them getting hurt because of you?"

We all look at each other. I shake my head, holding my finger to my lips.

She wrings her hands together next to me. "He's right. This was a mistake. I've made things worse."

I grab her tail. "That's not true, and you don't have to go back. This is what he wants. Your father thinks he can scare us into returning. There is no place for us in Pearlestria. It'll be more of a prison than ever."

Before Luna can respond, two large hands yank her from the spot next to me, pulling her from the pool and into the shallows of the cave. The water muffles her screams as she's taken from us.

The hands reach back down, aiming for me next. I reach up and dig my nails into the merman's forearms, scratching down toward his wrists. Carter thrusts me out of the pool, and I crash into Mateo. He skids across the rocks, hitting his back on the wall with a heavy thud.

"Go, Ava!" Carter yells, sliding up next to me. He doesn't even give me time to move my arms before he hooks his hands around my waist and yanks me along with him. We tumble out of the cave and into the churning water. The blurry bubbles disorient me, and my shoulder hits against rock. Carter scoops me back up and darts through the waves toward the open water.

But something jerks Carter back, causing me to fly forward without him. My heart pounds in my ears, and I spin around, trying to figure out which way to swim. My gaze falls on the merman I hate most in the ocean. Hovering a few feet away, the king holds his golden staff as it glows in the turbulent ocean.

"Swim, Ava!" Carter yells in my mind.

But I'm surrounded. There's nowhere to go.

Then the glow of the moon shining across the surface catches my attention.

So I swim up.

21

FINISH WHAT THE OCEAN STARTED

"WHEN YOU BREAK THE SURFACE, jump up as high as you can, okay? I'm coming." Carter's voice makes me flick my tail faster through the water.

Stretching my arms over my head, I use every ounce of my strength to breach, sending my entire body from the sea. A hard body crashes against me, but I see the spark in Carter's chest immediately as he grips me to him before diving under.

He bolts across the surface, away from the small ring of merpeople determined to catch us. But what they don't know is their determination is nothing compared to our sheer will to break free.

Carter breaches with me on his back, the moonlight sparkling off our skin. He swims us toward the sandy shore of the beach. At this point, neither of us cares we can't transform yet. If we make it to the beach, at least we might have a chance in the waves.

As fast as Carter swims, he's no match for the older mermen who were gifted with his same affinity. If he weren't carrying my weight, he'd probably make it. But he'd never leave me willingly. I wouldn't want him to either.

A pair of hands wrap around my caudal fin, yanking me hard, sending pain through my tail. I scream out, trying to flick it, but I'm injured. Two bodies crash over the surface, and Carter fights out of the grip of his uncle as he tries to keep him away from me. Using my arms, I freestyle through the water, heading toward the surface again.

A flash of light flicks across the surface, and I head straight for it. The king laughs from behind me, knowing I can't get away. I can barely manage to swim instead of sink. He lets me try though, probably waiting for me to exhaust myself.

But he doesn't know what I'm planning.

The silhouette of a boat blocks the glimmering ripples of the surface in the light of the moon. Grinding my teeth through the pain, I flick my tail as hard as I can before I hook my fingers to the back of the boat, keeping my distance from the motor while letting it propel me forward.

Giselle glances over her shoulder with a smile and steers the boat away from the cliffs and down the shore, heading toward the harbor. My heart slams against my ribcage over and over. The king will now realize my best friend knows of our existence. But Giselle can live her life away from the water. There are ways to make sure she's safe.

"Hang on, Aves!" she yells over the hum of the engine. "We're going to the harbor where the king will be outnumbered by boaters."

"Carter's still back there!" I scream.

"That's the least of our worries," she calls over the hum of the water. "Something is coming up fast behind you!"

I peer over my shoulder, catching sight of a golden tail darting toward me. Using all my strength, I do the only thing I can think to do. I yank myself up and into the boat. My tail flops in the wind as I pull it over, rocking the vessel.

My hands tangle in a small fishing net, and I pick it up and hold it just above the water. The king won't stop now, all his caution thrown to the wind. He'll do anything to catch the both of us.

"Go faster!" I yell.

"I can't! This isn't a speedboat." Giselle turns the wheel to take us closer to the shore. If we can't make it to the harbor, she'll take us straight to the sand. I might not be able to run, but at least she can make it. I'd risk my life to protect her.

"Ava," a familiar voice cuts through my mind. But it isn't Carter's. "You have to tell my son to run. Tell him he has to leave you. It's the only way to save him. The king won't kill you, but he will kill your mate." It's Mateo. His words send tears bursting from my eyes. The last thing I want in this world is for any of the people I love to die on my behalf. And right now, the two people I love most are risking everything.

"Carter?" I send my voice through the water, focusing on his presence that is just out of my grasp. "The king is chasing me. This is your chance to go."

"I'm not leaving you, Aves."

"Your dad said the king will kill you. My life isn't worth your death. You can't expect me to live the rest of my life without you. Please, just go. I'll figure things out."

"Ava, don't do this."

"Please," I beg. "Someone needs to take care of Giselle for me."

"Ava." His voice nearly causes me to break.

"I love you, Carter."

With those words, I bring myself back to the present, readying the net. Giselle growls in frustration as the king comes up under the boat and pushes it up, trying to flip us out. She grips onto the steering wheel, fear in her eyes, and I know if the king gets to us again, he'll be successful.

"Giselle, thanks for being my best friend. Please, tell my parents they were everything I could've asked for. Make sure they know I'm not dead, okay?" I push myself higher to look over the edge at the king ascending toward us.

"Don't talk like that, Aves. This isn't over."

As the words leave her lips, the boat surges above the water.

I thrust the net down on the king, tangling him in it, but it's too late for me. I fall overboard into a swell, flailing as pain erupts in my injured tail. Breaking the surface, I spit out water and peer around to get a better idea of where I am. Giselle turns the boat around, heading back toward me.

"Just go!" I scream.

The water swells next to me, the king breaking the surface, cutting through the net with his sharp fingernails. Giselle lifts her flashlight, aiming it for the king's eyes, and he jerks back in the water in surprise. I guess he's not used to battery powered light. Who knows how often he has ever come to the surface.

Giselle rams the boat into the king, knocking him away from me. His voice, much angrier than the thoughts he sends in my direction, cuts through the air. With a flick of his powerful tail, he flips the boat, sending Giselle overboard and into the churning water. He heads straight for her as she gasps for a breath, swimming away.

I fight through the pain to swim to my best friend. If King Attilonious reaches her first, she'll be dead.

Giselle yells out, thrashing through the water, heading in my direction. A flash of gold shimmers beneath her and my screams ring out as she's pulled under by the biggest predator in the ocean.

Diving down, I jet through the water, sticking my hands straight out in front of me. Giselle's panicked eyes meet mine. She fights in the king's grip, digging her thumbs into his face. I stab my nails into his back, but he shifts too quickly for me to injure him.

King Attilonious raises his staff at me, pointing it in my face. Light glows from the diamond on top, and I find myself locked in its magic, unable to move. The water heats around me, bubbles surging toward the surface at the sudden change in temperature.

A figure darts through the water toward my best friend, and I meet Starla's blue eyes. She wraps her arms around Giselle, pulling her back.

"We've won, my king," Starla says. "No need to hurt Ava. I'll take care of the human."

The fire in the king's eyes fades away, and he nods his head at Carter's mom. Giselle's bronze hair floats around her face. She continues to struggle for her life as Starla keeps the air from her. She'll drown in another minute, and there's nothing I can do about it. Once again, this woman rips apart my life all in the name of the ocean and the king.

The king closes the distance between us, hooking his arm around my waist, forcing me to stay by his side. Starla swims away with my best friend, and I watch as one more bubble escapes Giselle's lips as her eyes close.

Then they're gone.

My heart shatters into a million pieces, threatening to stab through my chest to cut out my own spark of life that keeps me a mermaid. King Attilonious drags me deeper into the sea, the world flying by until I can no longer glimpse the full moon slowly setting.

I've never felt so powerless and alone. At least the last time I was taken away from my life on land, I had Carter by my side. I had people who cared about my happiness and wanted me to love the life that was given to me.

But now, under the king's arm, all I can hope for is Carter got away and the king will leave him alone. He's won, and he can live happily knowing he's broken all the hope left in me.

"I've never met someone as brave and determined as you are, Ava," the king says as he descends into the pearlescent glowing colony. "I admire that, you know."

I don't respond to him. Compliments aren't going to change the fact that he saw to it that my human life, my future, my happiness is all over.

"You have something in you no other mermaid in all the world has," he continues. "Something I haven't seen since I chose Luna's mother as my mate."

I still don't answer him. I don't give a crap about what he sees in me. Because apparently whatever it is, it wasn't good enough to fix things, to save my best friend, to save me.

"And that's why you will be my queen."

What the? Oh, God. This can't be happening. I think I'm going to be sick. The king is like a million years old, mean, and not someone I want to have near me. He's tail-flippin' insane if he thinks I'd ever agree to be his queen. I'm not royalty. I'm not fit to rule. All I want is my freedom. I've already paid the cost for it. I deserve it.

I pound my fists into his shoulder. "No! I won't do it. I'd

rather die than be your queen. My heart belongs to Carter. I won't betray him."

The king grabs my hands, locking them in his strong fingers. He leans over, his salt and pepper hair veiling over us, and then he thinks, "You will obey me, Ava. If you want your mate to live to see another day, you will go through with this and vow your loyalty to me. If you don't, I will search both the land and the sea until I find Carter, and then I will break your bond. You'll have no choice but to be my mate."

I cringe at the thought. Being queen is bad enough—but being forced to be the king's mate? That's unthinkable. I didn't even know it was possible. Merpeople choose mates for life. Their bond is eternal. But now, the king threatens to rip that away from me, too.

Then I realize why all this is possible. Carter and I never went through with the coupling ceremony to make things official. While I have Carter's spark in my chest and he transformed me, I never vowed myself to him on the full moon. And now, I'll never be able to.

Voices echo through my mind, pushing away my thoughts, as we're greeted by the entire colony waiting for the arrival of their king. In the small valley, just outside the entrance to the castle, lies a rock platform with four pillars decorated with coral and sea plants. The water sparkles with glowing bubbles, the magic of the moon filtering through Pearlestria.

Without having to ask, I know this is the spot I was supposed to vow my life to Carter. This is where we were supposed to officially couple. And now, this will be the spot where King Attilonious will force me to pledge my loyalty to him as his queen. This is where my life as I know it will end. Because whatever magic stirred in me before—whatever affinity that lies within my body that can control the sea—remains dormant and untouchable as grief consumes me.

The king raises his gold staff into the air. He descends toward the platform, his sharp nails puncturing my side as he tells me to smile. I grind my teeth through the pain. I refuse to act like this is supposed to be the best day of my life. All I want to do is curl up and drown in the despair settling in my soul.

I want to finish what the ocean started all those years ago when it swept Bailey out to sea and rocked my world. If I could go back and change things, I would. Regret holds me by my spark and squeezes my heart. Had I just gone along with things and officially coupled with Carter, had I just sucked it up and dealt with the life I'd been given, if I'd just been the good mermaid and did what I was told, I'd have never been in this mess. But like the sea calls me on the full moon, the earth, the sky, the air—that call is just as strong. And now, King Attilonious will see to it that I'm broken beyond repair.

King Attilonious stops on the platform, still holding me at his side. My hair veils my face, blocking the dozens of onlookers, the ones who came to watch the coupling of me and Carter. Mateo's parents, Grandmer Oceana and Pops, float a few feet from the stage, both frowning when they realize I'm alone.

The rest of Carter's family sends thoughts to me, asking me

what's going on. They shoot me a dozen questions, worry and fear in their eyes. I close my eyes. I can't bear to face them with the grief in my heart. I can't bear to face the family that was supposed to be mine.

"Ava," a soft voice says from the crowd. It's Grandmer. She swims up behind her family, her blue-streaked hair pulled back into an intricate braid. "Ava, please hold it together. I'm here for you. I'll help you through this."

But the only one I want to help me through this is the one person who can't.

Mateo slides up beside Grandmer and hooks his arm around her shoulders. My heart swells as I look at Carter's dad with hope in my eyes. Just seeing him, knowing if he's here then that means my mate—my soul mate—must still be out there. As long as Carter is alive and safe, I'll live an eternity of misery for him.

Mateo meets my gaze and nods. "Carter's safe now. You're doing the right thing."

My lip quivers. "Then why does it feel so wrong?"

He turns away with sad eyes without answering my question.

A soft hand touches my shoulder, and the king releases his painful hold on me. Luna pulls me to her, brushing my floating hair from my face. I press my face into the princess' shoulder and let her hug me.

"This isn't over," she whispers into my mind.

But it is.

The king bangs his staff into the rock platform, sending a jolt of energy into the water to quiet the merpeople of Pearlestria. The muffled thoughts disappear as all eyes fall on us, some in excitement, others in confusion, and the few people who were supposed to be my family stare on in utter melancholy.

King Attilonious pulls me away from his daughter to spin me to face the crowd. "Tonight I have gathered you here to celebrate a great union—one that will empower us all and bring everlasting fortune to our home and to the entire ocean. For tonight, under the full moon, the enchanting Ava Adair, human-born, ocean-chosen mermaid will officially vow her loyalty to me, King Attilonious, as my queen."

The edges of my vision darken with his words. Gasps sound out from the crowd and into my mind, his announcement sinking in.

Then, to my despair, everyone cheers.

THE VOW

A FEW MERMAIDS PULL ME away to ready me for my sudden coronation as King Attilonious' queen. Luna hovers by my side, holding my hand in hers, as a mermaid strips my bikini top away to replace it with a bejeweled top woven from the softness algae-like material I've ever felt.

It's not until this moment I realize this was supposed to be my outfit for coupling Carter. It sends a shooting pain straight to my heart, and I push the mermaid away. She comes right back toward me to stick her fingers into my hair. Ignoring my cries, she yanks hard enough to ripe my hair free as she braids it into an intricate pattern around my hairline.

Another mermaid swims up behind me and sets a crown of silver on my head. Eerie light reflects from the ruby stones, casting a bloody haze through the water. They adorn my neck with ropes of black and white pearls, and the weight of everything sends my head bowing forward.

I sink to the glittering floor, bringing my fin up to my chest. But the mermaids still don't leave me alone. One scoops some sort of paste from a jar and dabs it across the patches of missing scales on my tail. New scales sprout up as the healer mermaid works some sort of magic on me. Next, she massages my caudal fin, sending pain through me. I flick my tail, knocking her back, but all she does is look at me with curious eyes. It takes another mermaid holding my arms, and Luna whispering for me to calm down in my mind, for the healer to wrap the top of my fin in tight kelp bandages with speckles of rainbow sea glass peeking through to make the bandages look pretty.

I hate to admit it, but it stops the shooting pain up my tail. I despise it though. I should be completely miserable as I face my fate.

When the mermaids leave me with Luna, I finally meet her sapphire eyes for the first time. "Why did you return? You could've escaped."

She pouts her bottom lip. "I promised Carter."

"You spoke to him?" My heart hangs heavy with the light of his spark.

She nods. "I vowed to keep you safe, so I am. It's my fault

you've been dragged here. I should've expected they'd use me to get to you. I'm sorry, Ava."

I throw my hands up. "It's not your fault your father is out of his mind. Queen, Luna? I'm going to be his queen. Th—"

"Better than him killing you."

I grimace. "It's worse."

I cover my face with my hands, though the water doesn't let me cry as much as I want it to. Luna rubs her hand over my back, comforting me the best way she can. But she doesn't understand. To her, being queen isn't so bad. Deep down, though her father angers her, she still loves him. She'll forgive him.

"We'll make it through this," she says. "It won't be so bad as long as you stop resisting. You have to get my dad to let his guard down. You have to make him trust you. And when he does, that's when we'll fight to get out of here."

"That could be years," I say. "And Carter—"

"He'll be safe and alive."

But he'll be without me, and I without him. It's like fate wants me to repay him for saving my life, because if I go through with this, I'll be saving his life in return. But what kind of life can we have now? This isn't life. It's just living.

"His majesty is ready, my queen," a mermaid says, sending her thoughts to me. "The moon will be setting soon, and the king will not wait another month, so you better hurry."

I don't move. If the king wants me to appear before him, he'll have to make me.

"Your sadness is killing me, Aves." Carter's voice whispers

into my mind.

My heart flutters with hope as I sense him near. "What are you doing, Carter? The king will kill you."

"I'm not letting him take you from me," he says.

"But Carter—"

"Just follow the king's orders."

"He's making me vow to be his queen," I say.

Carter growls in my mind. I can feel his anger in my very bones. "I won't let that happen."

The mermaid, who has come to collect me, swims down and grabs my hand, pulling me toward her, forcing me to move. Luna trails behind us, and we exit the tunnel and into the grand room.

The hum of voices rings loudly in my mind. I push them from my head. No one is going to get to me now.

"Straighten your shoulders. Don't look so defeated," Carter says like he's standing by my side.

A smile crosses my mouth. He whispers his love for me through my mind. The spark in my chest pulls me forward, and I let Carter fill my every thought, forcing away the darkness threatening to consume me.

King Attilonious mistakes my smile for something meant for him, but I don't let him think differently. Luna was right. The best way to fight him is silently, like a good little mermaid who'll answer to his every beck and call.

The king bows deeply and so does the rest of the crowd. I peer over them, and that's when I see him. In the very back, a small sea of faces away, awaits Carter. He smiles when our eyes meet, and I have to force myself to bow back at the king.

As much as I know how dangerous it is for Carter to be here, I'm relieved he didn't abandon me. If we're going to fight, it's going to be together. Because he's my true mate, and I'd rather see the world end, see the ocean dry up, than give up what my heart desires no matter how selfish that is.

The king offers his hand out to me, and I force myself to let him take my hand. My fingers disappear in his large palm as he pulls me closer to wrap his arms around me. It takes everything in me not to reel backwards and gag.

"You look absolutely stunning, my queen," King Attilonious says, bringing my hand to his mouth to kiss my knuckles. *Stay calm. Keep smiling.*

The crowd coos, breaking through my mind shield for a moment before I push them away. The king stretches tall, towering over me by at least three feet, and he slams his staff into the rock platform, making the water quiver around us.

A moment later, he holds out the end of the staff to me and places my hand on the brilliant diamond.

"I've waited so long to have someone like you by my side as my queen, Ava. And as our kingdom looks upon us under the magic of the full moon, I vow to be your king, your protector. I vow to stand by your side as we rule the ocean together..."

I push his thoughts from my mind. I can't listen to them. He acts like he's been waiting his whole life for me, when he just wants me to fill the void created by the mermaid who had abandoned him.

"Ava," Carter says into my mind. "In front of the witnesses of our colony and under the glow of the full moon, I hereby promise to share the very essence of my being with you, the mermaid who completes me. I vow to always keep you safe and happy, to kiss your pain away, to hold you when you're sad. I vow in the name of the ocean to never stop loving you as my love is greater than the sea, the land, and the sky above. My love for you is unconditional, unending, and eternal. I vow my very soul to you, to be by your side, always and forever."

I turn my gaze away from the king as he continues to drone on, but I don't let his voice reach me. Instead, I project my voice out through the ocean for all to hear.

"Carter, in front of the witnesses of our colony and under the glow of the full moon, I hereby accept your vows as my eternal mate. I promise to share my very essence with you, the merman who promised his life to me to live as part of the great sea. I vow to cherish the gift of life with love, loyalty, respect, and thankfulness."

The king's eyes widen, my words settling in his mind. But I don't stop.

"I vow to stand by your side as your mate through even the roughest storms, for my love for you is greater than the sea, the land, the sky, and every star that shines above us. I promise to protect you with my life, to follow you wherever you lead in the form that you choose to be in. I vow to love you for the rest of my life and beyond. My love for you is unconditional, unending, and eternal. I vow my very soul to you, to be by your side, always and forever." I turn my gaze away from Carter. "And I won't ever let anyone stop me."

The king jerks out his hand to grab me, but I swim back, raising my hands up to protect myself. Carter darts over the crowd in my direction, pulling me to him, before he plants his lips to mine to complete our ceremony.

The king rips Carter away from me with fury blazing in his dark blue eyes. He throws Carter to the rock platform, holding his staff over him, aimed at the spark in his chest.

"No!" I scream out into the water. The ocean vibrates around me as a shockwave knocks the staff from the king's hand.

Rushing from my place, I link my hands around Carter and tug him back before the king can impale him with his sharp nails. Carter flips through the water, pulling me by my hands, but the king grabs onto my tail, dragging me away from my mate.

King Attilonious glares at me, hovering over me, his chest heaving as he inhales the salty ocean water. His staff floats back to his hand, pushed by the water, and he aims it at me. Death has never felt so close in this moment, but the king isn't aiming to kill me.

"You *will* be my queen!" His voice roars through the water instead of in my mind. Turning away, he throws his staff like a spear, and it cuts through the water heading toward Carter.

There's nothing I can do as the staff smacks Carter in the

chest before he even has a chance to move. The water shudders with turbulence, his body flying back and crashing into the sandy floor.

"Carter!" I scream. "No!"

With every ounce of strength in me, I dart forward, cutting through the churning water and throw myself onto my mate. The spark in his chest flickers as he struggles to live. The power of the sea had given him his spark, and it's the sea that can steal it away.

"Carter," I beg, sending my voice into his mind. "Hold on. Please. You can't leave me."

"Ava..." His voice is barely audible in my mind.

"Don't say my name like it's the last thing you'll ever say." I cup his face in my hands, and his eyes close. My chest clenches, our hearts beating out of sync for the first time since I've become a mermaid.

This can't be happening. I can't lose him. Not after everything.

Closing my eyes, I lean forward and kiss him. I kiss him with all the love I have for him. Through our kiss, he sends me a single image. It's a flash of a memory from the first moment he saw me standing on the dock near the Ocean Jewel. My blond hair blows around me as the land sits behind me, the most perfect backdrop. My blue eyes shine in the bright sun, and in that moment, I'm so very human. I'm the girl I've craved to be the last few weeks. The girl I want to be now.

"Carter, I love you," I say into his mind. I send a burst of my own memories to him. I show him how he looked when we first met, his hair shining bronze in the sun, his eyes as clear and as beautiful as the sea that holds his soul. I show him how he looked when he picked me up on our first date and how he closed his eyes when he ate his dessert. Then, I show him as the boy I fell in love with—with his glorious aqua tail. I send him the memory he shared with me weeks ago when he told me I was a mermaid. I send him the image of what his spark looked like in the water, how good it felt when I touched it.

Carter lies still beneath me. I pull away, and my whole world is shaken when I glance down at his chest. The spark we had once shared has faded into darkness. The ocean stole it away.

But the spark still glows from my chest now. And I refuse to carry it without Carter. I can't do this without him.

"I'm not keeping this life. Not without you, Carter." I send the thought into the sea, hoping it reaches every merperson in the world. I want them to know I'm not accepting the gift the sea bestowed on me. I won't do it, not without my mate.

Leaning down, I brush my lips against Carter's, sending the spark he gave me back to him. Because I can't be who I am now without him. I can't let the ocean have me if it won't have him.

"Ava!" the king roars. "Stop!"

It isn't until this moment I realize I've created a whirlpool around us, protecting me and Carter from the entire world. And the king can't touch us. No one can touch us.

I turn back to Carter, his dark hair floating around his head in the current. "Carter," I whisper into his mind. "You once gave me a part of your life so I could live. And now, I'm giving you mine. Please, come back to me. The ocean can't win, remember? No matter how rough it is, we can swim. We'll get through this storm. Because the ocean doesn't control us anymore."

A bright light flashes in my closed eyes through my kiss with Carter. Warm hands wrap around me as Carter accepts my spark into him. It's something I gladly give him and something I'd gladly give up for him.

Leaning back, I smile toward the surface, feeling my life fill Carter's body. He shifts in my arms, and his fin splits apart. He starts transforming into his human form for all the ocean to see.

Flicking my tail, I push us toward the surface.

The sun rises on the horizon somewhere above, stealing the suffocating darkness away. The full moon no longer controls us. Tingles take hold of my body, and I stare in awe as the spark radiates from me, filling Carter whole again, giving him back the merman life that was stolen from him. Our hearts beat in sync in my ears, and then cramps take hold of me.

Giving my spark to Carter triggered my transformation. To give him life, I have to give up my own to the sea. Water burns my lungs as my body transforms back to human. Without air, I'll drown. I am drowning. We're drowning together.

"Ava," Carter whispers into my mind. "You have to let go. Let the sea take you."

And I do. With my last strings of life, I not only vow my

life to Carter, I vow my life to the sea.

~287~

EPILOGUE

THE LOST COVE

MY EYELIDS SHINE BURGUNDY, THE sun glaring brightly overhead. I don't want to open my eyes. My lungs scream in pain, but at least I'm breathing. The hum of the ocean crashes in the distance, and I can't move even though it calls to me.

A memory flashes into my mind. I drowned in the middle of the ocean above Pearlestria, but somehow, I'm still alive.

"Ava?" Carter asks, his voice wrapping me in familiar warmth. "Ava, can you hear me? Please, open your eyes."

I force my eyes to flutter open and gaze up at my mate. The sun halos him in golden light, shadowing his face. The spark in his chest shines more brightly than ever, and I reach out and brush my fingers against it.

"You're alive," I whisper, my throat burning. My body convulses as I cough, spitting out water from my lungs. "How?"

He smiles once before kissing my lips. A series of images flash through my mind, and I watch our bodies float through the ocean as it carries us from Pearlestria to spit us out on the shore of this island.

"When I died, my spark went to you. It shouldn't have been possible, but you gave it back to me. It was like you were born mermaid, choosing me as your mate like how I chose you. And the ocean allowed it." He runs his fingers through the wave that creeps over us. "The ocean protected us from the king."

I blink a few times, sitting up. "You're human."

He nods. "For now. I think until the next full moon. It's like I was reborn or something. I can't explain it."

I kick my smooth, unblemished legs. "You sure?"

"I can still feel the ocean's essence. I just can't transform."

It takes me a minute to realize I'm just as human as he is, and I'm without a sea stone ring. I hold my hand out and show him. "What about me? How is this possible?"

"I don't know, Ava. But there has to be a reason."

A million thoughts cross my mind, but I don't want to think about any of it. I just want to revel in the fact I'm on this beach with Carter and we both have legs.

Carter must feel the same way, because he pulls me into his arms and hugs me. I smile against his lips, showering him with desperate kisses. I have no idea what's going on, but it doesn't really matter in this moment, because we're both alive and free from the sea.

"We'll figure this out," Carter says. "But let's just enjoy it for now, okay?"

I nod. I'll enjoy it forever.

As the sun dries my damp skin, the events of last night start to settle into my bones. It's the first time I've had a chance to think, and all I can think about now is how Giselle lost her life for me—Carter, too. I was so close to losing everything.

Tears drip down my cheeks, and I start sobbing. Carter hugs me tighter, kissing my wet face as the tears spill freely. We might have won. We might have survived the storm. But it has left a trail of destruction in its wake.

"Ava, Carter?" A familiar voice sounds out over the waves, taking our attention from each other. "What are you doing here?"

Jerking up my head, I glare at Starla strolling down the beach to me. I fling myself from Carter and rush toward the woman. She wasn't there for the coronation. She was busy murdering my best friend. In this moment, I want her dead.

I ram my shoulder into her chest, and we both tumble to the sand. Screaming, I wrap my hands around her throat. "You killed her!" My yells echo through the air. All I can think about is hurting Starla for taking away my best friend in the entire world, even if it was because of the king.

Hands grab my shoulders, pulling me back, and I thrash to the ground.

"Ava! Ava, I'm alive."

I freeze in my place, bringing my gaze to my best friend.

Giselle thrusts her arms around me. "Starla saved my life.

She brought me here."

Carter stands with his mom, and I peer around the secluded beach. "And where is here?"

"Welcome to the Lost Cove," another voice says from behind me.

I turn in the sand, my mouth falling open as my eyes fall on a familiar girl. One I could never forget in my life. Shifting my gaze to Carter, he only offers me a shrug. It takes me a moment to find my strength, but when I do, I run through the sand and embrace the girl with all my might. She might be older, but I'd never forget her face or who she is.

She laughs. "Whoa. What's that for?"

I pull back and look into eyes the same color as mine. "What is this place?"

"A sanctuary for those lucky enough to escape death for discovering the truth about merpeople."

I hug the girl again. "I can't believe it. All this time you've been here."

Her eyes light up, realization taking over her thoughts. "Ava?" she questions.

"You know her," Carter says, coming to my side.

I smile through my tears. "Yeah." I grab my mate's hand. "Carter, this is Bailey, my sister."

I once thought the ocean had stolen everything from me—my sister, my best friend, my life—but as it turns out, the ocean had been protecting them all along. It's not the deep water that is my enemy. It's the king. The merman who thinks he controls the sea.

And now I know why the ocean has chosen me.

Because like me, it wants to be free.

And I'm going to make it happen.

For everyone I love, including the sea, I will finally beat the storm.

To be continued...

ACKNOWLEDGMENTS

FIRST AND FOREMOST, I WANT to thank the team of people who made this book and series possible. Sarah Collier, Amy Holliday, Katie Harder-Schauer, Jan Moran, Nikki Godwin, and Jamie Hall—from critiquing and beta reading to editing, proofreading, and blurb slaying—your help has been invaluable. I appreciate all the hard work, time, and effort you all put into my novels.

Second, I want to thank my BFF, Jazmin Garcia, for harassing me into writing a mermaid series. This has been such a fun world to explore, and I appreciate all your encouragement and support.

Thanks to my family and friends, who've been so supportive of my dreams. Thanks for being here for me and not getting upset when I'm lost in one of my imaginary worlds.

Thanks to the bloggers who have been so sweet and helpful to me. I appreciate all the hard work you do to help me out. You all rock!

Lastly, a special thanks to my readers. You have no idea how much I appreciate you. Thanks to those who reach out to me via email and social media or reply to my newsletters.

Thanks to those who leave reviews of my books online, and to those who just enjoy my stories. It's a big book world out there, so thank you for taking a chance on me. XOXO!

ABOUT GINNA MORAN

GINNA MORAN IS A WRITER from sunny Southern California. She started writing poetry as a teenager in a spiral notebook that she still has tucked away on her desk today. Her love of writing grew after she graduated high school, and she completed her first unpublished manuscript at age eighteen.

When she realized her love of writing was her life's passion, she studied literature at Mira Costa College in Northern San Diego. Besides writing novels, she was senior editor, content manager, and image coordinator for Crescent House Publishing Inc. for four years.

Aside from Ginna's professional life, she enjoys binge watching television shows, playing pretend with her daughter, and cuddling with her dogs. Some of her favorite things include chocolate, anything that glitters, cheesy jokes, and organizing her bookshelf.

Ginna Moran loves to hear from her readers so visit her online at www.GinnaMoran.com. You can also find her on Facebook, Twitter, Instagram, and Snapchat(@GinnaMoran). To stay up-to-date on new releases, sign up to her newsletter. You'll not only get a FREE story, but you'll be able to participate in monthly giveaways!

Ginna Moran is currently hard at work on her next novel.

Other Young Adult Novels by Ginna Moran

PARANORMAL
Destined for Dreams Series
Demon Within Series
Finding Nate Series
Going Ghostly Series
Spark of Life Series
When Souls Collide Series
Demon Watcher Series

CONTEMPORARY
Falling into Fame Series

STANDALONES
Life After Lila